STORMBRINGER

ALSO BY SHANNON DELANY

THE 13 TO LIFE SERIES

13 to Life

Secrets and Shadows

Bargains and Betrayals

Destiny and Deception

Rivals and Retribution

THE WEATHER WITCH SERIES

Weather Witch

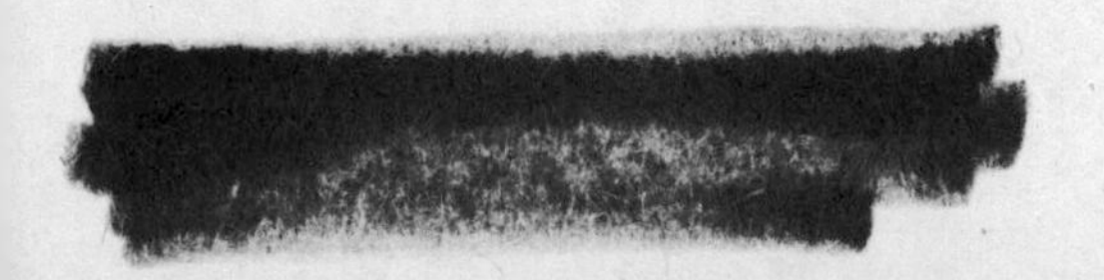

STORMBRINGER

A WEATHER WITCH NOVEL

Shannon Delany

ST. MARTIN'S GRIFFIN NEW YORK

This is a work of fiction. All of the characters, organizations, and events portrayed in this novel are either products of the author's imagination or are used fictitiously.

Printed in the United States of America. For information, address St. Martin's Press, 175 Fifth Avenue, New York, N.Y. 10010.

www.stmartins.com

Library of Congress Cataloging-in-Publication Data

Delany, Shannon.
Stormbringer : a Weather Witch novel / Shannon Delany. — First St. Martin's Griffin edition.
pages cm.
ISBN 978-1-250-01865-6 (trade paperback)
ISBN 978-1-4668-4092-8 (e-book)
[1. Airships—Fiction. 2. Witches—Fiction. 3. Social classes—Fiction. 4. Fantasy.] I. Title.
PZ7.D3733Sto 2014
[Fic]—dc23 2013032018

St. Martin's Griffin books may be purchased for educational, business, or promotional use. For information on bulk purchases, contact Macmillan Corporate and Premium Sales Department at 1-800-221-7945, extension 5442, or write specialmarkets@macmillan.com.

First Edition: January 2014

10 9 8 7 6 5 4 3 2 1

Stormbringer is dedicated to all who dream of a better, fairer world and, more important, to those who work with great passion and conviction to see that dream become reality.

Acknowledgments

There are always so many people to thank throughout the course of a series and I worry I'll leave someone out. The reality of publishing is that every book is the result of a team effort, starting with the agent who shops a story and the editor who acquires a novel and helps develop it into even more than the author imagined it could be. So I'm going to introduce you to my team. Many of them have been thanked in my previous novels, but each new book usually means a small change in the makeup of the team.

Stormbringer comes to you from: my beta readers, Patty Locatelli and Karl Gee, who ask the right questions and encourage most of my choices and listen when I rant or worry; my agent, Richard Curtis, who always makes himself available and answers all of my strange questions with great tact and vast quantities of knowledge; my editor, Michael Homler, who has a knack for making me reexamine my work so that it evolves; my cover designer, Ervin Serrano, who comes up with lovely images that encourage readers to give my books a try; Elaine Rothchild and Loren Jaggers, who do marketing and public relations and give great advice on what to try and what to avoid; my production editor, Lisa Davis, and my copyeditor, Christina MacDonald, who both make my stories stronger through their hard work and vision.

There are many others along the way who help make

my novels successful: my fans worldwide (I'd be nothing without your support), bloggers, other readers, and reviewers who love what I do, booksellers, librarians, and event coordinators—I cannot thank you often enough for what you do (not only for me, but to get books into the hands of people who will appreciate them and question or grow as a result of them).

STORMBRINGER

Prologue: 1844

The boundaries which divide Life from
Death are at best shadowy and vague.
—EDGAR ALLAN POE

Philadelphia

"I am not quite myself of late," Lady Cynthia Astraea, once ranked Fifth of the Nine, complained to her head servant, Laura. Not that a great variety of servants remained for a lady to choose from, as there were currently many better households to find oneself aligned with. Yet Laura had a mission and a mission was enough to keep someone rooted when others fled.

"Not *quite,*" Lady Astraea murmured, running a fingertip along her cheekbone and down the curve of her jaw to stop at the very tip of her chin, the whole while staring into her vanity's mirror from her place on its matching cushioned seat. Her more elegant dressing table had been sold and replaced following her daughter Jordan's seventeenth birthday party. Certain similar sacrifices had also been made since that disastrous evening.

Granted, the party had been what most hosts wished

their events to be: memorable. But not in the way the Astraea household hoped.

No party was more talked about on Philadelphia's Hill than that at which Lord Morgan Astraea, a leader in the country's Council, was accused of Harboring a Weather Witch: his youngest daughter, Jordan. The Astraeas' most recent event, society demanded it be their last.

Harboring a Weather Witch was one of very few things that resulted in a complete loss of rank and cut a household from the Hub—the centralized source of power lighting Philadelphia's fine homes, government buildings, and fanciest storefronts, all via stormcell technology.

It was a technology fed by the only magick the United States government allowed, and only allowed because it remained firmly within government control. The council knew by "making" Weather Witches they could do more than call storms. But how the Making happened—that was a secret to nearly all but the Witches and the Maker himself.

Cut from the Hub and shunned by respected society, Lady Astraea sacrificed things like the dressing table and the set of china that had come with her dowry as well as the family's fine silver tea service bearing Paul Revere's hallmark. Whereas Lord Astraea's investments abroad might secure the family home and property on Philadelphia's prestigious Hill a while longer, perhaps Lady Astraea looked toward the future of those still living within the estate's rambling brick and fieldstone walls. Laura hoped that was why her ladyship parted with such possessions.

But hoping something was true and something actually being true did not always coincide.

"Please shutter the windows and draw tight the curtains,"

Lady Astraea said. "I chill much more easily now." She tugged at her shawl.

Laura adjusted the shawl's finely woven fabric so it lay snug around her lady's shoulders before moving to do as she bid. Her ladyship raised a pale but commanding hand. "Wait. Light the candles first, please. But carefully."

Laura glanced toward the window. It was only now nearly dusk, and she imagined the lights of the Hill and the sprawling buildings at its stony foot would soon begin to rival the glowing summer sun edging toward evening.

Yet, with a polite bend of her knees, Laura curtsied and changed directions, knowing quite well that Lady Astraea had recently become particular about both light and flame.

Once the lady would have demanded the windows be open and the curtains thrown wide so she might watch the sun slip slowly down the face of the sky. Once she would have stepped to the window late at night to wish on falling stars. And once she would have kept a much different servant as her favorite.

But Chloe had been hanged.

And there weren't many ways to undo something as final as death.

Not *many.*

As she reached for a modest tin of lucifers, Laura's gaze drifted to the crystals peeking out of the shawl wrapped tight about her ladyship's neck. Beneath that shawl lay a sparkling system of jewels hanging like spiderwebs decked with fresh dew. The stormcells twinkled, nestled in her lady's hair, dangling from her ears, adorning her throat, her wrists, and even her ankles.

But the most important stormcell crystal of all was the

one Lady Astraea did not even realize she wore, the one slipped beneath her skin and as near her heart as the Reanimator could easily place it.

The soul stone.

If Laura had known where to find the Reanimator, she would have had some questions for him. First, regarding the fact her ladyship had trouble maintaining body heat. And what of her coloring—her complexion—which seemed a wee bit different if one saw her in a certain light?

And then, there were other things she would ask the Reanimator. Stranger and darker things regarding changes in her ladyship's attitude, her likes and dislikes. Both big and little things: a favorite dress was despised now for being a dreadful color and her favorite food no longer suited her taste. Would Lady Jordan recognize her own mother upon her return?

The question twisted and evolved in Laura's head, becoming *Would Lady Jordan return?*

Witches never came home. No one talked about it. Discussions of Witches and Weather were deemed petty things unworthy of discussion. The same way slavery was deemed a nonissue.

Laura struck a lucifer and lit the nearest candle.

Unless you were a slave.

Or an abolitionist.

John had been a slave and he talked about that far less than the night he brought Lady Astraea home from the Reanimator's—just this side of death.

Besides, the Reanimator might know more about the prophecy people whispered in quiet corners, about the Stormbringer—the Witch who would unite all the ranks and bring an end to the Wildkin War. According to the rumors she'd heard and the odd details she wheedled out of John, the Reanimator was precisely the sort of man to know the answers.

Another wick trimmed, another candle lit—soon the room would glow against the coming dusk and eventual creep of night.

Yes, Laura would have quite the list of questions for the Reanimator had not her coconspirator, John, kept the man's location from her.

For her safety, John insisted.

Still, Laura knew the Reanimator lived in the section of the Below that Philadelphia's Hill referred to as the Burn Quarter: the one populated area the battling fire companies would let burn if it ever sparked. *Nothing and no one worth saving in that shambles,* they claimed.

The Burn Quarter was no place for a girl to go looking for something. Unless she was looking for trouble.

Her back to her ladyship, Laura was still lighting candles (and missing the steady, clear intensity of stormlight) when Lady Astraea made her next request.

"Yes, ma'am, what else did you require?" Laura asked, turning to face her.

Lady Astraea's features pinched and sharp, her eyes narrow and lips thin, she spat her next words out, forcing them between her teeth. "Why must you be so tiresome? When I say *hand me the brush,* I do not mean for you to stand there gawking, but for you to *hand me the brush*!"

Trembling, Laura snatched up the brush sitting by her lady's elbow and snapped it into the woman's upturned palm.

Astraea straightened on the seat, pulling the brush up and behind her head to hit the girl, and Laura ducked, raising her arms against the coming blow. "You little bi—" But the insult stopped, the last word dying in the woman's throat as something changed in her eyes, left as fast as it had come. Some flame there extinguished, some flicker of hate snuffed itself out.

The brush clattered to the floor and, resting her palm flat on the dressing table, Lady Astraea struggled to catch her breath, her other hand on her chest and not far from the soul stone. "I . . . I do not know what happened just then. I am so dreadfully sorry," she whispered, her eyes soft, sad, and seeking Laura's. "I was going to say something that was quite uncalled-for. Something quite appalling." She shook her head. "Forgive me, Laura, I am not quite feeling—"

"—yourself," Laura said with a determined press of her lips. Her jaw set as her ladyship nodded. The strange malady brewing within Lady Astraea yielded the same complaint so frequently Laura regularly completed her ladyship's words for her.

No longer did Lady Astraea say, "Something ails me," or "I am not feeling well," but always it was "I am not feeling myself." It seemed an accurate assessment. There were many days Laura thought had it not been for the physical trappings of her ladyship's body, the familiarity of both face and form, she might have believed herself employed by some sharp-tongued stranger.

There were times, increasing steadily in number, when Lady Cynthia Astraea simply was not quite herself. With a care born of wariness, Laura shuttered the windows, pulled the curtains tight, and realized she too chilled more easily now.

Chapter One

Being human signifies, for each one of us,
belonging to a class, a society, a country, a
continent and a civilization . . .
—CLAUDE LEVI-STRAUSS

Aboard the Tempest

Rowen Burchette stood in the belly of the airship *Tempest,* his hands pressed flat to the glass of a window as cables hissed and zipped free of the bulbous boat, falling slack against Holgate's Western Tower and slapping as loud as cannon fire. The airship drifted slowly up and away from its place at the docks, carrying Rowen farther from his goal of rescuing Jordan Astraea.

He balled his hands into fists and slammed them against the window's wooden framing. It did him no good and it definitely smarted, so, thinking better of the action, he stopped.

He needed a strategy to get from this ship to the other. He needed a strategy to get to Jordan (whom he most certainly was *not* in love with, no matter what people suggested). He had a mission: he would rescue her and set things right in Philadelphia for both their families.

He needed a strategy that would give them all their happily ever afters.

But strategy was not his strong suit. His brother Sebastian was far superior in all things strategic. Sebastian could have outwitted the chess-playing automaton the Turk itself if he'd had the opportunity to play it! Rowen would have more likely sat across the chessboard from the mechanical man wondering who his tailor was.

Rowen's fists opened and closed again and he leaned forward, resting his forehead on one. He needed a plan. But planning was *also* Sebastian's strength.

Blood pounded in his ears.

He needed . . . to gather his thoughts.

He needed an achievable goal.

His focus at the window changed and he caught a glimpse of himself in the reflection. He backed up, swatting at his beard, trying to lessen the unkempt way it taunted him. No use, it still stuck out from his face like his jaw was covered in the ends of frayed ropes. He tugged a hand through his hair and got most of the blond mess to go in the general direction he hoped.

Most of it.

Dammit. The things he was known most for—his dashing good looks and ability to dress for any occasion—were also beyond his grasp.

How did one dress for abduction via pirate ship, anyhow?

He'd been forced into the hold of the *Tempest* by a group of large (and powerfully-smelling) men. Not that he couldn't have taken at least a few of them down in a brawl, but he submitted when watchmen appeared on the Western Tower's dock.

The watchmen had been, after all, looking for him.

So he let himself be jostled inside the rocking airship, because sometimes what seemed like losing was only a quiet way to win.

The men searched him without even a "by your leave, good sir," found little of interest upon him (having neatly disarmed him in the dark room beyond the Tower's base), and then they disappeared, locking him inside.

Piles of wooden boxes, crates, and trunks, most of them rough-hewn and similar in dimension, nearly surrounded him. The ceiling here was not much beyond Rowen's own height and the interior was spartan with only wood beams, floors, and walls held together by metal strips and broad flat-headed nails. Copper pipes ran overhead, snaking across the ceiling, crawling down the walls to the floor, and disappearing into each.

This was not a place one kept people, but *things*. Here the only noises were the creaks, groans, burbles, and hisses of a ship rising slowly into the atmosphere.

He peered out the window again, marking well the name of the opposing ship. The *Artemesia.*

It was a liner—larger than the ship he rode within, and far more fashionable with its sleek finishes and elegant trim. A generously endowed figurehead embraced part of its balloon, her wooden arms permanently thrown back as if against an oncoming wind, her skirt and hair flowing out and around the front of the balloon, its shape looking to him a bit like an egg tipped on its side. His stomach growled at the thought of food but he focused to scrutinize the *Artemesia,* wanting to be able to identify her easily again. Behind the figurehead's wooden shoulders hinged the great ship's folded wings, and in their current upright position he noticed wings painted onto the balloon's fabric as well—a stunning blend of technology and art. Cabins were integrated into the design of her long skirt, their windows flashing in the waning light.

At the *Artemesia*'s back sat her rudder and at the balloon's very top . . . Rowen squinted.

A door whined open and someone snapped, "You!"

Rowen whipped around, giving the approaching redheaded woman a wary look as he spread his feet and crossed his arms to better appear imposing.

It did nothing to slow her progress.

He doubted much could.

But she suddenly paused, saying, "Ugh. I cannot stand the parading about of supposedly modern women dressed in these—these . . ." She grabbed the wide flounces of her skirts and pulled at them as if making war with her outfit. "—skirts so broad, so cumbersome . . ." She reached for the belt buckle that bit into her clothes just above her hips and Rowen stepped back as she gave the buckle a twist and with a *pop* her skirts fell in a puddle of fabric about her feet.

Beneath the skirting she wore tight leather leggings—*indecently* tight for a woman—and a pair of tall black boots. She wiggled the belt down across the broadest bit of her hips, declaring, "That is a great relief!" Kicking the skirts to the side, she stared at the newest addition to her crew.

Rowen swallowed.

The woman, a few years older than him if the lines edging her eyes and curving by her upper lip were any measure, pulled an etched flask free of her belt and took a long swallow of its contents. Her eyes lost focus a moment and the ship bucked slightly upward. She reattached the flask to her hip, licked her lips, and her eyes, a startling green, snared him again, brighter and fiercer.

She wore a strange necklace of slender rope that wove in

and out making a knotted pendant with three loops. Removing an old-fashioned tricorne leather hat, its sides pinned up with gadgetry, she leaned over at her waist, shaking out the longest mane of coppery hair Rowen had ever seen. Sighing, she swept it back up with her hands and knotted it at the nape of her neck, its ends fanning out at one side like a golden pheasant's feather caught in the knot.

Straightening, she donned the hat once more, and loosened the front of something that was at once as form-fitting as a corset and as masculine as a waistcoat. Again she sighed.

Unsettled by her unseemly display, Rowen (with his vast quantities of time running wild with the lads and his adventures into Philadelphia's Below to explore a world beneath his rank) slapped a hand over his eyes, knowing there were things one did not get involved with.

Certainly not when sober.

He groaned. This had been a disaster from the start. The loss of Jordan, the trouble with Catrina, the drunken argument that led to the duel in which he surprised himself (and many others) by *not* being the participant lying dead on the field.

He slid his hands back down to his sides, keeping his eyes closed. Perhaps the biggest disaster had been letting his family servant and dear friend, Jonathan, be his second at the duel. They were both made criminals the moment Rowen had fired his gun.

But Jonathan believed Rowen had the stuff of heroes—the stuff of legends—hidden somewhere within him. He believed Rowen's true worth would be shown, but only when tested.

Jonathan had never been wrong before.

Evidently it only took being wrong once to wind up dead

alongside some anonymous river, the victim of a Merrow attack.

Rowen knew little beyond what was expected of him. He never bothered with anything other than meeting everyone's expectations: use your strengths (he was handsome), marry up if possible (he had Jordan as a viable option until recently), be loyal to your rank and enter military service (his enlistment date approached too soon for his liking). But that was all.

Meeting the basic expectations meant one born of a good household prospered.

The irony was being born Sixth of the Nine, a military rank, he knew he was no hero, no fighter, no leader of men. He'd heard it said by men who were all those amazing things. *He could keep the troops laughing,* they claimed, *but he'd never lead them.*

He was as good as cannon fodder.

The woman tapped her foot and, opening his eyes, he saw her lips twitch in his direction, pointing up into a smile. "Elizabeth," she said by way of introduction. "And, you, what was it?"

"My name matters not one whit, as I shall not be staying aboard."

The smile fell from her face and her lips tightened. "You will stay aboard until I see fit to release you. This is my world, my kingdom, my realm, and you—"

"—are your *serf*?" he asked with a snort.

Changing the sound of only one letter, and only slightly, she replied with a smirk, "You may certainly *serve* me."

Rowen snorted and scratched at his beard.

"Give up your name, lad, or I'll have the naming of you myself," she warned. "And you might be a pretty thing beneath that mangled mess of facial hair, but if I name you something less than flattering, I guarantee it will stick whilst you're aboard the *Tempest.* Perhaps even after you leave. Ask Wee Willy Winky if you doubt me."

She touched the tip of her index finger to her lips and rolled her eyes up, beginning the process of assigning him a new name.

Wee Willy Winky? Well, at least that name was taken . . . But she seemed the inventive type and he did not like that at all.

He groaned, admitting, "Rowen."

"Aye, *Rowen . . .*" A grin split her face. "See there, lad, how difficult is it to go along rather than be headstrong? There is a time stubbornness serves, that I guarantee. But stubbornness best serves man—and by *man,* I mean *mankind,* which of course includes the fairer sex," she added as disclaimer, "but, as I was saying: stubbornness best serves man in matters of either love or war."

Rowen grunted.

"Now be a dear, will you? I need all of these crates—" She strode across the narrow space not occupied by the boxes filling the bay, and rested a hand on a substantial stack of them. "—moved over to . . ." She paced a few feet and tapped her foot. ". . . here." She widened her stance and tapped her right foot definitively. "Not here," then slid it back, tapping once more, "but here. And the sooner the better, of course."

He looked at her blankly, rubbed his ragged mess of a beard, blinked once, and turned back to the window.

She tapped her foot again, resting one fist on an outthrust hip. "Darling," she cooed, "you appear absolutely stunned!"

"It isn't every day I get kidnapped by a crazy bitch to work on a pirate ship."

"Such language," she said, scowling. "You will certainly

need to mind us better than that. I shall not suffer to hear any aboard referred to by *that* term." She shook her head. "We are most certainly not a *pirate* ship, nor a *pirate* vessel . . . nor a *brigand's* boat . . . none of those things. We are a *trading vessel,*" she specified. "We are traders (the latter sound being a 'd,' not a 't,' mind the distinction well). We are purveyors of fine goods and the occasional provider of unique services." She paused, fanning out her fingers to examine her nails. "We operate under strict guidelines and within the boundaries of important legal codes and laws. Just not all of the legal codes and laws the government might like us to observe . . ."

He blinked at her again. "I did not fathom *pirate* being the most offensive term in my sentence."

She shrugged. "What is it I've heard said: when I see a bird that walks like a duck and swims like a duck and quacks like a duck, I call that bird a duck . . . ?"

Rowen pawed at one ear, and, raising his chin, tried once more. "It is even less often, I daresay, that I find myself kidnapped by *traders.*"

"More appropriately, you were *shanghaied* by *traders*. Or *crimped* by a captain. Or *impressed.*"

Rowen snorted, "And yet I am not impressed by being impressed."

Elizabeth clucked her tongue and said, "Darling, you must go adventuring more frequently."

His brow lowered, combining with his already prominent jaw in what he hoped was an intimidating mix.

She winked at him and sprang forward, grabbing his arm to tow him away from the window. He stood still as granite. "Whatever is wrong with you?" she laughed. "I saved you from the Holgate watchmen—"

"—you *kidnapped* me," he reminded her.

"Technically, we call it something else . . . Remember? *Shanghaied.*"

"And you expect what—*gratitude*?"

"Perhaps rather than gratitude you should simply give me less *attitude* than the watchmen hunting you deserved, eh?" She cocked her head, eyes sharp as flint. "Exactly what *were* they hunting you for? They seemed quite determined pounding on that door." She pursed her lips, watching him. "What is your crime, Rowen?"

He turned away to watch Jordan's ship slip into a haze that grew, thickening on the other side of the window.

"There are crimes not even I will tolerate aboard ship . . ." She dropped his arm. "Have you hurt a child?" she asked, her voice thin. "I'll gut a man for that." Her hand dropped to a spot on her belt behind the flask.

Rowen Albertus Burchette, unarmed, recognized the threat as it went from words to potential action.

"Tell it true, lad," she said, squinting. "I'll know in my heart if you're lying."

"No," he replied. "I would never hurt a child."

Her eyes roved over each feature of his face, making his heart hammer beneath her scrutiny. Her hand fell back to her side, her shoulders dropped, and her lips slid back into something just shy of a smile. "Good. Not that at least." She nodded, urging, "Come, come. This," she waved at the crates, "can all wait a bit longer."

"That was the only crime you wanted to ask about? What about stealing, cheating at cards . . ." He swallowed, avoiding the one crime that damned him.

Murder.

"No," she said. "Little else matters. But harming a child

is like cutting off a rose's bloom before a bud's yet sprouted. Other crimes are too frequently understandable. We all run from something whether we're in the air or one of the Grounded population." She shrugged. "Besides, the truth will out. Now come. I would not be a proper hostess if I did not show you more of the ship on your first day."

"So you are a *hostess*. On a fine *trading* vessel." He rolled his eyes, taking in the room. His tone proved him to be less than impressed.

"I've brought you aboard the most talked-about ship in our fleet and I am ready to make you privy to many of her secrets out of courtesy—and the fact I could gut you in a heartbeat should you prove less than amiable." The smile never left her lips even as she threatened him. "And yet . . ."

He shook his head.

"You care not—"

"—not one whit," he agreed. "I was supposed to be on *that* ship." He jabbed a finger in the direction the *Artemesia* had disappeared in.

"No, you were not," she returned, her tone flat. "You are precisely where you are supposed to be at this moment in time. Everything happens for a reason, and for some reason you were not fated to be aboard *that* ship—at least not *now*." She crossed her arms and stared at him with a fierce focus.

He twitched, looking away.

"I thought as much. For some reason Fate is keeping you from that ship right now. You must allow Fate to do its work."

"Wait. You're a pirate but . . ."

"*Trader.*" She said it more slowly, rolling out the *r* at its end as if instructing a child in the word's pronunciation for the first time. "A *liberally aligned trader.* What? We—"

"*—liberally aligned traders—*" he inserted for her.

She mock-curtsied, turning up her fingers at her sides and bending her knees. "We cannot believe in predestination? You suppose our kind to be the guiding light and standard for all free will and liberty, is that it?" She snorted. "You probably think I'm some Robin Hood and my crew's my merry men. Well, I'm no one's hero," she corrected, arching her eyebrows. "I take from the rich—so I might someday *be* rich. And my crew?" She looked toward the door in the ceiling at the bay's far end and the stairs disappearing into it. "They are mostly surly. They are only merry when they are quite drunk. And then only before the vomiting ensues. So. Buck up," she demanded, a true smile coloring her tone. "Life is short, choices are made for us, and the best we can do is roll with the punches. Perhaps avoid a few punches landing on our face if Fate feels kind."

He heaved out a groan, glancing away. Wisps of white edged around the window, transforming the haze into a gently rolling fog.

The captain . . . hostess . . . *Elizabeth,* he finally decided, pulled out her flask again and took a few quick gulps of whatever liquid resided within.

It was bound to be sturdy stuff to satisfy such a woman's thirst. She recapped it, shoved it back into its carrier on her low-slung belt, and reached for his arm once more.

Outside the window the fog boiled up into dense clouds, drawing tight against the *Tempest*'s body.

The *Artemesia* was gone, enveloped in the weather its own Conductor cast, and camouflaged against the late-afternoon sky.

Feeling her hand warm on his arm, Rowen did not twist away; he no longer protested. Perhaps she was right. Perhaps Fate or Destiny dragged him from Jordan even though he had come so close. Perhaps his life as a ranking gentleman on the way to military service and a future of security—a future that included Jordan—was already over. He had, after all, seen his best friend murdered and killed a man and several of the Wildkin's Merrow on the way to this very moment.

Jordan most likely hated him. He had failed her by not mounting a timely (or successful) rescue. Why would she want him now?

Things could never go back to what they had been before with the money and the parties and so much promise ahead of him. There was no returning to life as he'd known it when he was simply another cog fitting comfortably in the wheel of Philadelphia's wealthiest society, the social ranks living high on the Hill.

Holgate

Hearing a knock at his door, Councilman Stevenson set down his teacup. He took his time rising from the comfort of his sofa, having decided to take his supper in his personal apartments again, though his gut warned him he should be eating with the other men involved in Weather Working. He should be seated at the high table in the main hall watching the Wardens, Wraiths, and Testers interact, and more importantly, listening to the rumors.

He should be playing this most dangerous of social games.

But he wanted none of the drama, none of the posturing and positioning. He wanted to go home to Philadelphia, to be more involved in the Council. But going home meant returning to his new and young wife, so he stayed in Holgate and frequently dined alone. He opened the door to glare at the watchman disrupting his solitude.

The large man looked down to meet Stevenson's eyes, a ragged scar marking his face in the space between hairline and beard. He shuffled his feet and cleared his throat.

"Well," the Councilman demanded. "Why are you interrupting me?"

"I bring news, my lord. News from Philadelphia."

Stevenson's right eyebrow quirked. "Good or bad news?"

The watchman's jaw went slack, his mouth a vacant space between both beard and mustache. "I—"

"Good God," Stevenson muttered. "It's subjective, one supposes." He growled and the larger man stepped back. "Tell it true. What is this news from Philadelphia?"

"Your stallion?"

Stevenson blinked.

"King's Ransom?"

"Yesss." Stevenson drew the word out. "My stallion, King's Ransom, who is in the care of the military stables under the control of Gregor Burchette, *is* . . ." He tilted his head and leaned in, trying to draw the information out of him.

". . . gone."

"Gone?"

"He has been stolen." The watchman stepped back.

"What?!" Stevenson hopped back as well, his fingers darting into his hair as he tried to keep his brain from bursting out of his skull. "King's Ransom has been stolen?"

"Yes, my lord. Along with one other horse."

Stevenson released his hair and rubbed his forehead instead. "I care nothing for any other horse. King's Ransom is . . . was . . ."

King's Ransom was the only reason he married his new

wife. King's Ransom was the best bit of her dowry. King's Ransom was the reason he tolerated her simpering existence and returned to Philadelphia as often as he did.

"King's Ransom has been stolen," the watchman repeated.

"How could things get any worse?" Stevenson rubbed his forehead. "And what precisely is Gregor Burchette doing to find the horse thief?"

"Lord Burchette has given his assurance that all his men are watching out for the thief and that you will surely receive the justice you deserve."

"Good enough! We all eventually get our just deserts." Closing the door, he muttered once more, "How could things get any worse?"

Aboard the Artemesia

Shuffled aboard the *Artemesia,* Bran had kept a careful eye on his daughter Meggie as well as on Marion Kruse, the only escaped Weather Witch, whose hand wrapped tightly around Meggie's upper arm. Bran and his lover, Maude, followed with quiet caution, knowing the man who controlled the little girl's fate controlled them all.

It seemed to take so little for a Witch to brew a storm: concentration, passion, moisture in the air connecting with the moisture in their body—and it took so much less for a Made Weather Witch, like Marion, to call one element of the weather and cast it.

Anywhere.

Any Weather Witch in living memory Bran Made was quite a commodity.

And quite a liability.

There were reasons Witches were kept under tight government control.

Could they call a storm to dampen rebellious spirits? A simple task used in the May Nativist riots! Bring the rain on only certain days, at certain times, and for preset durations to optimize crop production? Of course. Feed the power of the weather itself into double-terminated quartz storm crystals to act as batteries for everything from lights to hot running water? Yes!

Toss lightning into a government building in protest?

Destroy crops by withholding rain from a region?

Drown an entire town?

Yes.

There were a multitude of reasons to maintain Witches, and even more reasons to maintain control *over* Witches.

Marion Kruse had a more subtle ability than gathering thundering storm clouds. He had a keen understanding of cold. Bran bet the Philadelphia newspapers had nicknamed him the Frost Giant—a man who killed prize-winning roses and most recently a tree near the Council's gallows—killed with a cold that grew from the inside out.

Bran's gaze remained pinned on his kidnapper's hand. Marion could summon a cold so powerful it would freeze the child's heart in her chest. So Bran and Maude kept their heads down and their voices silent. There was no way to win against your abductor if winning meant losing your recently discovered daughter.

Nearby, a masked man, his face hidden beneath the finely wrought carved and painted leather face of a gazelle, horns sweeping out behind him, paused. He brought with him a large and well-adorned trunk on wheels, a carpetbag and two boxes strapped between atop it. At his feet a fox the black of a starless night stopped, her tail curling around his legs.

Even as the crowd pushed their way through the *Artemesia*'s hold toward the grand staircase and their cabins beyond, the masked man was noticeable.

An authoritative voice said, "Come now." Everyone in the liner's bottom level turned toward the speaker, who fell silent and forced a smile when he realized he had been noticed. By a row of windows facing another docked ship the captain stood, his hand on Jordan Astraea's arm much the same way Marion Kruse's hand kept hold of Meggie.

The bag at Bran's side quivered, and, licking lips gone suddenly dry, he slipped a hand into the bag, past his journals, and rested his palm on its curved contents. Sybil's skull remained cool beneath his touch but Meggie jerked up straighter, pale blond curls quivering.

She turned and looked at him. "Papá?" she asked.

He leaned over, whispering into the crown of her head, "What is it, little dove?"

"Someone called my name."

"No," he whispered, blinking. "I heard nothing."

Her eyebrows drew tight together and he chilled when her gaze dropped to his hand hidden in the bag. "Are you certain?"

"Yes, love," he said, choking the words out. "Most certain."

Marion pulled Meggie around, moving from their planned path up the stairs and to their cabin beyond. Instead, he guided Meggie toward the captain and the beleaguered young woman.

Bran closed his eyes a moment, wishing for stillness, for silence, for peace. Did Marion sense what Jordan was? Had they met before? It didn't matter as Bran followed obediently, chin dipped down, eyes on the hem of Meggie's dress and the dangling feet of the stuffed dolly she'd dubbed *Somebunny,* which she kept wrapped in her free arm. Avoiding all eye contact, the last thing Bran Marshall of House Dregard wanted was to be recognized by the captain he had presented a Conductor-in-training to only a brief while ago.

To have any chance as someone other than the Maker, Bran needed to leave Holgate unnoticed—whether at the hands of an abductor or otherwise. The Maker never traveled, that was known by all. If discovered, he would be forced back into Councilman Stevenson's control. But if he shook free of his grim past and survived his association with Marion Kruse long enough to truly know freedom . . .

Marion made his way directly to the captain and Bran drew in on himself, becoming as small, as inconspicuous, as an adult could. Moving forward, quiet and unobtrusive, once one of the most powerful men in the New World, Bran focused on being disinteresting and utterly obedient. Still he noticed they were not the only ones weaving their way through the crowd to reach the captain and the Witch.

The masked man and his sable pet fox also pushed in that direction, arriving at nearly the same time.

Marion, coldhearted and hotheaded, spoke first. "Captain? And who might this disheveled young woman be?" he asked, thrusting his chin toward Jordan, who stood with her back to them all, staring out the window. "Surely not our Conductor . . ."

Bran turned away, hiding his face, and listening.

"Surely not," the captain said with a laugh. "But she is the apprentice *for* Conductor."

"She looks a bit rough." Bran imagined the new voice belonged to the masked man. It was a strong, smooth voice with the quality one expected from an orator or performer—a voice crowds traveled miles to hear.

A pause—perhaps the captain cocked his head, looking the man over. "Do I have a well-reputed illusionist aboard my liner?"

"Is there such a thing as a *well-reputed illusionist*?" the other returned. Bran heard a smile lighten his words.

The captain chuckled. "Has Fortune graced me with the Wandering Wallace?"

"Yet another question that only time may tell," the other teased. "Has Fortune graced you with my presence? We shall see how *graced* you feel when we eventually part ways. Am I the Wandering Wallace? Most definitely I am!"

Someone clapped their hands together, approving the announcement.

"But this Conductor-to-be," the Wandering Wallace continued, "she seems quite . . . unraveled."

The captain sucked a breath back through his teeth. "She ate something disagreeable and should be feeling better soon. She was provided by the Maker himself. And we all know that the Maker Makes marvelous things."

"Hear, hear," Marion responded, his tone dark.

"She will complete her training here? Aboard the very ship I ride?" the Wandering Wallace asked.

"Yes, and quickly, I hope," the captain said.

"I have never seen how such a thing transpires," the Wandering Wallace said. "I have heard rumors, but . . ."

"Rumors are simply that—rumors."

"Would it be too much to ask . . ."

"That you come to watch part of the process? Why, it would be my honor!"

"I would also be fascinated to witness the process," Marion said.

The resulting pause was measured in the rapid throbbing of Bran's heart. He heard and felt nothing else.

The captain's tone changed, stiffened. "Certainly. You and your companions shall join me for supper Topside, so long as the Wandering Wallace promises to entertain us," he added. Another pause. Bran remained entranced by the carpet running the length of the *Artemesia*'s hold. "Good! Then find your cabins, settle your belongings, and have a staff member bring you up. Training a Weather Witch to be a Conductor is quite a thing to see!"

"Of that, I am certain," Marion replied.

The captain led Jordan from the window and Bran's group wound their way to cabin number 145 with little issue and far fewer words. Having few possessions to settle in with (as a good kidnapping seldom allowed one to pack much) they waited for Marion to take them to supper, Bran's bags and their tragic contents never slipping from his shoulder.

Philadelphia

Catrina Hollindale sat with her knees and ankles pressed as tightly together as well-proportioned petticoats allowed in the parlor of her former best friend's home. Her left hand rested neatly in her lap while her right kept her fan twitching to and fro to better properly punctuate the emotion of her words. "And you have heard nothing from Jordan? Nothing at all?"

Lady Astraea sat across the small table from her, a teapot (certainly not Revere's work and, sadly, not even silver) steaming out a blend of floral and herbal scents between them. "No, nary a word," Lady Astraea confirmed. "Oh. Dear me. I do believe I have allowed it to steep too long . . ." she murmured, squinting at the teapot. Her mouth tightened and she reached for the pot's handle, carefully pouring tea into cups for them both.

Cups of lesser-quality china, not even good ironstone, Catrina noted with disdain. It seemed everything about the Astraea household had depreciated since their fall from high society—everything except the extravagant strands of crystals sparkling all over Lady Astraea in a garish display. It seemed more people wore similar jewels of late—far more than last year or the year prior.

Lady Astraea continued her apology, "Chloe used to . . ." She fell quiet and a crease dug into the narrow space between her eyebrows. "Well. I guess I must learn to manage with less. I must learn greater independence as the result of having fewer servants."

"Yes," Catrina agreed, looking around the parlor—empty now of everything but a fallen woman with doubtful taste in jewelry, the remnants of elegant decor going dusty from disinterest, and herself. At least *her* presence brought a sense of class to the place.

The estate once bustled with servants. Before, the household seemed to belong more to the staff than the Astraea family, considering their sheer numbers and the way the servants were treated—nearly like out-of-town cousins come for a visit!

Now there was hardly a maid to be found.

But, if Jesus Christ could sit among prostitutes and tax collectors then Catrina Hollindale, ranked Fourth of the

Nine, could pass a little time with the devastated Lady Astraea.

"I am certain Jordan will become a fine Conductor and live out an adventurous life in the skies high above us. Had you not Harbored her, things might be quite different now. Surely you knew . . . Why not turn her over to the authorities?"

Through her sniffling, Lady Astraea straightened. "She is no Witch, Catrina. That much you must know, as close as you both were. And . . . Even if she had been—the idea of giving up one's child . . . What sort of a parent would do such a monstrous thing?"

Catrina swallowed and glanced away. "I could not believe it myself," she assured her. "Though, what is it they say? The best liars maintain the deepest secrets?"

"She was—*is*—neither liar nor Witch. We did not Harbor. Things would be far different if they had not falsely accused her. We expected Rowen to ask for her promise that night."

The tea went bitter in Catrina's mouth. She swallowed. "Oh. One cannot be sure of the intentions of a boy like that," she warned. "Your Jordan may be much better off where she is. You do know Rowen is wanted by the law?"

"No! I have heard so little true news since the party. You, dear girl, are one of very few who still call upon us. *Me,*" she corrected. "You are one of very few who still call upon *me*. And I am *so* very grateful for your company."

Catrina inclined her head and forced a smile before she continued. "I should tell you: Rowen Burchette is wanted for murder. Dueling, to be precise."

"Why, whatever would have sparked such a passionate response within Rowen? What could he possibly argue over to get entangled in a duel?"

Catrina flicked her fan open wide, proclaiming, "I have absolutely no idea. So you have not seen him either? Have received no word of him?" She leaned closer, her fan causing the steam to swirl and dance out from the broad teapot's spout.

Lady Astraea shook her head. "I have not seen Rowen since the night Jordan was dragged away. I do hope he is faring well, no matter where he is."

Catrina's golden curls bobbed as she nodded. "I as well."

"May both Jordan and Rowen fare well."

Catrina nodded again.

"And may Fate bring them together once more."

Catrina blinked, regarding her teacup in silence.

"And your parents?" Lady Astraea asked. "How are your parents? They've been gone so very long, it seems."

Catrina immediately brightened. "Oh, they are keeping quite well."

Lady Astraea smiled.

Chapter Two

I beheld the wretch—the miserable monster
whom I had created.
—MARY WOLLSTONECRAFT SHELLEY

Aboard the Artemesia

At what seemed the very top of the world the *Artemesia*'s captain greeted his supper guests with a broad grin and a wave in the direction of two well-stocked tables. One was long and rectangular, the other (only a short distance from the foot of the first) was small and round. Stormlight lanterns lined the larger of the two, their bright and steady glow a testament to the Conductor who created the weather and through his witchery fed the ship its power.

"Do sit, do sit!" the captain urged them. "The soup is on its way and the worst thing is when hot soup catches a chill."

As if at his mention a breeze swept around the ship's body and ran a soft caress around the edges of both their collars and their shirt sleeves to better hurry them to the table where their Christian names were neatly written on tiny cards. They settled into their places.

"The *Artemesia* is one of the oldest ships in the fleet. She's seen service in both war and peacetime. Some even say she has a personality all her own," the captain said, stomping his boot down hard on the wood planks. He laughed. "If you ask me, though, I'd say she's just bits of wood and metal destined to eventually end in a destructive tumble. But for now, she is well captained and well Conducted." The captain raised an elegantly carved cut-crystal goblet to toast to the company he'd gathered. "To my most illustrious guests: the Wandering Wallace and his remarkable companion Miyakitsu, Marion Erendell—"

Bran startled hearing the wrong last name used for Marion, but it was sensible he would not travel under his real surname. No wanted man would dare. No escapee from Holgate's Tanks and Tower would risk being returned. Especially no man who evaded capture for years and had begun slyly harassing the wealthy inhabitants of Philadelphia's Hill.

The captain introduced both Meggie and Maude, also under fabricated surnames, and said, "And the most amazing of all my guests to date—the Maker himself, Bran Marshall of House Dregard!"

Bran's heart stopped. He swallowed—it seemed an uncomfortably long time for a motion made in so short a space as a throat—and he tried to regain his composure knowing even more certainly that he was a dead man.

Marion Kruse might not murder him after all—not if Councilman Stevenson found out where he was and got to him first.

Having the Maker aboard an airship was quite the coup. There would be talk.

The captain leaned over him, punching his shoulder, and

said, "Did you truly think I would not recognize you? Yet have no fear! I understand why young men often go abroad under false names." He winked in Maude's direction. Even in her Sunday best it was apparent Bran outranked her. The story of her birthright was written in the less delicate features of her face and the humble way she presented herself. "Some adventure is best to be had with a little less truth to muddy the fun."

Seething at the implications, which, although accurate, should not be brought up in polite conversation, Bran forced himself to maintain a smile.

To be obedient.

Bread was brought to the table, dense and dark and full of bits of grain. "Lamb's head soup," the server announced, ladling the rich-smelling broth out of a large white ironstone dish another servant carried. A fruity-smelling wine was poured for some, and a weak ale for others.

Often reserved for the Witches, here water was presented for diners as well—giving the impression it was from a well-regarded spring.

"Ah, yes," the captain said, noting Bran's interest. "We are the first to serve Ricker's Waters straight from Maine. They seem to have curative properties—that is if you ask Hiram Ricker himself, of course."

Curative or not, the water tasted remarkably clean and fresh.

Bran and the others consumed a lovely meal many men would have appreciated both in fare and in the company. But not many men found themselves in Bran Marshall's predicament.

The wind trembled across his arm, racing down his sleeve and over his knuckles to cool the soup in his spoon.

Lightning flashed overhead, illuminating the fob and watch chain that ran from buttonhole to pocket and made his waistcoat sparkle with the sizzle of illumination. The expected boom of thunder was muffled, a nearly omnipresent purr in the distance, held at bay by the power of the ship's Conductor for the pleasure of the passengers.

The Maker of Weather Witches, and a relatively obliging hostage, Bran nodded from his velvet-upholstered chair on the broad wooden platform that denoted "Topside" on the airship. He bobbed his head when the conversation's tone changed significantly and did his best to look as if he listened, while truly, he kept his eyes on the others numbered among the captain's guests for this evening's dinner.

To his immediate right sat Marion, tall and twenty-one or twenty-two years of age, slim and broad-shouldered with a mop of dark curls softening his perpetual scowl. On Marion's knee he dandled Meggie, Bran's newly discovered "nearly six years old" daughter. Her mother dead, Bran was practically all she had.

And vice versa.

Seeing her in the grasp of a Witch . . .

Bran killed the thought, unable to consider all Witches the same now he knew at least one Witch should have been impossible to Make, and that his only daughter—his dear little dove—was a Witch as well.

The bag hanging off the back of his chair shifted, contents rattling, and Meggie stiffened where she sat as if someone far away shouted for her attention. The soup in Bran's bowl popped with tiny bubbles and his water effervesced. He choked down the spoonful of soup, chased it with water, and reloaded his spoon as if in self-defense.

The child, Sybil, might be dead, but her skull gave lively

reminders of her past existence. He would give her skull a permanent resting place as soon as he could. He had promised that much and he would keep his promise.

The bubbles popped, dissipating.

Leaning forward for a piece of the still steaming hearty brown bread, Bran slid his gaze down the table and around Marion and Meggie to meet the eyes of the plump and previously jovial Maude, his lover and fellow kidnap victim. He mouthed, "I promised to take you on a grand adventure," in her direction.

Her lips fell into a sad smile and she inclined her head. This was not what either of them had imagined. Of course, it was only recently that he had imagined Maude returning to his life at all.

Marion reached in front of him for the salt, knocking Bran away with the force of his glare.

Bran sat back, pulling his bread apart bit by bit and speculating on the couple seated across the table from him: the Wandering Wallace and Miyakitsu.

The man, long of leg and with the supple grace of a professional dancer, wore a strangely twisted lion's-face mask constructed of leather and metal, its jaw articulated with tiny springs and gears so it moved up and down in mimicry of his own mouth. He consumed bread, he downed the wine that filled and refilled his crystal goblet, and he had more than his share of the soup that the serving girl ladled into their bowls.

Bran tilted his head to observe him more discreetly from beneath strands of his own blond hair. He doubted anyone knew what the Wandering Wallace looked like behind the mask and the hood that attached to the crown of its head, trailing down his neck and throat to his collar. Bran could tell little of him, not his facial features, not his hair's true color or style.

Certainly not his age.

The Wandering Wallace carried himself like a man who had seen it all and done most of what he had seen. But experience seldom equated to age.

His stature and array of haunting masks made the Wandering Wallace recognizable. Few types of people wore masks as regularly, and all of those types made Bran twitch. Seeing people's faces, identifying them—meant you could find them.

Bran's eyes dropped to stare at the Wandering Wallace's fingers. Hands offered clues to a person's age or livelihood, much like a person's neck or the areas around their eyes. The Wandering Wallace's hands were nearly smooth except for a fine down of light hair on the back of each hand and knuckle.

Bran glanced at his own hands. At twenty-six, his hands were already much more lined than the other man's—the other *younger* man's.

His gaze slid away from the Wandering Wallace to Marion's hand, resting on Meggie's ribs. Judging by hands alone, the Wandering Wallace was younger than Marion, too. He thought briefly of other hands he'd taken note of—men's hands—and their ages.

The bread in his mouth crumbled, dry, and he struggled to swallow. Hands were such telltale and fragile things . . . especially the hands of a musician.

He looked away, thinking of the young pianoforte player in the Tanks at Holgate, subject to whatever treatment those in Bran's stead deemed worthwhile. *Caleb.* He'd had the most elegant and perfectly shaped hands and fingers—masterpieces that looked as if designed by God to make nothing but fine music.

Fingers the Maker had taken exquisite care to methodically destroy so the boy would embrace his abilities as a Weather Witch. Nothing had worked. Now the boy's life was much like Bran's own life: far beyond his control.

But those fingers—before Bran had gotten to them—looked remarkably like those of the man seated across from him now. The man who, based on the tilt of his head, knew he was being watched. His pose mimicked Bran's, adding to it the subtle twist of a smile obscured by the mouth of the mask, frozen in a snarling roar yet mobile. The Wandering Wallace shook out his mane, long locks of differently colored yarn and ribbon intermingling and catching in the breeze.

Beside Wallace, small enough to be mistaken for barely a woman, was the brunette beauty who clung to him like his shadow. Her eyes were filled with stars—like the universe had fallen into two dark pools and lived there, planets spinning, surrounded by a forest of long lashes. She was surely the Wandering Wallace's wife . . .

Though they rode an airship and Bran was certainly not traveling with a woman who was legally bound to him . . .

He wondered about their arrangement—not that it changed anything between him and Maude; still, he was curious. He had not yet even heard her speak. Where had she come from? Surely the Far East, thanks to some trade or religious mission, or . . . He looked back at the Wandering Wallace, searching his masked face for some clue.

Military mission?

The Wandering Wallace pulled his linen napkin from off his lap, rubbed it between his hands, and dabbed both corners of his mouth with it. The fabric was blotched with dark spots of broth and wine, but the Wandering Wallace deftly folded the linen into the shape of a bird. His lion's head tilted, he speculated a moment before he tossed the napkin overhead, declaring, "That one's dirty, may I have a fresh one, please?" The napkin held its place in midair before exploding into shadow-filled wings that sprouted black feathers, and, bristling, a raven darted away.

The serving girl reappeared, her mouth flat, expression absolutely unimpressed, and she shook out a perfectly white napkin to replace the Wandering Wallace's previous one.

Graciously he took it and, grinning, responded, "I'd wager you lose more linens that way . . ."

She snorted, and Bran tilted his head. It was an odd reaction for a servant girl to have when dealing with the guest of a captain. The girl spun on her heel and stalked off to stand, waiting, by the wheeled cart that held every need the kitchen staff could anticipate for a grand dinner Topside.

"Not everyone is fond of trickery," the Wandering Wallace stated, looking to the young woman at his side. "Nor of illusion, are they, Miyakitsu?"

She shook her head, long black tresses glowing in the lightning that formed a flickering net around the ship, weaving about their vessel with a system of living light.

"I must say, Maker . . ." The captain addressed him directly, and Bran pulled his attention into a more narrow focus to listen. "I had no idea you would be a passenger on the *Artemesia.* Why, to hear the boys below tell it, you've never ridden an airship, you merely provide us our most valuable power source!"

Bran glanced at Marion and the little girl balanced on his knee. So blond her hair was nearly silver, she had a heart-shaped face and big eyes that took in everything.

Much the child's senior, Marion also drank in the details, controlling every action of his three unwilling guests like a puppet master tugging strings. He dipped his head in a small nod and the Maker spoke.

He chose his words carefully even in common conversation. "I rode an airship once as a boy. But Making is a tedious and taxing business and a Maker seldom has time for vacation."

"True, true," the captain agreed, "more the reason to be glad when Lightning's Kiss yields a Warden or a Wraith. Leave the Gathering to them and the Testers and focus on what needs your skill set so someday you might go on a grand adventure!" He opened his arms wide to envelop the entire journey.

"Yes," Bran agreed. "One never knows when travel might beckon." His gaze drifted back to Marion.

The Frost Giant's eyes were as cold as the bits of the weather he so easily summoned.

Bran dropped his gaze, again raising the spoon to his mouth and swallowing its contents. Its warmth did nothing to lessen the chill crawling through his innards at the captain's mention of his special skills. Would the captain, so merrily supping on fresh bread and soup, be so cheerful if he knew what talents Bran readily employed to Make a Witch? If Bran told him about his selection of fine blades, or his cat—Bran fought to keep the soup down—would he approve of his violent methodology? Would anyone outside the Council members controlling the Weather Workers approve?

Aboard the Tempest

Rowen followed Elizabeth up the stairs from the cargo bay and through a hatch in its ceiling. They emerged in a curving hallway far narrower than the bay below. He turned, looking behind him. "It encircles the entire ship?"

"Aye, nearly," Elizabeth said, smiling. "It enrobes nearly the lower third of the ship in three levels—all above the cargo bay. And, note the doors to our right?"

He nodded, noting in particular how no two doors matched.

"Cabins, closets, and assorted other necessary spaces, including the map room and library." She paused, again taking a sip from her flask. It would have been in good taste to offer some of whatever she was drinking to him, too, but it seemed the thought never crossed her mind.

Perhaps pirates simply did not share.

"A library?" Rowen asked, squinting.

Elizabeth rolled her eyes. "Just because we are liberally aligned traders does not mean we are uneducated or uncivilized. The thing that most accurately demonstrates a person's cultural value is the quality of that person's library. Here," she motioned for him to follow, "see this?"

Portholes were spaced at fair distances one from the other all along the inner wall.

"This is the true beauty of the *Tempest,*" Elizabeth confided, bending to peer through the thick glass of the nearest porthole. She wiggled a finger at him and he leaned close, looking through the same window. "The Mech Deck." Light drifted and swayed inside the dimly lit room, giving Rowen the sickening impression everything he saw was sunk in a large lake.

He braced himself, having only been underwater once before. He would never be caught that way again. That dare hadn't been taken in a water body where Merrow—slinking and supple beasts leading the Wildkin War—swam, but the Merrow had allies. Swaying under the memory's force, he shut his eyes a moment, condemning the thought to the darkest regions of his mind.

When he opened his eyes, Elizabeth was staring at him.

He looked back into the heart of the Mech Deck. In its center sat a large, glowing metal box bristling with tubes, rotors, and gauges. They shot out of it, joining with pipes aplenty, soaring and snaking into the surrounding walls, ceiling, and floor. The faint scent of smoke set Rowen's nerves jangling. Deep inside him something primal stirred, insisting there should not be fire on a ship, not on *any* type of ship, neither water- nor airborne.

Elizabeth leaned so close Rowen smelled mint on her breath. "*That* there's the truth of the *Tempest*'s magick," she confided. "And an excellent reason for our kind and the government to be at odds. We have the thing they want us least to know about, and we know how to hide it and hide it well."

Two men flanked the stove; one sporting large green goggles leaned over and yanked the metal box's door open. Orange light poured out, and even at a distance Rowen stepped back. Vents hidden in the Mech Deck's side walls whispered open, releasing the sudden flood of heat.

Flanking the stove, the men improvised a rhythmic chant as they loaded it with coal. Rowen pressed his ear to the glass and, closing his eyes, listened.

The *Tempest* is our vessel
The sky is our domain
Our mission just to live our lives
And seek out better days

We ride the winds that carry us
Wherever we intend

And shun the war and miseries
That plague all them on land.

"We have steam power," Elizabeth announced. "And the wits to hide that fact from the authorities. No one aboard *my* ship is enslaved."

"Just kidnapped," he reminded her.

A grin slid across her face. "Shanghaied. Crimped, Impressed," she corrected. "Fair enough. But I daresay this is one of the finest crews to be taken by. Until the vomiting ensues." She shrugged, and, turning away from him, opened a box built into a recess in the nearby wall. Unfolding a metal handle topped with a small wooden knob, she gave it a crank. She spoke into a horn mouthpiece, asking, "What's our altitude?"

The men standing by the ship's hot, glowing heart leaned around the stove, glancing at a system of gauges and dials and then the taller of them jogged to the wall. "Just about right," he shouted into a similar device.

Even though she was out of their sight, she gave a quick nod of approval, adding, "Keep her clear of other ships if you can, boys—saves me a headache." Uncapping the flask, she took another drink.

"We'll do our best," he returned.

The smaller of the two adjusted his goggles and shouted, "We'll direct-line you if there's a need for cover."

"Good enough," she said. She flipped the handle flush, closing it back into the box. "Follow me."

Opening a wide blue door with two white panels, she ducked out of the hall and into a nearby room. Rowen's curiosity piqued, he followed.

Inside, Elizabeth stood before an open window through which a rope ladder extended, its lowest portion pinned beneath a decorated plank that clamped onto the floor with grandly molded brass fittings.

From there, the rest of the rope ladder extended out and *up.*

Elizabeth slipped a leg out the window and, resting her rump on the windowsill, leaned out and reached around, grabbing the ropes.

"We're going to climb . . . ?"

In answer, she began, hand over hand, to climb up, until she was completely out of his sight.

He went to the window and looked up, his hands tight on the window's frame.

"Grab a ratline and come along," she called, waving an encouraging hand. "There's a great deal more to be seen before I settle you into your quarters."

He grabbed a vertical line of rope.

She laughed. "That's a shroud, not a ratline."

"I'm getting to it," he growled, snagging one of the thinner horizontal ropes.

Thinner.

Rowen was suddenly aware of every bit of his bulk and, for the first time ever, was glad he had not eaten recently.

The ladder shifted in his grasp.

"It takes a little getting used to," she told him, "but surely a man of your fine form can climb. Unless heights scare you . . ." The last phrase an obvious tease, still Rowen responded by hefting himself up the ladder, and not—no, *not at all*—looking down.

The air rolled around him, tickling the hair on his face as if a gentle hand ran across it. He had climbed more than his share of trees as a boy. But no tree he'd climbed soared so high. Nor had any of the trees slipped loose as if ready to throw him to the distant ground if he took a single misstep.

Or sneezed.

The ladder shimmied across the fabric of the big blue-and-white balloon like a springy trellis. It slid only inches, but a few inches on an airship could equate to a fall of a thousand feet or much more, he imagined, to the ground below.

His stomach lurched.

Rowen kept his neck craned back so he was only looking up, but that had disadvantages. Peering up the ladder meant looking directly at Elizabeth's rump as it continued its merry ascent, giving a far different impression in breeches than in a skirt. He had never seen a woman's rump so clearly displayed while clothed—never seen one so close to wearing nothing and yet so definitely wearing just the perfect amount of *something.*

Tavern girls wore layers of skirts and petticoats that left much to the imagination. It wasn't as if he had never seen the rear parts of a woman unencumbered by clothing—he *was* eighteen. Still, he cleared his throat, distracted to be faced with a woman's rump so prominently displayed.

He tried looking beyond the back end of her—farther up the ladder that hissed against the fabric of the massive balloon.

She loosened her grip, looking down at him again. "Have a care," she warned.

He froze, seeing they were only halfway to the top, the ladder disappearing over the curving apex high above them, and he realized how insubstantial their cords were in relation to the rest of the construction of the airship. The *Tempest* was a floating mammoth. Both hands clutching the same rung, he hung there, doing his best to breathe and hang on. Hanging on seemed more important than breathing, and closing his eyes, he concentrated.

On *not* thinking.

It was usually not a difficult task for Rowen. On *not* thinking.

She shouted from somewhere above him, her voice light and silly for the captain she seemed to be. "What's the problem, boy? What are you—a cat stuck in a tree?"

He felt the ladder shift again and heard the rhythmic creaking of the ropes as she approached him.

"Well, darling, it seems you have again been taken by surprise. Stunned to stopping! Here, attach this to yourself."

A cord slipped between his arms and slapped against his boots.

"Can't," he grunted, staring so hard at the balloon's silk he was certain he could count the individual threads.

"Scared stiff, are you?"

The ropes shivered. "Stay steady, boy, hold tight," she said. "I'm coming for you." Her boots passed into the constricted range of his vision, and then her legs and rump, her back, and finally the back of her head was flush with his nose.

"Keep a tight hold, we're about to become a bit more closely acquainted," she warned as she took the slack cable in one hand and turned on the ladder, hooking the heels of her boots in a ratline.

Her chest pressed against his and her arms encircled his waist as she wrapped the cable around him.

He squeaked when she ran the cable between his legs—twice!—and looped it back around his waist, cinching the entire system tight.

"Now you're secure," she said, her breath brushing his ear. "Keep calm and climb on."

He nodded and she spun in the space between his arms and ascended again.

He swallowed hard and pried the fingers of his right hand open, pulling them free long enough to snap them shut on the next ratline up.

"Atta boy—not much farther!" she encouraged.

He worked his way up the last yards of rope by staring at the balloon's fabric and willing himself to keep going for more than the sake of mere safety—for the sake of what was left of his pride.

He'd wrecked his honor in Philadelphia and nearly lost his life. But here they only knew him by what he did and how he acted. Here he might regain some of what he'd lost for Jordan's sake. Here he might reinvent himself and be something more.

Or at least be someone different.

If Elizabeth never mentioned this display to anyone else. He was even more thankful he hadn't given her any other reason to devise a new name for him.

He could impress the crew. At least the captain . . .

If only he kept reaching, kept climbing. Up. And up. And—

Her hand was in his face, reaching out to help him span the last bit. He took it, astonished by the power of her grasp and the strength in her arm as she hauled him onto a platform.

Her eyes searched his face. "Here." She grabbed his hand and placed it on a brass railing that ran the majority of the platform's perimeter. "Steady yourself a minute before we proceed."

"*Proceed*?" he asked, his eyes widening.

"Yes. Of course. Why did you think I'd bring you all this way if not to let you explore all of Topside?"

"For amusement," he snapped, not meeting her eyes.

She snorted. "You're far too pretty to be so bitter so young," she said.

Rowen ignored the statement, caught his breath, and brought the world into focus, slowly raising his gaze.

"This is it," she proclaimed, taking her hat off to shake her hair free and throw her arms wide. "This is the biggest lie we tell the government. And the only lie that keeps us free to be the way we wish and do the things we want." She spun on the deck, her hair falling free and flaring out around her and, brilliant in the slanting rays of the sun. She stopped suddenly, pointing to a woman who moved the gears and wheels and levers of the ship, Conducting its every move.

His breath caught and he staggered a few steps forward, his eyes darting from the deck's edge to the figure moving and jerking along at the whim of the ship—a woman tied—*bound*—to the ship.

Enslaved.

"You said no one was . . ." He stopped, swinging back to Elizabeth, aghast.

"Look again."

He leaned forward, squinting. Strings shot out from the hands and head of the woman and Rowen realized it was not the woman steering the ship at all, but rather the *ship* pulling, tugging, and yanking the woman about in an awkward parody of living movement.

He blinked, and laughed so hard he bent over and held his knees. "You have steam power hidden beneath the facade of a Conductor!"

"Aye. Is not Tara the finest puppet ever?"

Again Rowen laughed, looking back at the human-sized mannequin. "They wouldn't know unless they were nearly upon you. But then . . . How do you get enough lift to get away from docks—to get out of view and wait to start the steam engine? That early fog—the cloud cover . . ."

She chuckled, took a sip from her flask, replaced it on her hip, and put her two hands out before him. Something shimmered between her palms and wisps like cotton formed. A cloud grew there, cupped loosely in her grasp, and then she threw her arms open. The cloud split and skittered across the deck to pop off its edges and launch into the air. Lightning flashed and the little cloud swelled into a thunderhead, sizzling and popping before dissolving back into a clear sky. Elizabeth's already impossible grin spread farther and she bowed before him, saying as she rose, "Welcome to Topside on the *Tempest*! This is only the *beginning* of our potential!"

Aboard the Artemesia

The door's lock clicked, turning, and two guards entered Jordan's modest room, each dressed in the *Artemesia*'s signature crew colors of royal blue and gold, crisp jackets spanning strong arms and broad chests. Nearly matched in height, they wore short-crowned blue top hats. The darker-haired man with his carefully trimmed beard and drooping mustache stood an inch or two taller than the man with mousy hair who slouched beside him, holding something the same blue as the crew uniforms.

"Mouse" threw the wad of fabric onto Jordan's narrow bed, following it with a rumpled hat, saying, "Clean up and change. Be quick about it."

The taller one tipped his hat at her and they both stepped back out of the room, closing the door and turning their backs to the small window in her door to allow her some privacy.

The moment the door shut, Jordan reached into her neckline and pulled out the tiny blue crystal she'd found in the drain of her cell in Holgate. Her brow furrowed as she turned it to catch the scant light afforded in her room by the ship-powered stormcell lantern. In the crystal's depths light flickered, shimmering like a butterfly testing its wings. It was lovely, but she sensed it was not for her to keep. Holding the sparkling gem, Jordan slipped out of her golden ball gown, its edges frayed and its beauty savaged by filth and harsh wear.

She poured water from a pitcher on a stand in her room into a nearly matching basin, setting the tiny crystal down by the basin's bottom. Her space aboard ship might be nowhere as grand as her rooms on Philadelphia's Hill, but it was far finer than the straw-strewn floor of Tank 5 at Holgate. She snatched up a small towel they'd provided her and dabbed it into the cool water, wiping off her face and hands and then the more private bits of her before she wrung out the towel in the water and worked on her feet. She had tried to stay somewhat clean in the Tanks by using the water from the bucket she, as a member of the Grounded population, did not need for Drawing Down.

But if cleanliness was next to godliness, then God kept far from Holgate's Tanks.

"Hurry up," Mouse shouted, banging on the door.

She jumped, dropping the towel into the basin, where it muddied the water. Jordan wrinkled her nose and, shrugging into the provided blue gown, looked back at the pitcher. There was no time to wash her hair so she smoothed it with damp hands, tucking wisps behind her ears and doing her best to wrap it into a tamed mess. She looked at the provided hat. Wide-brimmed blue straw, a touring hat with a fitted satin crown, it had been beautiful once.

She sighed. Now its ostrich feathers drooped and the large satin bow was faded from sun. With no hatpin, the odds of keeping it on her head were not good. Still she pressed it over her unruly hair and retrieved the stormcell crystal and slipped it into her neckline.

Her basin of water full and filthy, she paused. On the Hill the servants either threw washwater out the window or carried it to the privy and dumped it. But, on an airship? She glanced at the windows in the room's sky-facing wall. "What do I do with the water?"

"Oh, for Christ's sake," Mouse muttered, shoving through the doorway and snatching the basin. He strode to the window, grabbed a hooked handle at its edge, and cranked the window open, sloshing water against both window and wall, but mostly into the cloud-filled sky. He turned, setting the basin down with a *thump,* and grabbed Jordan by the arm.

The other guard—she decided to call him Stache because of his most noticeable feature—stepped forward, resting his hand atop the other man's hand. "She is only a girl."

Mouse pulled away, rolling up to his full height. They were matched after all. Jordan shrank back but Stache stood his ground while Mouse spat out, "You *must* be new. She is no *girl.* She is merely a Weather Witch—not even a *Conductor.*"

The two squared off, gazes locked.

Jordan whispered, "I need shoes," and their attention snapped to her again.

"You won't need them where you're going, *Witch,*" Mouse snarled.

"Where am I going that I do not need shoes?"

"To supper."

Stache blinked but said, in a low and even tone, "Someone will be sent to get you shoes. Later. We must not be late," he explained. For a moment Jordan thought he sounded apologetic.

She ducked her head and allowed Mouse to take her arm again, leading her out of her cabin and into the narrow hall.

A door across the hall from hers opened, sliding like the pocket door leading to the linen closet in her family home. After shoving her inside, the guards squeezed in beside her. The door shut, confining them in a warm darkness. The entire room lurched, beginning its rumbling way up. Not many Witches could say they'd ridden in an elevator.

And only Jordan could accurately claim the elevator in her home—metal and glimmering glass—was far finer than the one in the airship *Artemesia.* But riding the tight elevator Topside, she remembered that the promises her future once held meant nothing now. Not here.

Above them the ceiling pulled apart; air and a soft light seeped through the opening it left. They continued up, Jordan glimpsing the glossy Topside deck first at eye level and then, in a moment, the floor of the elevator drew flush to the polished wood of the deck and all that remained of the elevator were three seemingly misplaced walls.

Jordan of the fallen House Astraea, a freshly Made Weather Witch, was escorted onto the deck.

To her right was a raised wooden platform surrounded on three sides by wooden posts capped by a sweeping railing and topped at each corner with stormlights. In its midst stood a dark-skinned man with straight hair cropped short and as black as the stormclouds he called. His eyes half-closed in a strange state of ecstasy, the hint of a smile twisted his mouth. His hands moved in jerky motions, fingers flicking out at odd intervals to send cogs turning, wheels flying, and a dozen different spinning devices chattering in their orbits as a storm burgeoned around and beneath them, encircling them in a nest of blackening and roiling clouds.

Before him was a large capped glass tube filled with clear liquid and crystals that looked like suspended snowflakes, and behind the Conductor was mounted the largest stormcell crystal Jordan had ever seen. The size of her fist, it balanced atop a metal-wrapped wooden post mounted in a thorny crown of jutting copper and silver wires. Jordan froze, mesmerized by the lines of light glittering in its faceted depths.

The Conductor reached a hand into the air, snaring a snap of lightning that made Jordan jump, and turning, he opened his fist and pressed the living light into the crystal, where it danced, trapped.

He summoned the storm to feed the stone . . . There was a brief flash of light and the large crystal dulled faintly, but all the other stormlights brightened.

Jordan blinked, understanding. The Conductor grew the storm to feed its energy into the crystal and disperse it through the ship in a Pulse.

Mouse grunted and pushed her forward, but not before she saw one last detail of the workings on the dais: the man who perched on the rail behind the sparkling stone and its webwork of wires, a man who rested the snout of a gun on a stand and yawned, judging every move the Conductor made.

The Conductor powered the airship, but he did not set its course, that right was the captain's. Nor did the Conductor guarantee he followed the course. That job belonged to the sniper at his back.

As there were layers of ranks, so there were layers to the power structure aboard an airship.

A place for all was more than their young country's motto.

Jordan mistepped as the ship bobbed, and Stache reached out, steadying her. She heard a growl and a grind and glimpsed the ends of the the *Artemesia*'s wings as they popped into another position. The sails spanning their steel-and-wooden fingers snapped taut, filling with air.

The stormlights mounted on top of each Topside banister post and lining the skeletal metal-and-wooden frame of the wings shined star-bright, building a constellation in the thickening dark.

Led to the smaller of the two tables, Jordan waited as Stache tugged the table forward, and Mouse shoved Jordan onto a chair that would have toppled had it not been bolted into place. A belt was run around her waist and cinched tight, pulling her snug against the chair's back. Mouse snatched her right hand and slipped a leather strap around that wrist; no, Jordan realized, not a strap but a slender belt. He adjusted it so it was tight on her wrist, and Stache did the same to her left.

Then both guards dropped to their knees and raised the hem of her dress.

Jordan shouted and everyone at the table turned to look at her. Her eyes narrowed, seeing the Maker there, so near the head of the more finely adorned table. She kicked when she felt a man's hand grab her calf.

A curse answered when she connected with a guard's

head. "Hold her," Mouse growled to Stache, and she felt another belt snare one ankle and they switched their grip and repeated the action.

The whole while she stared straight ahead, her gaze skimming the array of fine foods, hard as the glint coming off the ironstone dishes and polished stormlights. It was as cruel as she could make it, and her gaze latched to the Maker's face.

He looked away.

At the table's head the captain stood, one hand raised for the guards' attention. "Welcome, Witch," he said. "I am Captain Kerdin. This will be where you mark your days from henceforth. This will be where you spend your time and energy, and you will come to know this ship as well as any lover you might have someday had." He dropped his hand and Mouse pressed down on a lever. The hiss of leather across metal sounded and Jordan yelped as her hand was yanked suddenly to the right, knocking her tankard to the floor.

"But, as relationships inevitably are in the beginning, there will most assuredly be awkward moments." He walked around the table, coming to stand just between her table and theirs. "You are now connected to the *Artemesia,* your hands her wings, your feet her rudder and bowsprit. As she moves, so will you."

Jordan's hand whipped back and cleared the table of her silverware.

There was a gasp and Jordan recognized the child, Meggie.

"Keep your hands high," the captain instructed. "Pay attention and try to feel the shifts before they happen. Try to sense them, anticipate them—and soon enough the power will shift and you will *control* them. And here—" He produced a hatpin, securing her hat to her head. "You may have this. But only here." He motioned to a man standing stiffly by the server's cart and the man lifted a violin and began to play. The captain smiled, dancing his way back to his seat. "And mind you," he said over his shoulder, "this is the simplest stage of your training. This is the basis of all Conducting."

She stared at her wrists, blinking back the moisture burning at the edges of her eyes.

Her lower lip stuck out, quivering, as she tried to do what he said. She pressed her shoulders back and lifted her hands, doing her best to look somehow appropriate for dinner even dressed in the recently acquired blue gown with its worn and threadbare hems and edges. This dress was a far cry from the original elegance of her golden gown, but this dress . . .

At least this dress was not the trap the last one had been.

Everything *else* here was the trap.

Jordan listened to the air around her—the breeze that stilled and stormed at strange intervals and seemed sometimes a reaction to the mighty ship's wings and sometimes a result of the raising of them. She reached for the tankard, which had been righted and refilled, and nearly had it before her hand was whisked away again, only the tips of her fingernails making contact with the tankard's handle.

The Wandering Wallace rose, carrying a tripod with a box mounted on it. Jordan recognized a camera obscura—her family had a portrait made by one.

He stood it by the table, pointed the machine's capped lens at the diners. Except for Jordan. "Everyone please stay still," he requested as he removed the cap. "Dear Conductor," he called to the man who was ever in motion, "might I trouble you for sunlight?"

The Conductor and captain exchanged glances. "Set her to glide," the captain said.

The Conductor moved to the side of the dais, throwing his weight behind a large lever to thrust it forward. Jordan jumped as the ship's gigantic wings fully unfurled with a boom that outstripped the muffled thunder. The clouds overhead peeled away and sunlight slanted in to brighten Topside beyond the power of its bright stormcell crystals.

The Wandering Wallace stepped around the camera obscura and again sat beside his woman, looping an arm around her shoulders. She smiled and he said, "Perfect! Everyone smile and look at the lens. This will only take a minute . . . or seven . . ."

The diners and even the violinist stayed still, posing, while the machine caught the sun's rays. Only Jordan and the Conductor kept moving—and she knew that meant only she and the Conductor would be excluded from the picture. If they were caught at all in the image they would seem to be ghosts. She took the time to eat a few bites.

"That should do right well," the Wandering Wallace said, moving back to reclaim the device. "Thank you for indulging me."

The captain threw his hand into the air and the Conductor dragged the lever back with a grunt, adjusting the wings. He raised his eyes to the hole in the clouds and Jordan thought she heard him sing something as the hole was stitched shut and they were again entirely enclosed in the brewing storm.

Before Jordan the violinist picked up playing again, his music punctuated by the constant and varying click-click, clatter, and whir of mechanics from the Conductor on his raised dais behind her as he powered the storm and all within the ship through the large and glittering stormcell behind him, tweaking the movement of the ship that threatened to draw and quarter his eventual replacement.

Philadelphia

John finished his work as quickly as he could after Laura had come to him with her concerns about Lady Astraea's behavior. His first stop hadn't been to clean up after a long day of tending the yard and moving things of significant size, but to find Laura and make his way to Lady Astraea's room with an appropriate escort.

Laura surprised him with the announcement that her ladyship was occupied hosting a guest for a late tea, as the woman no longer had much appetite even for supper. It was strange. Nearly no one called on a household fallen from grace. Few people bothered with the Astraea household at all. No deliveries were made—not ice, not milk . . .

A small crew of servants that remained, stubbornly against Lord Astraea's wishes, gathered everything in from the markets—either from the market that ran by day featuring fresh fruit and vegetables or the Night Market, which specialized in darker and more dangerous fare. The staff accepted a cut in already modest wages, but they had good beds for sleeping and fair quantities of food filling their bellies. That was more than many of his kind could boast of. A freed African in Philadelphia, John knew that though things seemed bad, they could be far worse. So John, and a select few members of the staff, stayed on.

Laura turned the key, opening Lady Astraea's door for him. He stepped inside the room—the first time since he'd climbed up the treacherous rose trellis with her ladyship slung unconscious over his back. The night of her reanimation he had slipped her into bed, closed her in for safety's sake, and sought out Laura. His original and most well-versed coconspirator in the saving of her life had been arrested, embroiled in a multitude of accusations. And Chloe had been summarily executed.

John was determined not to depart this world as Chloe had—neck snapped at the end of a rope.

Or, if that was what God determined his lot in life to be, John would at least hold it off as long as he could, because what waited for him on the other side of death was not something he looked forward to any longer.

His would not be a homecoming to the pearly gates, nor was he expecting a welcome from some low-swinging chariot "coming for to carry him home."

No. He'd saved someone's life and was fairly certain that meant the damnation of his soul.

"The soul stone should glow differ'nt," he said, looking round. "Should be in the lantern nearest to where Lady Astraea tried to do herself harm. Should glow differ'nt." He nodded. "With color."

Laura stared at him, her mouth agape. "Her soul stone is still here? Why on earth didn't you get it when—" She looked around and dropped her volume. "*—he* needed it?"

"Didn't know nothin' 'bout none of this. Not exactly preached about in church or on street corners . . ." He peered at each lamp near the broad bed. "I shoulda done this weeks ago," he muttered, shaking his head. "But tragedy has a way of building. Never did seem the right time."

Laura stared at him. He rubbed his forehead, his scuffed

knuckles nearly pink with scars from hard labor inside and outside his beloved household.

"It done near slipped my mind . . ."

She patted his shoulder. "We'll find it. Wc have to. Something's not right with her. She knows she's not herself, and her new self—well, she's meaner than a rabid skunk."

"Shouldn't be. Picked a good stone for her. A new-to-her soul from a real nice lady. Here." He dug in the pocket of his dusty trousers, pulling out the small namecard that had rested beside the soul stone he chose in the Reanimator's house.

She took it from him and read it aloud. "Lady Caroline of House Amalthea. A fine and noble lady of good breeding and manners with a kind heart and a fine disposition." Laura shook her head. "That sounds not a whit like the woman she becomes sometimes. Not one whit."

He rose to his full height and looked down at her, frowning. "Not a blessed soul stone here. When the Hub men reclaimed the stormlights . . . They take all of 'em?"

Laura opened her mouth to explain, but a noise behind them stopped her.

"Why, whyever would you want to know that, John?"

Laura stepped back, her hand flying up to snare John's arm in warning. In the doorway stood Lady Astraea, the foreign fire back in her eyes and her features their cruelest-looking.

Chapter Three

Bravery is being the only one who knows you're afraid.
—FRANKLIN P. JONES

Aboard the Tempest

Laughing, Rowen and Elizabeth turned back to the ladder to descend, but she stopped him, resting a hand on his arm. "Look," she said softly. "We have steam power secreted away and we are working on obtaining a thermo-acoustic engine. But this is the other advantage we have." She pointed off the ship's port side, her finger aimed at the mountains they'd crested, rising like the purple spine of a sleeping dragon.

The sun was sinking behind the glowing ridge, orange and yellow threatening to set the mountain range's back afire as color saturated the mountains, filtering through the distant trees until the colors blurred and blended and the entire sky grew soft with the promise of coming night.

Elizabeth sighed, her arms swinging at her side. "They never get to see it, you know? The airships. We get the occasional fart of black smoke from the engines, but, like any gas, it passes." She winked. "I whisk it away if another ship is near and bring in clouds. But their airships—their Conductors—control the weather and almost never get free of the clouds they build long enough to see either sunrise or sunset. Imagine."

Rowen tore his gaze away from it, his chest tight. "I'd rather not."

Elizabeth cocked her head, peering at him with sparkling eyes. Then she punched his arm.

"What the hell was that for?"

She grinned at him. "Buck up! Your girl—it is a girl, right?" she asked, quirking one eyebrow. "I mean, you said *Jordan* and that might be a man's name . . ."

He did not answer, but watched as she sputtered on.

"But your name's *Rowen,* which might be a girl's name, and, love being what it seems to me what it is (which is rather annoyingly indiscriminate—not that there's anything wrong with that) it seems to me I best not presume that *your* Jordan is female."

His left eye pulsed in his skull.

"Or male."

His eye twitched again.

"Or human. Or even reallll," she squeaked out before bending over, consumed by laughter. She stayed frozen like that a moment, doubled over and wheezing between giggles, and he wondered how this woman could possibly be an effective pirate captain.

Trading hostess.

He snorted. "Jordan is most certainly real. And human. And quite definitely female."

Straightening, she grinned at him again. "Well, all of that is *quite* a relief!" She wiggled the toes of one boot and pointed to it, saying, "It's small, and it's a good thing."

"What? Your foot?"

"Aye," she said. "Easier to get it back out of my own mouth." She winked at him, saying, "Your real, human girl, Jordan, is most likely propping her feet up and relaxing aboard the *Artemesia.* Most likely enjoying herself."

"That's highly doubtful."

"Why, she doesn't enjoy travel by airship?"

"Likely not, as she's the source of power for it."

Elizabeth winced. Her gaze dropped to the deck and her lips pressed together, sliding back and forth across her face. "Oh." She hooked her fingers into her belt and swayed a moment before her eyes settled on the rope ladder attached to the deck near her feet. She cleared her throat. "I was thinking . . ."

He took a breath and made a conscious effort to be more positive. Rubbing his ragged beard, he asked, "Do you believe you should? Be *thinking*? Might you not strain yourself?"

Her head snapped up, and catching his overly dramatic expression of concern, she snorted. "You seemed . . . *worried* coming up the ropes. There is an alternative for the descent . . ."

"The only alternate method of descent I can fathom is over the edge of the ship," he said. "Given that option, I'll climb."

"There is another way." She gave a little cough. "There are other methods of down—and up." She fluttered her eyelashes.

"You were testing me."

"I must test you to better know your abilities. You are part of my crew now."

"*For* now," he corrected. "I have other goals."

"Of course. Come with me."

At the far end of Topside, behind Tara-the-dummy, was

the lip of a broad tube with a cap securing its top. Elizabeth slapped it lightly with her palms. "We don't generally use this," she explained. "It's more of a safety precaution to get us from Topside to the other gun decks as fast as we can."

"*Other* gun decks?" he echoed.

She winked again. "Perhaps you'll never need to know. But," she redirected his drifting focus back to the cap with a tap of her fingers, "we'd best go." She grunted, pulling the heavy metal cap back on its hinges. Stepping inside the broad tube, she rested her feet on one of four rungs he could see. "I'll disappear, you count to three, climb down to the last rung, pull the cap shut," she touched a handle that was attached to the cap's concave interior, "let go, and step off."

He noticed there were several other capped tubes dotting the Topside deck. He leaned over the mouth of the tube, his hands tightly gripping its edge as he squinted into the dark beyond her feet. "I think not."

She rolled her lips together and furrowed her brow. "It'll all be over in just a moment."

"That phrasing is supposed to reassure me?"

She patted his hand and descended another rung. "Count to three, step in, close the lid, and step off."

He shook his head. She nodded in return and went down another rung. "Count to three, step in, close the lid, and step off."

He glanced from her face back to the rope ladder all the way across the deck.

Stars began to glitter faintly in the sky and Elizabeth peeked over his head to see them better. She sighed again. "That, too," she commented. "They miss that, too." Then she said, "Rowen." She winked. "Count to three, step in, close the lid, and step off," she instructed, clapping her hat to her head. Disappearing into the dark of the tube, a final pair of words reverberated back to him: "Be brave!"

He blinked. They were the words he had so frequently said to Jordan each time he tried to widen the horizons of her life with his bolder experiences.

Be brave.

So he had no choice but to follow the instructions he'd previously given. How could a man expect anyone to follow his words if he himself did not?

He stepped inside, feet cautiously fumbling down rung after rung, handle firmly in his hand, the lowering cap squeezing out the remaining light as he made his descent.

Be brave.

His left foot swept down finding no more rungs. The lid snapped shut above his head, sealing.

"Come down already," Elizabeth's voice echoed from somewhere in the darkness below.

Rowen took a deep breath and stepped off.

He was not proud of the fact he screamed. *Like a girl,* he thought as he snapped his jaw as tightly shut as his eyes already were. His rump and back connected with the tube, knocking the breath out of him. His hair blew back as he rocketed down, fast as a cannonball mid-flight.

His eyes peeled open at the brush of cooler air cutting across him, and light shocked his senses nearly as much as landing in the old strawtick mattresses did. He lay there a moment, stunned. And trying to get his lungs working again.

Elizabeth stood over him, laughing so hard she was crying.

He rolled slowly into a seated position. "I thought I was going to die," he said with a chuckle.

"I heard," she wheezed out.

He rubbed his head, trying to fix his hair. "But, to your credit, I didn't die."

"I see that."

"This is all . . ." He rose, looking around. They stood in a small and absolutely unremarkable room. A wooden floor and four wooden walls butted together with only two doors to break the monotony. "You said the tube led to the gundeck?"

She nodded. "The Aft Gundeck, more precisely. Many airships line parts of their exterior with stacks of cabins. The view of the storms is spectacular and the right people pay a pretty penny for those rooms. As a trading vessel we aren't expected to have as many exterior cabins, so most of ours . . ." She stepped over and pulled open the nearest of the two doors, stepping through.

Rowen followed.

Cannons lined the wall before them, wedged into place with triangular blocks and pins. Their thick black snouts were mere inches from the closed gun flaps. On them were stamped initials: S.F.

Elizabeth stepped forward and gave one an appreciative stroke. "Our heavy horses," she said with a smile. "I know you had little time to observe the beauty of our ship as you were welcomed aboard, but the *Tempest*'s exterior is painted to look like cabin windows thanks to an artist who, like many of his ilk, does not necessarily agree with our government."

Rowen nodded. "Nicely done."

"I do many things nicely," she said, straddling the gun and winking at him.

A door snapped shut as someone else entered the room behind them. A throat cleared and Elizabeth stood up and tipped her hat.

Rowen turned to see who had joined them.

Two men stood side by side.

The shorter of the two—a year or two older than Rowen and with red-gold hair—was already talking, and viciously disinterested in Rowen's existence. The man wore an unremarkable shirt, trousers, and boots. Across his chest was a belt with two pistols unlike any Rowen had ever seen before strapped to it. ". . . So what was that light show all about, eh, Evie?" he asked Elizabeth. In his hands he worked something metal back and forth. "Seemed a bit unnecessary, do you not think?"

Elizabeth—*Evie*—pursed her lips and looked down at the shorter man.

"Just who exactly were you trying to impress, eh?"

The other man, long and thin and all arms, legs, and Adam's apple, cleared his throat again, jabbing an elbow toward Rowen.

The shorter of the two stopped worrying at the mechanical thing he held and gave Rowen a glance and rolled his eyes. "I asked who, not *what,* Toddy. That there's not a person but a walking tree trunk."

Elizabeth's eyes crinkled at their edges. "Do you not have something of mechanical import to tinker with?"

"Tinkers tinker," the man said with a squaring of his shoulders. "*I* am an *engineer.*"

"Then is there not an engine you should be near, *engineer,*" she teased.

He bristled, stepping back. "No more fireworks. We do not wish to have attention drawn to us. Especially considering our current cargo."

She frowned but nodded, watching them both go.

The door shut once more and she announced, "The illustrious Ginger Jack, ship's engineer and constant thorn in my side."

"Seems like a . . . *passionate* relationship you two have."

"What? Ha!" She laughed, but color rose in her cheeks and she would not meet his eyes. "Nay. Not Ginger and I." She shook her head.

"This is quite a different world. I must admit, on Topside I was quite worried seeing Tara. I thought you'd done something utterly insane—*reprehensible*—like made a person into some puppet simply to fly your blasted boat!"

For a moment she was absolutely still, watching him, her breathing shallow, eyes sad. "Oh, Rowen. You've never been on another airship before, have you?"

Rowen staggered a step, bracing himself against a cannon at the insinuation. "No. I need to get to Jordan," he insisted. "And fast. I had no idea things were like that."

"The people on the top never know what it's like for those on the bottom—*ignorance is bliss*."

Philadelphia

It was Catrina's uncle who opened the door to the family home for her.

She sniffed. "Whyever do you not let the servants do that much at least?"

He closed the door behind her and bolted it. Brushing his hands down his shirt's front to neaten it, he responded, words slurring, "We all should endeavor to do *something* at least. And you, dear niece, have done more than enough already."

"Good God. Here. You want to do something? Take my shawl. You are constructed wholly from drama and a guilty conscience, are you not?" She undid her shawl and thrust it at him. "And here. My hat." She slipped free her hatpin and laughed when he jumped back and flailed his arms wildly at her attempt to jab him with it. "Oh, but you are so amusing. Absolutely worth the hassle of keeping you around."

Tentatively, he reached for the hat and snared the pin as well. "People would wonder if both your parents *and* uncle were gone," he whispered. "A lady must have a chaperone . . ."

"And how you benefit from that fact!" Glaring at him, she stalked from the foyer to the hall. That only the echo of their footsteps returned to her ears was not lost on her.

"I dismissed the servants for the evening."

Catrina spun to face him. "But I am hungry!"

He raced to get around her, saying, "I can surely make you somcthing lo eat . . ."

She blinked at him and tossed her head. Perfectly spiraled gold curls bounced around the crown of her head, interspersed with satin ribbons. "Let us see if that is so." She pointed in the direction of the kitchen.

With determination she strode forward as he scampered ahead—a bit unsteady on his feet as always. But that was easily explainable when one realized where much of the monies she allotted him went—to drink. It was an expenditure she did not discourage.

He held the kitchen door open and, skeptically, she stepped inside, giving a little sniff. "Well, perhaps you will succeed in finding me something to eat."

"I do my best to keep you happy."

"That is wise, indeed."

He rushed about the room, going from cabinet to cabinet and examining the assortment of meats, cheeses, and herbs strung and suspended from the ceiling's open rafters.

"Perhaps a bottle of wine?" she suggested.

To anyone else it seemed an innocent enough suggestion. But Gerald paled. "From the cellar?" he asked, his voice more squeak than manly baritone.

"Why, of course. I just so happen to have the key!" She dug into the narrow space at the top of her corset just between fabric and skin to where a perfectly-sized pocket had been secreted away. "Perhaps there is something on ice that might interest me." She smiled, seeing his Adam's apple slide down and back at her suggestion. "Here. You do the honors." She handed him the key, and, shaking, he stuck it into the lock and opened the door. "When is the next delivery of ice?"

"Monday next."

"Oh, good." Descending the four steps into the wine cellar, she turned left and came to the set of ice blocks that formed a frozen table, sawdust packed around them and sprinkled across most of what rested atop them.

Most.

She stepped closer, the smile on her lips stretching to a nearly painful grin as she leaned in to inspect the faces peeking out from the wood shavings. "Well, hello, Mother. Father. Did you miss me?" She turned toward Gerald, who stood as stiff as her parents but by the door. "Come here," she demanded. "Take a good look. This is exactly why it is important you keep me happy—that you do not question my decisions nor disagree with me over . . . anything. Not which boy I wish to pursue nor what hours I keep . . ." She paused. "And never, *never* threaten to tell the authorities the truth about my nature. Never suggest you would hand me over rather than be accused of Harboring. A loving family would *never*!"

He looked away and, darting forward, she grabbed his face, fingers sinking into his dark brown beard as she forced him to meet her eyes.

"Because betraying me betrays our cause. You understand?" Her grip fierce on his face, she moved his head up and down in a slow nod. "And soon enough everyone will know what I am. And they will all be thankful for each move I made because they will understand I did it all for them, Gerald. All for the Witches and every type of slave there is. I am the one they have waited for. I am the one prophesied. And they will *love* me when they realize." She released him and clomped her way up the stairs. "They will *love* me. Unlike my dear, departed parents."

At the top of the steps she paused, her hand on the doorframe. "Oh, Gerald. You look positively dreadful. Perhaps a drink to calm your nerves?"

He nodded, brushing past her and heading straight for the cabinet where the liquor was stored.

Aboard the Artemesia

Bran sneaked another look at Jordan Astraea, trussed as she was in the thin leather lashings that connected her wrists and ankles to four key parts of the airship *Artemesia* as part of an initial Conductor's training exercise.

He'd Made her into a Weather Witch, forced her to become something both she and he knew she never should have been, but he had never witnessed the next stages of a Witch's evolution. What a Maker did was never discussed. Nor was *this*. He had never dined where one was being trained.

It did nothing to improve his appetite.

Her long, dark hair was pulled into a simple twist that wrapped into a bun held tight near the nape of her neck.

Her butterfly-wing pendant hung suspended and glittering from a black velvet band around her narrow neck.

The memory of a song drifted to Bran and for a moment it played in his head, rivaling the violinist's haunting tune, as he watched her.

> Her eyes were dark as the raven,
> You'd think her the queen of the land
> With her hair bound high behind her
> Swept up in a black velvet band.

But she was no queen of any land. When he realized this, the tune spiraled, deflating, every note falling flat as it died in his head. Here was no queen. Here was nothing but a slave of the lowest order. A slave of his Making.

She cried out as her left hand was wrenched violently to the side and bread flew from her hand, bouncing across the floor, between the brass banisters, and over the ship's edge.

The captain groaned, growling in her direction, "You're not anticipating the ship's moves—you have to feel her, know what she wants, begin to use magicking to convince her that what you want is the *better* thing!" He shook his head and stood. "Because there's one thing and one thing alone that this bitch of an airship wants! And that's the ground." He slammed his fist onto the table, rattling the dishware.

"It seems far more like riding an entire team of horses all at once rather than merely steering a ship," Marion muttered. His eyes left Bran only long enough to alight on the captain and dig his gaze into him.

"Or saddling a whole school of fish with Merrow on your tails," the captain laughed. "But that is precisely why we are here and they," he cast a look to the edge of Topside, his gaze going east, toward the Western Ocean, "are down there. In the briny depths. You couldn't pay me to captain a Cutter. And those poor fools who thought Clipper Ships would be enough? Merrow chum. It's no wonder Baltimore fell." He raised a cut-crystal wineglass and motioned they all, even Jordan with her modest pewter tankard, do the same.

Hesitantly she obeyed, watching the weak wine in her tankard slosh. Her hand was pulled left, then right, then forward as different bits of the *Artemesia* steered their would-be Conductor. Her tongue stuck out between her lips in concentration and Bran realized this young woman of once fine family no longer cared much about her looks or her beautiful clothing.

She cared about survival.

She cared about not being hurt anymore.

Jordan moved forward with the pull of her leather leashes as the ship's wings rose up beside its bloated balloon and she snatched up a second roll and waited. There was a shift in the wind that allowed her hands close enough that she could snatch a sip of drink and tear off a bite of bread. She chewed quickly, there being no art or grace to her eating, but rather a sense of grim determination. Her gaze flicked across each of them with cool disinterest and then flitted away to skim the odd bits of technology that made up the *Artemesia*'s Topside.

Bran watched, torn between obeying Marion's subtle commands, observing Jordan, and observing the ship's current Conductor, who moved like a mechanism himself not far beyond her.

He should remember the Conductor's name, having Made him. But he did not remember his name any more than he might remember one cog more than any other in a crate filled with its duplicates.

The captain cleared his throat and glanced over Jordan's head and to the Conductor. "New York City before nightfall, yes?"

A soft grunt answered, the Conductor's hands sending flywheels spinning. The Conductor leaned heavily against the main wheel—the one used for steering—and gathered himself.

"Not long, not long," the captain said, peering into his soup bowl.

"Not long for New York City?" Meggie asked, her eyes glittering. Surely she had heard of New York City—only during her short lifespan having surpassed Philadelphia in population.

Marion bounced her on his knee once and she settled, her large eyes downcast. He began, "A child should not—?"

"—speak unless spoken to," Meggie whispered.

But the captain smiled at her. "True, true, child," the captain agreed. "But, in answer to your question, I meant *not long for this world.*" His thick eyebrows slid together. "If you grasp my meaning."

Meggie's head tipped to the side but Marion bounced her again and said, "Speak not unless spoken to. Is that not the proper way for a young lady?"

Her tiny mouth drew into a pout.

Maude spoke, but softly. "What the good captain means, I do believe, is that our Conductor is not at all well."

"Very true," the captain agreed. "A good, good thing the Maker saw fit to provide us with a new trainee. Your timing was impeccable," he declared. "It seems some things are meant to be."

Bran ducked his head, trying not to think about the multitude of dark things he'd done to boil down to such impeccable timing, especially considering Jordan should have been impossible to Make into a Weather Witch. She was an anomaly—at least he hoped she was . . .

God, let her be an exception and not the rule . . .

He looked away from his bowl of soup, away from the table of diners, and off to the clouds that seemed to mimic his own rumbling gut. The darkness coalesced, spinning and bubbling like a murky swamp and only occasionally illuminated by a flash of lightning.

"I expect a week—a month at most—from this particular Conductor. He was much more energetic when he first came to us a year past. A trade, you know? Worked six months on another ship prior to coming aboard as ours."

Only a year and a half of service. Bran worked to keep control of his stomach. To be Made and Burn Out after only a year and a half of service—to only have a year and a half of life left in you . . .

All eyes were on him. Not just Marion's, Meggie's, and Maude's, but also Jordan's.

He looked down, surprised that Maude's hand rested on his arm. He hadn't felt it. He barely felt anything beyond a swimming darkness tugging at him like the clouds slowly dragging each other into shape like hands pulling taffy.

"Most of them last a bit longer," the captain said, rubbing his stomach with an appreciative hand before reaching for another piece of bread. "Some don't last nearly so long. Ah, well. We all have to die eventually, now, don't we?"

Bran felt the heat of her glare pierce through her eyelashes as Jordan forgot about the leather binding both ankles and feet, putting her at the ship's rough mercy as she knocked items off the table without a care for decorum. "You see it now, do you?" she asked, her voice rising in volume and pitch with every word. "You see what your tinkering with lives does? How you doom people—entire families?"

Bran barely began to form the word "no" before the long-legged man in the meticulously detailed leather lion mask flicked his eyes to the captain and the Wandering Wallace stood, leaning across the table to pluck a coin from Meggie's ear as the captain sprang up with a growl and knocked Jordan unconscious with the butt of a tankard.

The Wandering Wallace winced as Jordan collapsed, her head clanking into her soup bowl and spilling its contents across the table and down her front. But the Wandering Wallace kept one hand extended, a living blinder to Meggie's vision, and with his other produced a silk flower.

With a flourish.

The child saw nothing.

Jordan lay like a broken puppet, the animation that enlivened her body lost. Her guards stepped forward and undid her tethers.

Bran put down his spoon, no longer caring enough to even feign hunger. Dragging his gaze from Jordan's limp form, he contemplated his bowl.

Marion bristled beside him.

But the Wandering Wallace smacked his hands together, calling for their attention. Bran supposed he never had trouble getting attention.

He watched the masked man beckon to the slender black-haired beauty beside him.

Whereas he could not determine the Wandering Wallace's

age, Miyakitsu seemed to be approximately Jordan's age. Somewhere between sixteen and eighteen. But with features like hers—the planes of her face so mild, low, and foreign, with gentle curves as if her profile had been washed by a river for centuries—it was hard to judge.

Graceful as a green willow, she stood. Her eyes darted to the Wandering Wallace.

He nodded. From within the holes in the mask, his eyes smiled, welcoming her. "My lovely assistant, Miyakitsu!"

Around the table a smattering of applause echoed, the most eager of which sounded from Meggie's small hands.

"It is my duty to remind you all before I truly begin this evening's spectacle that the things you will see—things that will astound and amaze—things that will dazzle your eyes and turn your brain to butter—these things are not magickal in nature—no, not a single one! Every bit of trickery that you see performed by both myself and the lovely Miyakitsu is nothing but simple sleight of hand and basic illusion embellished and made more elaborate through our methodology. Neither of us are Witches nor Magickers nor Conductors. Not anything of the sort! And, so, though there is plenty of magick in this world, we utilize none of it!"

The captain leaned across the table toward Bran, whispering, "He does the finest legal disclaimers ever."

Bran nodded and watched the mysterious man and his woman as they easily took command of Topside to entertain the guests.

"This evening we have brought with us an intriguing trick from the Old World." From a carpetbag at the feet of his chair he removed an ornate box. "This box will help us show how truly flexible the amazing Miyakitsu is."

Miyakitsu stretched her arms over her head and bent back at her waist until her fingertips walked their way to her ankles. She kicked out her feet, heels flying over her head, and she popped back into a lithe standing position, her colorful silk robe with its ocean wave design barely fluttering.

Meggie was already clapping.

"I will obscure Miyakitsu's beauty—but only momentarily," the Wandering Wallace promised, "because I cannot bear much time without the sight of her. Sit, my darling girl." She withdrew her chair from its place at the table, sat, and rearranged her silk gown across her lap quite modestly for a contortionist.

The Wandering Wallace stepped up behind her and said, "Gather up your hair, my love—up off your dainty neck."

She swept up the long black locks and twisted them together, piling them high atop her head. She settled her hands in her lap and smiled as he rested the edges of the box on her shoulders so that her head was inside, her eyes peering out the opening.

He leaned on her shoulders, grinning at his audience, his chin resting on the top of the box as he explained. "It is said that owls can turn their heads all the way around. I, myself, have never seen such a thing. But I have seen Miyakitsu do what owls are only rumored to. Shall we watch her do it?"

Meggie's voice came out, a shocked whisper. "Twist her head all the way around?"

The Wandering Wallace nodded.

Her eyes wide, she asked, "Does it hurt?"

Miyakitsu shook her head, a silent *no*.

Meggie smiled then shouted in a voice far bigger, fiercer, and deeper than Bran thought she had within her, "Do it!"

"Watch carefully," the Wandering Wallace instructed, placing his hands on either side of the box. "Are you ready, dear heart?"

She nodded and he began to twist the box around just above her shoulders.

Meggie squealed, watching as Miyakitsu's head turned to her right. She turned, twisting her neck . . . The side and back of the box hid her head then, her face only reappearing as the hole in the box came back to the front, carrying her head again to its proper position.

Meggie screeched and they all clapped as the Wandering Wallace removed the box, declaring, "I must make sure all the parts still work!" He looked at Meggie, tapped the chin of his mask, and asked the child, "What are the five senses?"

She screwed up her face in thought, answering, "Sight, sound, smell, taste, and touch?"

"Very good!"

He clicked his fingers by both of Miyakitsu's ears.

Miyakitsu twitched away from each noise and the Wandering Wallace wiggled his fingers close to her eyes, making her blink in response. "Now smell," he said, reaching for a piece of bread. He waved it under her nose, her nostrils flared and she nodded. "Taste?" He tore off a tiny piece of the bread, setting it on the tip of her pink and pointing tongue.

She smiled, nodded, chewed and swallowed.

Finally he leaned forward and admitted, "My favorite test—touch," and he leaned in, his mask obscuring much of the view, but Meggie giggled, knowing they kissed.

The captain laughed. "Spectacular! I have heard you also sing, Wandering Wallace. You must delight the ship with song tonight after my man delivers the evening's news."

"I would be honored to do so."

From behind Bran came sounds of movement. Of heavy boots moving on the deck. He peered out of the corners of his eyes and watched Jordan's guards sweep in, one picking her up unceremoniously and throwing her across his shoulder like a sack of rice. They carried her away, Bran staring as the three-walled elevator again sank into the ship's deck, taking her back to wherever Witches were kept.

Meggie did not notice Jordan's absence until Captain Kerdin plucked the hatpin from Jordan's hat, and then the elevator carrying her was gone—the child was still too absorbed in watching Wallace.

Captain Kerdin shook his head, his jaw clenched and disappointment clear, his gaze flickering to the Conductor who kept the ship afloat in the heavens, his days numbered.

What happened if a Conductor died mid-flight? Would the crew and passengers simply hope the wings fully extended and had the strength to glide them to a safe landing?

Meggie glanced around. "Where has the lady gone?"

"What lady?" the captain asked.

Meggie pointed to the vacant seat at the smaller table.

"Oh. The Witch," he said. "She went home."

"But . . ." Meggie's expression squeezed in, and her lower lip pushed out. "I did not tell her good night." She squeezed Somebunny tighter.

The bag at Bran's back rattled again and he knew without looking that his drink was starting to bubble. He slipped one hand into the bag and one out to Meggie, his eyes widening as a pulse of some strange power shot through him from the bag to his daughter.

Meggie sniffled and blinked.

In the sky above, lightning darted and sparkled.

"I'm certain we will all see the young lady tomorrow

evening for supper, as the captain is a generous man," the Wandering Wallace assured them.

The captain coughed but nodded, murmuring agreement. "Of course. I would be honored to have you return for supper—"

"—and entertainment for us all," the Wandering Wallace promised with a wink. "An open invitation, then?" the Wandering Wallace asked, his lion's-head mask tipping up so his eyes locked with those of the captain.

There was barely a moment of hesitation from the captain. "Why yes, of course! An open invitation from this most generous of captains for dinner Topside for all you fine folks!"

"Excellent," the Wandering Wallace said.

Meggie sniffled once more and Bran stroked her hair, Marion watching. "Be at ease, little dove. We have faced many changes recently," Bran said, his eyes snapping up to meet those of their captor, "but we will face them together and be brave."

Chapter Four

Power, alas! naught but misery brings!
—THOMAS HAYNES BAYLY

Holgate

There had not been a single time since Councilman Stevenson had taken over the Weather Workers and the maintenance of Holgate that a town watchman's appearance at his door had been a good thing.

Compounding the issue was the fact the Tester had popped by earlier and remained in Stevenson's apartments, reclining on one of his finer sofas. And flexing his metal contraption of a hand open and closed like a predatory bird testing its talons. A miserable man, he commented on everything—even criticizing the color palette of his apartments.

Stevenson rubbed his forehead and glared at the watchman. With the loss of his prize stallion, King's Ransom, he very much wanted to be gone from here—to be back in

Philadelphia, even if it meant sharing space with his young bride. "What do you mean the Maker is gone?"

The watchman looked down. With a creak, the Tester leaned back on the plush divan, stretching against it and kicking his boots out before him so their black tips peeked from beneath his long gray and silver robe's hem, and said, "I thought it quite easily comprehended, myself. Not much more there than a verb and a noun to ponder."

Stevenson ignored him. "Might he be in town?"

"No, good sir. And his little girl's gone. And Maude, his woman."

Halfway through the watchman's explanation, Stevenson's eye began to twitch. "His books?"

The watchman rubbed his beard in thought, his scar puckering the flesh as he rubbed it. "Desk's a mess, and there's some broken glass. Some other strange things, too." He glanced to the side and then back down as if worried something would suddenly appear.

"What other strange things?" Stevenson asked, his eyebrows pulling together as he followed the man's paranoid gaze.

"Bizarre butterflies . . ."

"Butterflies!" Stevenson drew back, rolling his eyes.

"Demonic butterflies, you ask me," said the watchman. "Damned things are everywhere, flying into your face, your eyes especially—Lord, how they like the eyes!"

The Tester laughed and then dropped his face back into its standard droll expression. "Open a window. Swat them," he said with a wave of his hand. "Crush them, drop a book on them, stomp them with a boot. Demonic butterflies!" he said with a laugh.

Stevenson leaned in and sniffed the man's breath. "Your

dental hygiene is suspect, but you do not appear to be drunk . . ."

"I am quite sober, sir. And the Maker is quite gone."

"Clothing?"

"Some's taken, yes. But there is good news, as well."

"Oh. Excellent well. Do tell me this good news."

"Your stallion?"

Stevenson nodded.

"King's Ransom?"

"Yes, yes, we have previously established that my stallion is named King's Ransom—what news of him?"

"He's been found, my lord, and in fair condition."

"Found where and in whose possession?"

"Here, my lord. But the man riding him escaped. We suspect he boarded a ship."

Stevenson frowned. "But the stallion is penned, tended, and under guard?"

"Yes, my lord."

"That at least is some small victory. What says Gregor Burchette of this new development, as the horse was under his watch?"

The watchman cleared his throat and straightened his shoulders. "And I quote: *Well, that is an interesting bit of news.*"

Stevenson sighed. "Intriguing. I shall make my way to the Maker's apartments and judge the situation for myself."

The watchman nodded, taking a long, slow step back and out of the doorway.

"Not so fast!" the Tester said. "You had best take a force of watchmen with you, Councilman. To," he laughed, "guard against," he sputtered, "*demonic butterflies*!" He snorted, shifting the sound into a clearing of his throat. "They might . . . *viciously* . . . bring color into your drab existence!"

Philadelphia

John straightened, hearing Lady Astraea in the doorway. He turned to face her and rubbed his hand across his forehead.

Laura stepped closer to him—or perhaps farther from her . . . He wasn't quite sure how to judge.

"What exactly are you looking for?" Lady Astraea asked, her eyes scanning the room and her servants' faces.

"Well, milady," John began, the words coming slowly, "we's in need of another lantern down in the library. Seems one's been broke and Laura and I, well, we recalled that you don't bother with reading up here no more so we thought, if we could just find an extra lantern up here, we might replace the other, set it up with a candle, too, and keep the library lookin' mighty fine."

Lady Astraea's eyes narrowed. "A lantern in the library broke, you say?"

"Yes'm, I do," John said with the most earnest nod a lying man might muster. He had never been one to lie but it seemed that was all he did now—as if one lie grew into another and another, always rolling and growing like a snowball starting down a snowy winter slope on the Hill and rocketing toward the Burn Quarter.

Lady Astraea reached up and rubbed her gown's low neckline, not far from her heart, and her expression changed, softening. "Well, John, as I have never known you to lie, I will gladly give you one of my finer lanterns . . ."

She glanced around the room, and, her eyes settling on one, she scooped it up and handed it to him. "I do hope this serves the purpose."

"Yes'm, milady, 'tis most fine and will look right well in the library—begging your pardon for disturbing you with such a trifle." He gave a little bow and stepped around her and into the hall.

"Just a note for the future, John," her ladyship said. "It is highly improper for a lady to return to her room and find a man in it unexpectedly. Mind it does not happen again."

"Yes, milady. I shall mind, never you fear."

She smiled at him and for a moment it was truly his lady who smiled out at him. He smiled back.

Laura curtseyed to her ladyship and slipped into the hallway, too, walking a brief distance with John. When he was certain they were beyond anyone else's hearing, he said to her, " 'Tis not there, Laura. The soul stone is most certainly gone. And . . ." He paused in the hallway to look her in the face. ". . . as much as I hate to cast aspersions on our lady . . ."

Laura leaned toward him, setting a hand on his arm that she quickly pulled back, remembering her place. "Yes, John? Tell it true."

"I'd swear to you that there was another lantern or two in her room before this."

Laura nodded. "So it's worse than we feared? Our lady is not our lady, does not act like the lady named on that card of yours should, and our true lady's soul stone is . . . gone?"

"I fear so."

"Oh, John . . . This is bad. You must find the Reanimator."

He dropped his head. "I shall go there shortly," he promised. "There's just one thing I must do first."

"Yes, yes, of course. Do what you must," Laura agreed.

They parted ways and he walked to the library. Surrounded by shelf after shelf of books—in an entire room filled for the pursuit of knowledge and truth—he looked at the lanterns. They were beautiful. Carefully crafted. They lit the search for knowledge nearly as much as the books they illuminated did. And they were not merely lights, but pieces of art that hours of a craftsman's life had been traded away for in their making.

His stomach twisted and soured.

Setting Lady Astraea's lamp down, for a moment he let himself truly consider the ramifications of their actions. Of the danger they were all still in. Of the lies he'd told already and the ones he'd likely need to tell in the future.

He was surely and most definitely damned.

With that thought in mind he reached out to a lantern and discovered smashing it was not as hard as he expected.

He set the other in its place and cleaned up the broken bits of the first, his mind seething at what circumstances had brought him to.

With blind purpose in his heart, he strode from the house in search of the Reanimator.

Aboard the Tempest

His hand still resting on one of the many cannons in the Aft Gundeck, Rowen closed his eyes a moment before he looked at Elizabeth. "I need to find Jordan," he insisted. "I need to get to her—rescue her."

"It's not that easy, love," she said, reaching out and taking him by the arm again.

"Important things are seldom easy to do."

She led him back out of the room and down a winding set of stairs. Together they slipped through a narrow, twisting hallway where sculptured brass hands held stormlight lanterns away from striped walls. Up another staircase, down a new hall. When they again stopped, this time in a hallway lined with brightly-painted doors, Rowen felt utterly lost within the maze of the ship's belly.

They stood silent, regarding each other, outside a bright green and yellow door hung with garish golden hinges. She pressed her lips together until they were merely thin pink lines. The crow's-feet that crinkled at the edge of her eyes were a memory and she looked older, lines showing on her face that he hadn't noticed before. Still beautiful, with high cheekbones and a bold nose, she seemed suddenly tired.

With her right hand pressed to the door, she examined the floor between them and the narrow rug that ran this particular hall's length. She dug at the fibers of the rug with the toe of one boot. She sighed. "The men holding your Jordan? They will have guards and guns," she said, again meeting his eyes. "They will keep her at all costs, protecting her as staunchly as their kind guard a Hub. Especially with so many rumors of the prophecy."

"The prophecy?"

Elizabeth blinked. "Of course you wouldn't know . . . Prophecy, rumor . . . It's all a matter of perspective, I suppose. It is said a great Witch—the Stormbringer—will rise and unite all the ranks and bring even an end to the Wildkin War."

Rowen snorted.

"As unlikely as it sounds it is far more likely than the government uniting us and ending the war."

"I'll agree to that, at least," Rowen said. "You think they believe Jordan's the one the prophecy was written about?"

"It doesn't matter if they think she is or not. Witches are more than mere Witches now. The right one could be a symbol to unify the masses, and no government wants anyone unifying their people other than them, Rowen. They'll give no thought to killing you. And anyone with you."

"They are *enslaving* her—making her nothing but a piece of some airborne transport," he protested.

"It could be far worse. She is on a liner—a passenger ship. At least she didn't pull cargo duty." Elizabeth looked away, swallowing.

"It is still enslavement. They are making her a human cog in their sick machine . . ."

She rested a hand on his arm and this time when she looked at him a fire sizzled, flashing copper in the depths of her eyes. "As they have made many others as they prepare them to receive Lightning's Kiss."

He shook off her hand. "What is that?" he asked. "Lightning's Kiss?"

She leaned forward to slip a slender chain out from her blouse's neckline. A key glimmered on its end. Placing it in the door's lock, she gave it a twist. "I will tell you everything I know," she promised. "And I will let you go if that is what you wish—but *after* you know what I know. Only . . . promise me one thing in return."

"For my freedom and the chance at winning hers I'll promise you anything."

"Then promise that you will maintain an open mind and consider that perhaps Fate placed you here on more than a temporary basis." She shoved through the door, leading him. Stormlights came on in a rising glow and he was temporarily astonished at what he saw. She patted his arm again. "I will send for you in the morning. There is nothing else to be done tonight but worry. Or live for yourself."

She disappeared out the door and down the hall, leaving Rowen to his quarters.

Philadelphia

Councilman Loftkin was in a rare joyful mood. "What great fortune we got you, Councilman Yokum. The law is a bit loose about these things—nearly anyone of rank four or better could have slid into old Astraea's position on the Council if he'd been nearby and expressed an interest—we really must fix that for the future."

The younger man sputtered, "Surely not *anyone* . . ."

"Truly—this republic is quite loose about elections. The idea so many may vote is frightening when you consider the lack of education of the masses." Loftkin paused, looking at Councilman Yokum. "Did you really think politics was more than being in the right place at the right time and knowing the right people?" He ran a hand through his graying hair, adding, "And having a dashing smile. I daresay that's why no ugly man will gain true power here. It is our kind who should lead."

"Are those beliefs not the reasons we broke from England?"

Loftkin snorted. "Is that what they say now? Is that what you young ones believe?" He shook his head. "That is a highly romanticized notion! Why no, of course not. We did *not* establish this government this way so we'd avoid being like them. We made it this way so we'd avoid being *led* by them. At the heart of the matter, we broke with them because our families all those years ago knew King George was an ass and that *we* could govern better."

Aboard the Artemesia

Jordan woke in her small cabin to a throbbing headache and a thirst that dried her throat to the point of rattling. A modest lantern lit the room through a stormcell, allowing her to see a few feet in any direction from its glowing case.

Another lantern nearby housed a double-terminated quartz crystal that New Yorkers called "Herkimer diamonds"—a double-terminated crystal allowing the capture of power such as hers. She could provide a steadier, brighter light with her own energy—if she focused and harnessed it.

She prowled the small room, touching the sparse items placed there: a cup and pitcher of water, two lanterns, a basin for washing and a few accompanying rags, the bed with one thin pillow and a thinner blanket. She grabbed the cup and filled it, downing the contents, refilling and emptying it again. Hanging across the foot of the bed lay the tattered ball gown her best friend Catrina ordered for her seventeenth birthday party. Webbed underneath with thin metal thread that conducted energy, the gown allowed Jordan to be accused of witchery.

She retained the butterfly-wing pendant—a frequent reminder of her inability to break free—and the grimy but still precious paper star, but the thing that never left her sight—more appropriately the thing she never let far from her touch—was the brass heart pin Rowen Burchette gave her as a parting gift at her ill-fated birthday party. That present nearly earned her escape from the dreaded Tanks of Holgate.

She shouldn't have been able to be Made into a Witch, but she broke under pain and exhaustion and the knowledge that the precious little girl Meggie, the Maker's own daughter, was a Witch in need of Making.

The idea of the little girl being hurt as Jordan had been broke something in her like a boot crushing a dry twig.

She wandered to the small window. Outside the sky sparked and rumbled, tiny veins of lightning bursting into flickering existence and vanishing. Brilliance faded to near-black again and again like hope being snuffed out over and over.

It was disheartening.

Disgusting.

She snatched up the dress, her lip curling as she wadded it and paused, holding it balled in her arms and seeing the wounds marring her hands and arms—wounds still healing from her Making. Her skin had been nearly flawless—never so porcelain nor fine as Catrina's, but it had been free of cuts and scrapes and puncture wounds before she'd been dragged from her home on Philadelphia's Hill and ruined. Her mouth opened and a noise burbled up from somewhere deep inside her—a strangled cry like she'd heard a beast in a menagerie make when, panicked, it ruined its face against the bars of its manmade prison.

She'd been known for her hospitality—the Astraeas being known for their lavish parties—and her looks. Now, her family fallen from grace, and her body battered, she had nothing.

Nothing but hate and hurt.

Nothing but pain and disappointment.

She hurled the dress at the window with a shriek and

watched it slide down the glass and crumple on the floor, a once fine ball gown with no belle to wear it.

She stepped across it, her bare feet twisting into its folds and crushing it beneath her toes as she pressed her palms and face to the window.

She had *nothing.*

Nothing but potential—crumpled and twisted far worse in her aching gut than the dress beneath her feet.

The Maker triggered her only once. She'd called in a storm that dogged the one drawn to Meggie. It should have been impossible to Make her. Weather Witches were born years before they were Made. Everyone said Witch bloodlines bore a taint traceable through family and tied to intermingling lower ranks.

Or so they'd believed. That was one reason their society held so rigidly to established ranks. Everyone was born into a set level and although one might move rank through marriage—or lose it through the scandal of Harboring—ranks were established and firm.

Slaves and Witches were the whipping boys (sometimes quite literally) lining society's bottom level.

Jordan Astraea tumbled quickly from her well-regarded rank of Fifth of the Nine to Witch and took her entire family, including her father, Councilman Morgan Astraea, down with her. Their name ruined, their power was gone. If she had been taken away a little more than a year earlier, the additional drama and shame would have been avoided. She would have been forever lost to her family, but she would not have brought them down. If a Witch was discovered before sixteen, the family was generally not found to be Harboring, but by sixteen a Witch's powers manifested. Someone would have noticed and that someone should have told.

Whoever plotted to bring down the Astraea family (there must have been a plot, of that Jordan was certain) had waited for the perfect time.

The moment a Witch was discovered, he or she was turned over to a Ring of Wraiths or a set of Wardens. A Tester removed any doubt, doing the thing for which they were named.

Testing.

Jordan flinched at the memory of the first time anyone had intentionally hurt her.

At least that she knew of.

Her hand had only recently lost all trace of her Test wound. Many other marks—from a variety of different implements—took its place.

The greatest wounds couldn't be found on her flesh but marred her heart and soul—wounds that made her wonder how her family fared since her false imprisonment. Were they still living on Philadelphia's grandest piece of real estate, the Hill, or had they been forced into the dark and grim neighborhoods of the Below? Were they just one more bit of living insulation keeping the wealthy politicians from the war against the water-dwelling Wildkin?

What of her sisters? Had the fact they were older and already married—not even in attendance at her seventeenth birthday party—had that saved them from the fall?

The dress had come from Catrina (who had been closer to her than her own blood sisters) and been a carefully constructed cage conducting all the things that made a Weather Witch test true. But why would Catrina commission a dress to harm her? It was designed and manufactured by the odd little seamstress in the city, a woman who was as creative as she was churlish.

Did it matter who brought them down? Down they went. And if society and social protocol had anything to do with it, they would be kept down permanently.

The Councilman had been right—never had a Witch gone home having been found innocent. If there had been such a Witch, he or she would never have lived to have their story heard. An embarrassment to the Council, murder would have been the best way to avoid scandal.

Jordan knew what she was: an anomaly able to shake the very foundations of a society built firmly on the bent backs of others. Societies crumbled when bent backs straightened and people stood unified.

Or such a society might be bolstered by hardworking people's well-worn hands—bolstered and puzzled back together in a fresh, new way.

Her head ached with possibility.

She rubbed it, massaging and gently probing the spot the captain had hit her with the tankard. A small lump had risen. She went to the dented and beaten box serving as her armoire and reached into its back, pulling free the folded paper star. Tentatively she unfolded it, running her finger along each crease to better mark in her mind the moments it was created.

Little good remained of that party besides the star. The evening's entertainer, the Wandering Wallace, told how Betsy Ross faced down the men of the early American government when they told her the use of perfect five-pointed stars on the nation's flag was too difficult.

She merrily proved them wrong, folding a piece of paper and cutting an example much the way the Wandering Wallace had. Without any tools but a pair of scissors.

It flew in the face of reason, an affront to their expectations. And some might have said that a woman—a *woman*!—proving the gentlemen of the American government were wrong was disrespectful, too.

Jordan stared out the window, wanting to be the same as Ross, her mind swirling like the clouds, to fly in the face of established reason. Maybe she should shake society to its foundations and be brave enough to free herself.

She dropped to her knees with a grunt. What was that song Rowen and she heard in the Below when they sneaked away together—one Rowen made her swear never to mention or repeat? A pretty tune . . . something about courage being the key to freeing yourself.

She rolled the words around in her head, seeking the tune that bound them together.

No storm that ever strikes
Shall leave me helpless and afraid
And if darkness lingers heavy
I'll be fearless and brave

But if ever I am wary
If ever I am scared
I will listen to the wind
For the answer's always there.

Philadelphia

Lady Astraea closed the door to her bedchamber and slipped the stone out of her gown's neckline.

She remembered little from the night of Jordan's birthday

party. She recalled the party itself, the accusations, the smashing of her silhouette, the long walk to her quarters, and she remembered knitting something she could no longer find. But the hours after that? It seemed time had been stolen away from her that night—as surely as Jordan had been stolen by the Wraiths and the Wardens.

She had woken to find herself in bed, stiff and cold, in the darkest part of night. Her head throbbing, she had nearly fallen off the mattress in the effort of rising. Behind her eyes strange images had floated and merged: a man wearing an odd mask, her servant John, knitting needles so sharp . . .

And storms—huge sweeping storms that welled up from inside her and leaped into the sky.

She had clutched her bedcovers to stop from falling to the floor, but they only slowed her descent. She found herself on her rump at her bedside, staring at the closest stormlight lantern.

A stormlight lantern that still glowed.

The tiny crystal exuded a blue and steady light, a sweet and strong glow, and she had let go of the tangle of bedding and reached for it with trembling and hungry hands. Clumsy trembling hands . . . She had knocked aside the lantern's globe, shattering it on the bedside table, but she didn't care. All she wanted was that glowing blue crystal.

She pried it loose from the lantern, pressing it so tight in her hand it left an imprint when she uncurled her fingers.

But it felt good against her flesh, warming her. The cold of the storms growing inside her stilled at its touch and she felt peace instead. So she slipped it into the top of her gown, nestling it not far from her heart. With the utmost care she got rid of the broken bits of the globe's glass and hid the body of the defunct lantern under her bed.

She lay back down then and slept—her dreams warring with one another. But since that night the blue stormcell had not been far from her touch.

Aboard the Artemesia

Curiosity brought the *Artemesia*'s captain to the darkest region of the ship, the workers' quarters, and the place the new Witch was held. He intended to walk past her room on his way to inspect the sailors' quarters but the ship swayed under his feet, pitching him against the wall by her door. The ship rumbled around him, and he braced himself, his hands high and flanking the small window in her door.

As he looked down the hallway, his mind raced. Surely the Conductor was not dying at this very moment, the ship readying to plunge them all to their deaths . . .

He could risk a rough ride up the elevator behind him to see for himself or—his gaze snagged on the ship's intercom system. He could call the sniper and have him investigate.

A flash of movement in the Witch's room caught his eye and he froze, mind spinning as he understood why his ship was rolling and heaving in controlled airspace.

The Witch—Jordan Astraea—tore through her room, hurling things, stomping, arms flailing in rage. Her hair had come loose and her chest heaved with effort. He drew his gaze away from her to stare outside her cabin's window. The clouds had grown inky, the only light the shimmer of lightning as it raced through them, sparkling against the darkest black he'd seen in years.

She dropped to her knees, wrapping her arms tight around herself, and knelt in the middle of her room, rocking.

He pressed his face to the glass and shifted so it was his ear pressed flush to its cool surface.

She sang a snatch of a soft chorus, a thing he'd heard another Weather Witch sing once.

> When there is no one there to guide you
> And no one there to help
> Your courage is the key
> To freeing yourself.

The clouds changed from a soul-eating black to navy blue and then royal, the color softening and brightening. Pelting rain slowed to intermittent spatters on her window. The lightning slowed, the frequent booms of wild thunder coming with less intensity, softening as his Conductor regained control. One last bolt of lightning thrust a finger of searing white across the sky and fizzled, smacking against the far side of her window.

There were few things Captain Kerdin knew at that moment. First? That the most powerful Witch he'd yet seen was aboard the *Artemesia*. Second? She was beautiful.

And most importantly—third: she was his to do with as he pleased.

Chapter Five

The final end of Government is not to
exert restraint but to do good.
—RUFUS CHOATE

Philadelphia

The lighting in the Council's private chambers was some of the finest on the East Coast. There was no flicker or flare except during the brief period of the Hub's re-energizing Pulse, and the light remained ambient and perfect for both reading and writing.

Still, as warm as the glow was, it did nothing to alleviate the shiver crawling along the heavyset man's spine. George scratched his chin and shifted his weight, leaning on the cane he carried and listening as Councilman Loftkin reminded him of his mission.

"Wherever you hear rumblings of the existence of steam contraptions, whenever you catch sight or scent of it . . . If you hear of people buying large amounts of coal—uncharacteristic quantities . . . Or copper piping or . . ."

"If the people want to do it enough, you will not stop them," George pointed out.

Loftkin rounded on him. "The poor, the uneducated, they can do nothing without someone feeding them ideas. So we destroy the idea at both top and root. Everywhere we hear people mention the possibility of steam power we must remember that by destroying such fancies we insure the future of an empowered ranking system. You do your duty diligently and with a clear vision of our purpose. Never forget that what you do now determines the future."

"And my family?" George looked down, his fingers flexing around the cane.

"You will be provided for so long as you do your duty diligently and I remain in power."

"And . . ." George cleared his throat. "My son . . ."

"Ah, yes. An interesting predicament you find yourself in—supporting the Council so loyally and yet with a child exhibiting magicking ability. And he is so very close to sixteen."

George switched the brass-handled cane from one hand to the other, reassured by the weight of it. His eyes flicked around the room, marking each exit. And the lack of guards of any sort—human or automaton. He licked his lips and narrowed his eyes.

Loftkin watched him consider the softly spoken words. "Considering the good you do on the Council's behalf, certain things can be—*overlooked* with a certain amount of prejudice. Even forgotten."

George heaved out a sigh. "That is reassuring. My boy . . . He is all I have now his mother is gone."

"Yes, pity that," Loftkin said with a shrug. "And she was the one who passed witchery to your son?"

"Most certainly so. But—" He looked away, his knuckles tightening around the cane's head.

"But?"

"Nothing," George said, his gaze stuck to the floor between them.

"Mmhmm. I have found that lodged within the heart of *nothing* frequently resides a most important *something.* A something of substantial proportions. Sometimes incendiary ideas are couched in very small words." Loftkin stepped forward, examining the other man, his face lifting and lowering as if he sniffed the air around the man, scenting for lies.

George laughed, the sound sharp and unnatural. "There is nothing of import within my *nothing,* merely the passing thought that my son's mother was a good woman. Certainly nothing incendiary."

"She was a Witch. And a *good woman,*" Loftkin said, his eyes as thin as his lips. "One might think you approved of her being what she was."

"Approved of her being a Witch? Certainly not." He swallowed so hard the sliding of his Adam's apple nearly choked him. He took a step back from Loftkin and when he adjusted the cane in his hands it was to grip it in both, between himself and the man who suddenly seemed his adversary.

"Hmm. I see."

"But as a wife, she was a fine woman. Witchery was her ruin. As it was meant to be." George lowered his head.

"Well." Loftkin turned away with a sweep of his coat. "So long as it does not become the downfall of your son.

Do right by me, George, and I will do right by you and yours."

"Yes, Councilman Loftkin. Of course I shall."

Aboard the Artemesia

Back in Marion Kruse's cabin, four people sat, at once all together and miles apart. Bran kept his bags close at hand and Meggie sought solace burying her face in her stuffed oddity, Somebunny.

Marion pulled the blanket and finely stitched quilt off his bed, throwing them on the floor in front of the door and settling onto them. "That was quite interesting," he said of their recent dining experience.

Over the *Artemesia*'s intercom came the voice of the ship's announcer. The only news the airborne liner received readily came through his accounting of the day's events worldwide.

Marion leaned back, resting his head on the door's lower panel and listening as the announcer reported brief bits of what was deemed worthy. The war in Europe dragged on, magick devastating both wealthy families and the poor; another explosion of an experimental and illegal steam engine had blown apart a building in Philadelphia's Below—and were they all not fortunate the government actively sought to destroy such devices? In Washington, where Watchmen were less plentiful, a fire had started due to a steam mishap. And lastly, the Merrow had slunk out of the briny deep and slaughtered the worker of Boston's lighthouse, spreading what they didn't eat of him around the building's base as a bloody warning.

Meggie sank into Maude's lap, her eyes wide. "I remember the lighthouse's keeper," she whispered.

Maude looked to Bran, a strange expression passing between them.

"He came inland once," Meggie announced. "I met him at the Boston Museum with my papá. He wanted to see the Feejee Mermaid and so did I."

"No, love, that's not possible," Maude began, but Marion leaned forward, bracing his hands on the floor.

"And did you?" Marion asked, staring at the child fallen so deep into memory that her eyes had gone glassy. "Did you see the Feejee Mermaid?"

"Yes," Meggie insisted. "I saw her . . ."

Both Maude's and Bran's mouths dropped open but Marion ignored them and Meggie continued, her voice soft and halting.

"She was no mermaid, no—not like the beauty Hans Christian Andersen wrote of—she was dreadful, so stiff and scared and small. Like a baby . . ." Meggie shivered. "I remember."

Bran reached out and, grabbing her shoulders, shook her. "Impossible. You cannot remember something that never happened. Your mother was never in Boston and neither were *you*."

The bag holding Sybil's skull clattered at Bran's side and he grabbed it.

Maude took another tack, her voice shaking as she assured Meggie, "The Wandering Wallace will sing soon, pet, and I shall tell you a story, and then? Off to bed."

"But, Papá . . . I remember . . ." Meggie insisted. "The museum's tall columns, the sound of glass bells, the mermaid's huge and horrible head. Her teeth. The fear on her face . . ."

"Hush now, hush," Bran said, releasing the bag to put a hand on his daughter. Meggie had never been to Boston. But Sybil . . .

Marion sat back against the door, watching.

Bran shifted to block the other man's view. "You are only imagining those things, not remembering," he said.

Marion rose and stretched his arms wide. "Why say that?" he asked, rolling his head on his long neck, his dark hair falling across his eyes.

"The child's never been to Boston," Maude said. But she snapped her mouth shut.

Marion's dark eyes narrowed.

Maude stumbled over the next words. "She has suffered fright after fright and has surely heard some person's grim accounting and repeats it now. Dear fawn might shatter if you continue to feed her fancies and take so little care of her."

The rain outside drummed harder on the airship's windows.

"She is simply imagining a different place—a distant place, an escape," Bran said, eyes locking with Maude's.

"Well, if that is *imagining* Boston's museum then she has the most amazing imagination of anyone," Marion retorted, "because she describes it exactly as it, in fact, *is*."

Meggie's eyes widened. "Why do I remember if I was never there?"

"Yes, tell us, Maker," Marion said. "Tell it true."

"You *overheard* . . ."

"No," Meggie insisted, "Papá, I saw it. But with another—Papá?"

"Dear little dove, I am your papá—no one else. And you've

never been to Boston. And the Feejee Mermaid—she is a hoax—a fraud, a fake."

The rain ran loud as a waterfall over their windows, making even the lightning nothing but a distant smear of stuttering brightness. "No, Papá," she cried, "she was real. A real Merrow, but only a baby . . ."

"Why would you lie to your child, Maker?" Marion asked.

"See here," Maude said, her head snapping up and her eyes fixed and fierce on Marion. "It's that—*you*—who have done this to her. You scare her. You have us, every one, in your grasp. You have control. Why scare a child by buying into her fears?"

A storm brewed behind Marion's eyes, but he turned and stepped away from them, sliding down the door to slump on his blankets. "I was a child once, too."

Across the intercom came the voice of the Wandering Wallace as he sang *The Nightingale* to the *Artemesia*'s passengers as a lullabye.

"Gather in close, little dove," Maude said, wrapping her arm around Meggie. "Have I told you yet of the Frost King and the little princess?"

Sniffling, Meggie shook her head.

Maude brushed the pale curls back from the child's forehead and began the evening's tale.

Bran knew Marion watched the three of them: Bran moving to stare out the window, his bags on his lap, fingers back in some journal within them, Maude nearby soothing Meggie in her lap as she told her story.

Did Marion's stomach twist remembering how someone told him tales, seeing Maude do the same for Meggie? Did he hate his Maker more for ensuring that Marion would never again know that innocence, though he could watch it in the eyes of the Maker's daughter?

Aboard the Tempest

Rowen's room was modest: wood floor, ceiling, and walls with two lanterns flooding the space with light. Suspended between two of the walls like a giant spider's web hung a single hammock. Slung across it were a wool blanket and a thin muslin shirt. He closed the door behind him. A pitcher of water and an empty basin stood on a low crate in one corner and a chamber pot resided in the other.

Rowen moved aside both pitcher and basin and sat on the wooden box, tugging off his boots. He sighed and wiggled his toes, crossing one leg over the other to give the ball of one foot a solid rub. He scratched his chest and yawned. These were simple quarters, far simpler than any he'd stayed in before. He scanned the space again. At least the place was clean.

Snatching the pitcher, he sloshed some water into the basin. He stretched up and then reached down to his waistband to undo his belt and tug the tail of his shirt free. He pulled it up and over his head, bending over to toss it toward the hammock. It caught there and hung and he turned back to the basin. He scooped water up in his hand and splashed it across his face and chest, pawing at himself as he scrubbed with only water and the force of his own fingers. He moved on to his armpits, washing them with greater focus before he rinsed his hands off in the basin.

Grabbing the other shirt with damp fingers, he looked at it carefully. It would be snug, but clean, so he picked up the discarded one, turned it inside out, and toweled off with it. Still damp, he struggled a moment with the new shirt, feeling it stick as it crossed his broad shoulders. He worked it down and over the rest of him and then pulled off his trousers.

He stared at the wet and filthy shirt he'd just used as a towel. He had never done his own laundry, but he had dallied a few times with the girls he'd jokingly referred to as his washing wenches. He'd teased them as they worked and it had always resulted in laughter and wet clothing, which Rowen always felt meant it had been a successful day.

With a grunt, he crouched in front of the basin and pressed the shirt into the water, squeezing and swirling the fabric around. How had they done it? He pulled it up, wrung it out and then fished it back into the water, spun it around again, and once more wrung it out. Satisfied, he spread it out and hung it on a peg. He'd been on the road for too long without any true time to pause and refresh, and although this was not the place he had hoped to recuperate, still it was something. He couldn't get to Jordan without the assistance of the *Tempest*'s crew and Elizabeth was firm that there was nothing to even discuss until morning came.

He picked up the basin, looking for a place to be rid of the filthy water. In the corner near the chamber pot was a funnel feeding into a pipe. Above it was a sign scrawled with: *Water, yes, piss, no.*

He chuckled and sent the dirty water rolling out of the basin and into the funnel.

He scrambled up into the hammock and settled there as it swayed gently, pulling the blanket over himself. Glancing at the lanterns, he yawned again. Whether they were on or off he would sleep like the dead.

Philadelphia

It was a good thing the dead slept. John made the sign of the cross at the thought, but it was true—he no longer thought of Lady Astraea as being alive. Yes, her body still functioned—seemed normal as ever other than the slight change in her coloring. But Lady Astraea—the Lady Astraea he had been hired by and had come to know—no longer lived in that body.

He shuffled down the slate stairs that wound from the top of Philadelphia's Hill down the side of it, past real estate of continually decreasing value, descending into the dark and dirty depths of the Below.

The Night Market sprawled out across the candle- and torchlit streets, the music of violins and drums joining with raucous laughter and rolling out to fill the spaces between the slanting and awkward-looking buildings. The Night Market was an assault to the senses: firedancers puffed flames into the air, dancers made bejeweled bras and coin belts glitter and tinkle like a thousand tiny bells, the scents of flesh, food, and flame thickening the air.

The Night Market was one of the greatest temptations a man could face. In his case, it was a temptation he always somehow avoided.

He pushed his way past it—even more determined to be beyond the mass of staggering and rollicking people than he had been the night he rolled Lady Astraea's body into the Burn Quarter in a wheelbarrow.

He walked quickly, head down, eyes darting to avoid meeting anyone else's. There were places in the world where direct contact was considered disrespectful, and disrespect could be deadly. He coughed, realizing that in that way the Hill and the Below were much the same.

He passed beneath the bridge where the wounded veterans warmed themselves with dimming campfires and bottles of drink and continued to the worst of all the Philadelphia neighborhoods—the place even the gangs hesitated to claim—the place the fire companies had decided to let burn if a fire started there.

It was not long until he found the house again. He opened the gate and walked into the small yard with its rambling and wayward plants wandering their way across the walkway. He paused on the threshold. Something was different. No skull hung under the eaves with sparkling stormlight eyes. He reached out to rap on the door but it opened beneath his hand and he called out, "Hello?" as he stepped inside.

There was no answer and no lights. He held up the small lantern he carried, raising it high enough that its light fell across the entire room. This was where they had laid the body out and where the Reanimator brought Lady Astraea back to life. And there—he swung the lantern so the light focused on the room's far wall with row after row of shelves.

Empty shelves.

No papers, no stormlights or soul stones, none of the trappings of the Reanimator. He was gone. And it appeared he was not going to return. At least not for some time.

John scrubbed a hand over his short, tight salt-and-pepper curls, faced with a decision. Hunt the Reanimator now or return to his place on the Hill and guard the Astraea household from its own now-foreign lady? With a groan, he left the house and turned his face toward the Hill.

Aboard the Artemesia

The Wandering Wallace returned from Topside immediately after singing his lullabye. Exploring the liner's shops and intricately designed ins-and-outs held no interest for him. The only thing he cared for awaited him inside his cabin.

Miyakitsu sat on their bed, feet tucked up beneath her, and looked up at him, smiling.

He stood in the doorway, hands tucked behind his back. "I have something to show you," he whispered, giving Miyakitsu a lighthearted wink in direct opposition to the way he actually felt. "But only if you trust me." He paused, watching her. "Do you trust me?"

She nodded, almond-shaped eyes wide.

"Do you remember our most important rule?"

Again the slow nod came.

"And what is that? Tell it true."

Her eyes roamed their modest room and landed on the thing that might as well have been the Tree of Knowledge in the Garden of Eden, it was so forbidden to her. She spoke, her voice the caress of a warm spring breeze, gentle and welcome, and something she kept for him. "Never, never, open the trunk."

"That's my girl," the Wandering Wallace whispered, setting his hands on either side of her moon-shaped face to draw her in closer. "Such an amazingly good girl you are." He went to the well-adorned and oddly painted trunk, scooting around it so his back was to the wall and his face—his eyes—and the top of the trunk's lid faced her.

She folded her hands on her lap and sat primly, eyes on the ceiling, gaze far from the trunk's lid.

He grunted and with a few light touches the gears that made up the trunk's unique locking mechanism adjusted and allowed him to heft the lid open. He always paused a moment once the lid was up, paused to remember the things Miyakitsu would never recall. If he was lucky. He looked at the body in the trunk, lying cinched in place by a few well-designed belts and buckles, dormant, dead by some estimations, her ebony hair a cascade of black water shrouding a face that appeared to be sleeping. Beside her was his daguerreotype's developing box and the stormlight crystal collection that animated her. The most unique soul stone in the world lay among what looked like a fistful of broken glass strung into a half-dozen strands near her cheek.

Reaching in he moved aside a few items of clothing, withdrawing a small pillow that helped brace her for travel. Bruises, bumps, or scrapes were unacceptable, especially for a Fetch.

Miyakitsu sat on the bed, uninterested in what he was doing and Tsu slept in her box. He pulled out both the developing box and a smaller box, and holding them stacked high in one hand, used the other to secure the lid to the trunk.

This was the hardest part—other than the lies—and he grunted as he lowered the lid back into place, closing Tsu in once more.

Miyakitsu twitched on the bed, tempted to help him with closing the trunk, but he gave her a stern look and she settled once again, her hands folding, her knees together, ankles crossed.

The trunk's lock went through its standard relay of clicks and snaps and a small bell rang, signaling the lock's success.

He let out a breath and crossed the room to sit beside her, resting the dark blue satin box on his knees.

"Everyone likes a gift from time to time, you'd agree?" the Wandering Wallace asked, slipping the mask off his face to rub at the area beneath his eyes.

She adjusted her gaze from where it had been pinned to the ceiling to rest on him.

His eyes creased at their edges, a smile on his lips, and he knew the scars that covered a swath of his face barely adjusted, his appearance much like a damaged wax doll.

She stared at him a moment, then the edges of her eyes crinkled and she returned her gaze to the box, which he opened to reveal a selection of glimmering ruby rings. She touched the velvet beside each one, counting slowly and carefully. "Seven, my love."

"Seven? Still so many . . ." He pinched the bridge of his nose. "And so many families already gifted with them. Thirteen out. Seven left. Elections coming too soon, too soon . . ." he murmured.

"Three of the seven are aboard?" She cooed out the question and shifted toward him. Her long slender fingers closed the box's lid and she slid it onto the nearby table.

"Yes. And if we keep up the ruse of enjoying the captain's company for dinner we might gift him with one."

"What of the Maker?" She pressed her body against his side, her supple curves fitting into his lean lines.

"What of him?" the Wandering Wallace asked, blinking. "He was not even expected on this journey of ours."

"Gifted *him* . . . ?"

The Wandering Wallace straightened beside her, his eyes

locked with hers. "Gift the Maker with such a ring?" He laughed and Miyakitsu's mouth slipped into a smile. "You clever, clever beast, you!" he exclaimed. "Taking the fight to the man himself. Bringing the solution back round to the problem!" He nodded, steepling his fingers together before his nose and peering over them at her. "So which name on our list do we remove so there are enough rings to go round?"

She ran a finger from his forehead to his chin, her touch feather-soft. "Such a large decision," she said. She yawned and he glimpsed the beast inside her, the fox she was always a heartbeat from being, all flesh, fur, teeth, claw, and wilderness dressed up in the skin of his wife. "Some decisions are best when slept upon," she whispered, leaning into him once more. She gave him a soft, lingering kiss and her slanted eyes, with the forests and pools of Japan reflected in their depths, closed beneath a thick fringe of eyelashes.

She scooted closer to him, a beautiful dark-haired angel from a foreign land, and he knew he would give her anything: his heart, his soul . . .

"What if I told you we are going to take over the world? At least the New World . . ."

Yes, he would give her the world.

Her hand slipped down his arm, into his hand and she tugged him down on top of her.

He did not bother feigning resistance.

Chapter Six

Lost, yesterday, somewhere between sunrise and sunset,
two golden hours, each set with sixty diamond minutes.
No reward is offered, for they are gone forever.
—HORACE MANN

Aboard the Artemesia

The Wandering Wallace sensed the dawn though he could not see it from any window on the airship due to the thick bank of clouds holding them aloft.

Exhaustion would eventually take him. He knew that as well as he knew his own name. There was little a revolutionary could guarantee except for an early grave and a gnawing exhaustion only kept at bay by the fire in his gut that shouted at him to change the world. He yawned, but fought down the feeling, swallowing it up and watching as Miyakitsu stirred in her sleep.

A fitful night, one moment she was Miyakitsu, human, soft and supple, lying like the embodiment of temptation at his side in only her silk robe, and then she whimpered, dissolving away into her fox form, thick midnight pelt a cool tickle against his flesh. She had not flashed in and out of her forms so frequently since . . . He struggled to remember and nearly laughed at the dichotomy of it all.

Him—the one struggling to remember!

The sad truth was she hadn't acted this way since they first boarded the ship and left her home country and past far behind. The only things they'd brought with them were his trunk, his clothing, a few scant possessions he'd obtained on his strange quest, and her clothing, such that it was. She owned three kimonos, one for dress and two for everyday, a set of sandals that he felt impeded her keeping a reasonable pace, several pairs of socks that she was meticulous in keeping, and a delicate hand-carved comb. Easy enough to pack.

Few on board the Cutter they rode back then cared about their marital status. She was foreign, he was odd, and the crew just tried to make certain they all—or at least most of them—survived the voyage through Merrow-infested waters. On such a journey few people cared who kept company with whom in the wee hours of the morning.

It was as freeing as it was terrifying.

They stayed to the ship's center whenever on deck and watched every porthole and spot that needed plugging—and there were more than a few aboard that leaky Cutter. Merrow had never been known to tear straight into the bowels of a boat, but there was much about the Merrow none of them knew. So the Wandering Wallace kept her close and by day she was a beautiful young woman that cared only for his company and by night she was his pet fox.

On that ship he obtained his prize possession and learned how to use it. A technology only in its early and experimental stages, a premade camera obscura for the making of a daguerreotype was expensive to obtain and difficult to keep, but it was there and then that he had obtained his first image of the two of them together.

It was a modern miracle—proof of them together that went on beyond her falling asleep and him falling out of her memory. Tangible proof that she was happy with him—pictorial proof she was loved by him and he loved her back.

She stirred in her sleep and the small dark fox elongated, her flesh swallowing fur and her body stretching to fill the kimono. She yawned and he thought, as he so often did, that her teeth were just the faintest bit sharper first thing in the morning.

She rolled onto her left shoulder—always her left shoulder, he knew, and jumped up in the bed, feeling something hard beneath her arm.

She grabbed it, held it in her hand, and tilted her head. It was framed in copper with a thin protective sheet of mica covering the image within. An image of . . . She wrinkled her nose and peered at the picture. A man in a funny mask stood beside a young woman with long black hair. She straightened further and he knew even from the body language he saw sitting behind her that she was not sure.

Look up, he willed her, *look up . . .*

The light glinting off the glass caught her eye and she peered at the long-handled mirror that hung from the ceiling, suspended and slowly turning, one face carved metal and one—

—her own.

She grabbed the mirror, inspecting her reflection as if seeing it for the first time. It was all at once so familiar a scene and yet so unsettling that his stomach dropped. Would it be today that she no longer even knew herself? Would this be the morning he would never recover from?

She held the mirror in one hand and the daguerreotype in the other, doing a careful side-by-side comparison. Then her gaze fell onto the mask from the picture, sitting as he always left it by her bedside.

It was the same one in the picture. She saw another picture by the bedside and another. There was a stack of them she flipped through, frames clicking against each other. They chronicled their time together, showing him sporting each of his masks—each of the ones that he left displayed around whatever room they called their own on any given night.

She fumbled through the photographs, her curiosity in control until she came to the last one. The image only he and she were meant to see.

The face only they would ever share.

She gasped, seeing the truth there in stark black-and-white.

But it could never be said that foxes were not crafty—that foxes were not clever—and he hoped she knew the truth by reading it in his eyes. That was all that mattered. No scars, no marks could change the truth she saw all over again for the very first time each morning in that first photograph.

The truth of his love for her.

She always turned so slowly. Every morning it was the same. A slow and graceful pivot on the bed, barely disturbing the thin covers, as she followed the path of the masks, finally coming face-to-face with the man behind them.

The expression on her face said it all: I should remember you. The pictures prove that. But I cannot. Why can I not remember something so happy? So good?

Questions washed across her features in waves of varying degree and she reached a soft hand out to his battered and burned cheek. With one tender touch all his fear and hate from that night so long ago disappeared.

It was as if he was never found as a child with a steam contraption he refused to see burned and destroyed. It was as if he had never lost his mother and father in the ensuing blaze and never been taken in by the people of the Night Market who taught him many skills . . .

As if he never had been pushed to want nothing more than vengeance.

Beneath her ministrations he was whole again.

And each morning, like he had done so many times, he seated her beside him and told her his favorite tales as a magician—the tales of the potent magick making up their relationship and binding them together.

Aboard the Artemesia

Jordan woke in darkness, her lantern out, only the faint flicker of lightning in the clouds surrounding the *Artemesia* giving a pulsating glow to the room's interior. The sky outside was as thick and claustrophobic as her head felt.

Her brain pounded against her skull, the memory of the blow to the back of it a distant ache. Her head felt thick with the sizzle of fire. She licked her lips, hearing them rasp together like paper, her mouth sticky with the last bit of moisture. She swallowed, her throat threatening to close. Gasping, Jordan stretched out across the floor, her hand reaching blindly toward the stand on which was balanced both pitcher and cup.

Her fingers traced a path up the stand's leg and found the cool curve of the pitcher, wrapping tight around its handle. She pulled it toward her but it fell, her arm's muscles rubbery—barely strong enough to stop it from tumbling to the ground and shattering. She brought it down to the floor with a teeth-rattling thump, glad the thing was so sturdily built.

Reaching for the cup when a flare of lightning briefly lit her room, she knocked it down and heard it hit and roll away. Her hand walked across the floor trying to find it, but she swallowed again, fighting to peel her dry tongue off the roof of her mouth. Sitting, she dragged the pitcher to her and hefted it, her lips searching out its edge.

She tilted it only far enough for the water to tease against her mouth and she let the cool liquid spill into her. She had no idea how long she sat drinking—she wondered if she had even bothered to breathe—only that the pitcher was empty and still her tongue felt like a desert was spread across its top.

A drop of water rested at the corner of her lips and her tongue darted out to guide it in as well.

She rose, making her unsteady way to the door. Leaning against it, she pounded with her fist, shouting, "Water!" She coughed the word out, stroked a hand down her neck, and tried again. "Water!" she demanded, pounding and kicking at the door.

She ran the back of her hand across her forehead. She was not fevered so why did she feel such a thirst? Why did her head feel like a thousand bees hummed inside her skull?

Her hand dropped from the door, fist uncurling. A memory, like a shadow, floated behind her eyes and filled her ears. She remembered the sound of rain falling hard against her window. The invasive scent of minerals and moisture. Of wind whipping clouds into fresh shapes and lightning jabbing like accusatory fingers across the sky.

She had done it.

She had called down a storm. She had found her own

trigger and identified it. Her trigger had never been pain or sorrow.

Her trigger was blinding rage.

Hate.

Now she needed to control it.

The lock on her door clicked and the door opened, a young boy with a fresh pitcher stepping into her room as two guards pressed forward, filling the space between the door's frame.

A stormlight lantern was slung from the boy's forearm and he set the pitcher on the stand and adjusted her lantern so it flared on again. "The moment you start to Draw Down, call for water," he suggested, his dark eyes large and sparkling in the light. "It will keep you free of thc headaches. When the body loses too much water, the brain suffers."

He reached down and retrieved her wayward cup, filling it for her. "Drink," he said, taking her right hand and gently folding her fingers around the cup.

She did—not because he told her to, but because her mouth gave her no choice—her body compelled her to drink. When she finished with one cup, squinting over the edge of the glass at him, she asked, "Who are you?"

"No one important," he returned with a broad and gleaming smile. "But some call me Jeremiah."

"And some call you Powder Monkey," Mouse said with a snort. "Our names," he motioned with a crooked thumb to himself, Stache, and Jeremiah, "and your name, Witch, matter not one whit. We matter only because of our jobs."

Jeremiah agreed with a modest dip of his head and handed her the pitcher.

"Wait," she called as he stepped toward the door, "what is a powder monkey?"

Jeremiah flashed his smile again. "The one they send to help load the cannons. I'm small and quick."

"We have cannons aboard?"

He laughed. "Every airship has cannons," he said. "You have to have something to protect the ship."

"Protect the ship from what?"

"Pirates."

He squeezed out between the guards and the door closed before she could ask anything else.

Philadelphia

The boxes arrived the same morning and were presented to the councilmen while they took the first of many breaks for food, drink, and conversation. Seated behind the long table that served as their main base of operations, fresh tea steaming in their fine porcelain cups, the whir of gears and clicking of cogs signaled the arrival of an automaton. The hum of mechanics drew their attention to the large walking doll and the silver platter it carried. It strode to the middle of the table and, leaning, carefully set the platter down.

Seated at the edge of the room, waiting to address the Council, Catrina Hollindale balanced a cup and saucer in the palms of her gloved hands.

"Here now, what is all this?" Councilman Loftkin demanded, snaking a hand out to draw the etched silver tray across the mahogany table to him. He snorted, looking at the set of petite burgundy boxes—ring boxes—that faced him, each with a tag carefully written out in a delicate script. "Why, these aren't for us at all," he muttered. "These are for our wives." He tugged one box free and poked a finger into the folded tag to open it. He announced, " 'In an election year we appreciate the fine job you do in supporting the success of our people by being a complementary support to your husbands, the wise and wonderful councilmen.' " He drew back, chuckling. "Well. I daresay I agree with the sentiment. Shall we see what precisely is within the boxes, gentlemen?"

They nodded, passing the ring boxes around until each man had his mate's gift in hand.

Catrina straightened, focused.

Not one was left on the tray. "Hmm," Loftkin remarked. "I take it that whoever sent these keeps up well with the shifting membership of the Council. There is not one left for old Morgan Astraea's wife now that he's no longer a member."

"There is also not one for Stevenson," Councilman Mendelheim added. "Oh," he said. "Not that it matters much to the way my day shall progress, but I'm curious to know—as Councilman Stevenson is still away at Holgate on Weather Working business, do you suppose he too will receive a gift for his wife?"

Shrugs and indifferent nods were their responses as they carefully undid the delicate ribbon holding each lid tight to the top of each box and opened them. Tied onto a small satin pillow within was a ring for each of the wives set with a beautiful bloodred ruby that seemed to catch fire.

Councilman Loftkin held his wife's ring box high, turning it in the light.

Catrina blinked, looking down at the ruby ring adorning her own finger, its band snug over her lace glove and slightly loose on her naked finger. She was never without it. It was the only worthwhile gift her uncle had given her.

The men appraised the rings carefully, noting and commenting in turn on the delicacy of the band and the setting's design (Catrina's own was delicately crafted), mentioning the finely carved shapes that graced either side of the crown (Catrina's sported a tiny fox on one side and a lion on the other) that held each ring's rectangular cabochon (the same shape as Catrina's gem).

Her eyelashes fluttered, her mind racing.

"Who are these things from?" The newest among them, Councilman Yokum, asked the question also on Catrina's lips.

"Does it matter?" Loftkin responded. "They are lovely gifts. And I daresay it will save me from spending more on another adornment for my bride of oh so many long years," he added with a laugh.

"I think it must matter," Yokum insisted. "What if these are intended as bribes?"

"They are poorly devised if they are bribes," Loftkin scoffed, flipping the tag over and tugging the pillow out of the box. He peered into the box's bottom, into the lid, turned it over, untied the ring from its ribbon, and scowled at the interior of the band. "They are absolutely unmarked by any maker. If they are intended as bribes the one committing bribery traditionally announces himself as the benefactor in some way. Otherwise how would the one being bribed know on whose behalf to act?"

Yokum pursed his lips. "You seem to know quite a bit about how bribes work."

The older man reddened at the sly accusation. "It is common sense, Yokum, nothing else. I guess I should not be astounded by the fact such a thing escaped you," he added with a sniff and a tip of his chin.

"So what do we do with these?" Yokum asked.

"We have had anonymous benefactors in the past," Loftkin pointed out. He blew out a breath. "You, Yokum, can do with yours whatever the bloody hell you wish—I could tell you where you might as well stick yours, but I doubt it would sparkle nearly as nicely where the sun does not shine . . . For me, though, I shall be placing it on my wife's finger this evening over a nice dinner."

"Hear, hear," the others agreed. The boxes were again closed, the ribbons not as well nor so delicately tied, but done nonetheless, and the gifts put away.

"We have a guest with us today, gentlemen," Loftkin said, setting his box aside. "The young Lady Catrina Hollindale, ranked Fourth of the Nine." He extended his hand, motioning for her to rise and address them.

Catrina stood, holding her teacup and saucer before her, and cleared her throat.

"Why, yes, of course." Loftkin snapped his fingers and the automaton clicked its way to Catrina, bowed, and, taking the cup and saucer from her, stepped away with all the humility expected of an automaton.

"Good Council," Catrina began. "I come before you today to beg your mercy on behalf of a young man whose father is well known to you all. I beg you desist in your hunt for Rowen Albertus Burchette, ranked Sixth of the Nine and whose father serves your military with great ability."

Loftkin snorted. "I am sorry, my dear. Rowen Burchette, who was embroiled in a duel that he himself initiated, to defend the supposed *honor* of a Harbored Witch, the same Rowen Burchette who shot and killed Lord Edward?"

Instead of lowering her head, Catrina raised hers higher, tipping her chin up so she peered down her nose at the seated men. "The same. He was drunk the night he made his challenge."

"Imagine if we excused the behavior of every drunk," Loftkin muttered, shaking his head.

Leaning forward to catch the eye of the man at the table's center, another Councilman teased, "From what I hear of your Saturday evenings, Councilman Loftkin, it might be to your advantage to do so."

"Ha. Ha." Loftkin pressed his fingers together and peered over their tips at Catrina. "And do you have any other reason as to why we should rescind the hunt for this . . . this . . . murderer?"

Catrina pressed her lips together and clasped her hands. "Because, good sirs, sometimes it is better to have someone on your side rather than have that person against you, and showing mercy may create that effect in this case."

Loftkin laughed outright and Catrina's face reddened.

"Dear girl," Loftkin began, "if you believe that Rowen Burchette—the boy best known for his clothing and hair—"

"—and lewd jokes and riotous parties," Councilman Mendelheim added.

Loftkin nodded. "So I have heard. The boy is no hero or leader of men. Miss Hollindale, you are quite mistaken if you believe we should feel threatened—"

"—or frightened—"

"—by the idea of a lad of eighteen, this Rowen, coming after us because we are hunting him . . . The hunt shall continue." Loftkin stood, waving her away with a dismissive gesture. The automaton stepped forward, its intent clear. "You are greatly naive if you believe we fear Rowen Burchette."

Catrina turned to follow the automaton to the exit, beneath

her breath promising, "I would *never* suggest you feel threatened by *Rowen* . . ."

Aboard the Artemesia

Maude and Meggie were allowed to leave the room on their own recognizance when the *Artemesia* was secured in New York City, and Marion rested on the room's bed, his feet up, arms behind his head as he stared past Bran and out the distant window. "What would you do if you were I, Maker?"

Bran turned toward him and made a request. "Not Maker. Please. Not anymore. Just Bran."

"Why call you by your Christian name? It might give people the wrong impression—the impression we are friends. And that, dear Maker," he snapped, "is quite far from the truth."

Bran sighed.

"Still, I am curious. So I shall play along. Do tell me, Bran, what would you do if you found yourself in my situation?"

"You have other options. This, kidnapping us—and whatever grim thing might come next—is not your only choice." The circles under Bran's eyes were heavy and lined with fine grooves that spoke of little sleep.

"Do tell me, Bran, what numerous options are still available to me now that I am aboard an airship with one of the most well-ranked men in the United States as my captive? Where do you see this multitude of choices?"

"You wish to wound me, to punish me—in that you have already succeeded."

"So said Brer Rabbit to Brer Fox."

Bran continued, knowing Marion was at least halfheartedly listening. "You have ruined my ability to maintain my livelihood. From anyone else's perspective it appears I have abandoned my post. You have most likely encouraged a hunt to be initiated. When they find me, regardless of the damage you do, they will strive and succeed in making your efforts look paltry by comparison. The Councilman does not take lightly the disappearance of a man of my rank. You have, by association, destroyed Maude's ability to find employment. No household will employ her now she's gone off without reporting in. And my daughter . . . Meggie will never again know who to trust. She will live out her life looking over her shoulder and wondering who might try and uproot her happiness. So if you were seeking some long-reaching punishment, you have done more than achieve it.

"But if your goal is to do more than to ruin a trio of lives—if your calling is something grander—something higher—then you must adjust your course as surely as this airship shifts to avoid running aground in the mountaintops."

Marion glanced down and Bran held his breath. Something had made an impact.

"Rather than being the criminal the honest men dog and drag through the dirt with their righteous accusations, be like the men you seek to depose—find, establish, and hold your power *legally* so none may question your ascent," Bran suggested. "Do not give them more reasons to destroy you—they are politicians, they naturally desire to do that—lend them no aid through the committing of a greater illegal act against my family. Be as our country's leaders are: upright and merciful."

Aboard the Tempest

Rowen woke to a pounding on his door. Outside in the corridor the long, thin man he'd heard called Toddy stood. "Good Queen Bess wants to see you," he said, wiping his nose on his sleeve.

"Queen Bess?" Rowen rubbed at his eyes, puzzled.

Toddy rolled his eyes. "Queen Bess—Captain Elizabeth?"

"Oh. Oh." Rowen pawed at his head, briefly trying to rub his hair into some semblance of order.

Rowen followed Toddy back through the winding halls. They came to a long room filled with slender tables and matching benches. Men lined the benches, bent over small bowls of steaming food, bickering. At the end of one long table sat Elizabeth or Evie, depending on how well one knew her. Seeing them enter, she stood, waving Rowen in her direction.

Leaving Toddy, he strode across the room to join Evie. She set her hand on his arm. "Go get yourself something to eat from the galley and we'll talk." She pointed to a nearby door and window and he obeyed.

From the window he could see a wooden table at the end of which a fierce-looking female snapped down a knife, slicing into some fruit he didn't recognize. She was a fleshy tree stump of humanity, built with short legs, heavy hips, a sagging bosom and jowls that reminded him of a prize-winning dog he had once seen. He hadn't found the dog visually appealing, but he had seen it work a troublesome escaped bull back into its pen and appreciated its power as he appreciated this cook's skill. The fruit she handled was covered in spikes and—Rowen's nose wrinkled—pungent. The woman's brows knit together as she handily whacked off both its stem and butt while the fruit spun between her hands, and she swept each piece into a bucket by her feet with a wet slap.

She grunted while she worked, but it was not the sounds nor the looks that held Rowen's attention—nor even the odd fruit which was quickly being peeled and pared down—it was her sharp and efficient movement, her economy of motion. Had she been a warrior on the field of battle she would have made quick work of an enemy. As a dancer such skill would have translated into a methodical grace. But as the cook on a pirate ship? She was unmatched. A greasy, thick-fingered, knife-wielding, flour-covered goddess.

"Eh," a man grunted from the opposite side of the window, shoving a wooden trencher towards Rowen. He grabbed it, mumbling a "Thank you" as the other man shoved a spoon into it.

What "it" was Rowen wasn't quite certain. Lumpy and thick it had a color that was somewhere between beige and ivory. It was studded with bits of something—he raised the bowl as he turned and took a deep whiff—spiced apples and raisins? His stomach rumbled in response and he decided, hungry as he was, he would make the best of whatever food was provided. He glanced up and made his way back to the table where Evie sat, watching with amusement as she kicked another crewman further down a bench so Rowen was seated at her left hand.

Then, as he began to shovel the porridge into his mouth, Evie opened her mouth and began to disappoint him.

She explained that rescues were not always possible or prudent and seldom cost-effective. She suggested he put the wind to his back and move forward with her crew. And she leaned over, placing a hand on his shoulder as if that would relieve what twisted and turned in his stomach, gnawing at his guts. Mentally he measured the distance from this ship to where the *Artemesia* might be and realized he had no idea where their ports were or how he could reach Jordan.

And knowing the little he did about how she was being treated, he felt sick. Not quite finished, he pushed his trencher away.

Evie glanced at him and then rose, saying, "Come along. There is a little left to see of the *Tempest* before you face your assignment."

Rowen stood, still stunned by Evie's attempt to dissuade him but she set a hand on his shoulder and steered him out of the dining hall.

Never had he been around a woman who was so willing to put her hands on him. On his arms, on his face, on his chest and his stomach. She had no sense of appropriateness. No sense of decorum.

He glanced down at the captain and realized it wasn't far down to glance at all. She was nearly his height in those thigh-high boots of hers. The only other woman who had been so willing to put hands on him had been Catrina. And a few of the women of less repute at the local tavern . . . but that was to be expected. Jordan would have never been so free with her touch. Why was it that the touch he wanted most was the one he got least?

Young men of his rank grew up knowing what was appropriate in settings like churches, taverns, gentlemen's clubs, and tearooms. That was not to say that because they knew what things were deemed appropriate and inappropriate that they actually acted in accordance with those expectations . . .

But, had there been a chapter in *Gertrude's Great Book of*

Ultimate Etiquette on how to behave aboard a pirate vessel, Rowen's instructors had either chosen to forgo it or it had been taught on one of the days he'd remained in his room nursing a hangover.

In the hall not far from the galley, a man with a face pockmarked in stunning black spots removed his hat and gave a curt incline of his head to the captain. She continued moving Rowen along, only leaning in long enough to whisper, "Powder blowback," in his ear as explanation for the man's odd marks.

She stepped out ahead of him then, saying, "As much as I enjoy putting my hands on you and making you do as I wish, I fear I am more apt to lead than to follow, and so, at this point I do hope you keep pace with me as I show you the rest of my ship and set you to your assignment."

"My assignment," Rowen murmured.

She laughed. "Why, yes. I do not kidnap handsome young men to simply be my boon companions." She stopped suddenly and, so close behind her, he bumped up against her. "Well, not of late at least," she corrected. "So, like any good sailor you must be assigned a proper duty."

She turned and, not for the first time that day, appraised him with open interest. "You appear to be physically fit, so I expect you will be capable of nearly any physical task I assign. And I expect with clothing like what you boarded wearing—although it is a bit worn—that you came from money and have some small bit of a proper education. Though I hold less stock in book learning than I do in real-world experience," she admitted, "I'd wager you have a decent head on those broad shoulders."

He merely watched her. She had stolen him and kept him

from his heroic mission and now would assign him some petty job, trapping him aboard her ship forever. He might never see Jordan again. He stared at her, hoping to stare her down. "I cannot stay here."

She shrugged. "We are too far above ground for you to go."

She turned on her heel and strode forward, pointing as she went, and announcing with each thrust of her arm the designation of each room. "You've seen the galley," she pointed back the way they'd come, "the *kitchen* as your kind would say. To our left we have the library, to our right, the chart room, and here, the water closet."

He raised an eyebrow and she grinned.

"Water closet, privy, waste room, whatever you prefer. The place one goes to thoroughly relieve oneself while aboard ship. In the days of water passage you'd just swing your bum out over the water and let fly. But those who are Grounded," she pointed down toward the distant ground, "tend to frown upon plummeting poop." She wrinkled her nose. "Poor senses of humor, the lot of them." She winked. Rowen was equally disgusted as he was intrigued. "Nowadays, of course, if you were to make a water passage and put your bum out bare to the air you'd—"

"—have it chewed off."

"Aye." She grinned. "Bastards the Merrow've become."

"Have *become*?" he asked, his eyes wide. "They've always been that way. They're savages. Little better than beasts."

"Let me guess," she said, crossing her arms, cocking her hip, and tilting her head to examine him again. "Strong jawline, firm mouth, broad brow, and sharp eyes . . . You were ranked Sixth of the Nine? Military, aye?"

He squared his stance and nodded.

"Then, you, m'dear, have been fed the same line of lies the rest of the Grounded have been."

"What do you mean?"

"The Merrow—they couldn't give two shakes of a fin about our kind. They never cared for us or bore animosity against us. Not until the last couple generations. My pappy used to tell such tales of them . . ."

"And who was he to know?" Rowen demanded.

"A fisherman. He worked the waters as his livelihood. He knew the truth."

"And that fisherman pappy of yours . . . did he ever tell you marvelous tales of the one that got away—a fish so huge it could be saddled and ridden, or so large it could swallow a man whole? One he had on his line—or in his net once but . . ." He laid the back of his hand across his forehead and swayed on his feet, "alas and alack, the beast busted free?"

She snorted. "Of course he told tales of the one that got away and he exaggerated—all men do."

Rowen blinked. "All *men*?"

"Yes, all men," she said with a smirk.

Rowen blinked again and pushed past the jab. "Then perhaps, before you accept his word on the Merrow as gospel truth, perhaps you should recall that he was in the habit of . . . embellishing."

She straightened. "Oh, love," she whispered, her tone low, her voice staying deep in her throat. "I wish you hadna' gone and done that. Casting aspersions on my pappy's character—that's nearly the worst you can do," she said, slowly shaking her head. She seemed to make a decision then and, sighing, she raised her hand, and pointed down the way they had yet to travel. "Continue another three doors down and turn left.

Yell: *Ginger!* And you'll meet the one who will handle the details of your assignments while aboard this ship."

"You're leaving? Now?"

"Yes. I just remembered I have so many things of greater importance to do than dealing with you directly."

She brushed past him, not caring how harshly she smacked into his shoulder as she left him behind.

"Huh," he muttered, brow furrowing. "Three doors down . . ." Hesitantly he made his way toward his future aboard the airship *Tempest.*

Philadelphia

The Council chambers of Philadelphia were not only used for the business of governing. "She is a hearty servant from sturdy stock," Councilman Loftkin said. "I would keep her myself except that our household is overflowing at this point and I resent the idea of sending a past staff member packing to something as dark and grim as the Below."

"Of course, of course," Councilman Yokum said. "She is a lovely-looking girl. And sturdily built. You do not shy from hard labor, do you, child?"

"No, sir," the girl said with a proud smile. "Never have shied away from work of any sort. My hands are steady and strong as my desire to make good in life. I work hard, sleep little, and listen closely so I serve well."

Yokum chuckled. "That is wondrous. And you are certain you will not keep her?" he asked Loftkin.

Loftkin smiled like a man who had already devoured too much of a good thing. "No, no. I simply cannot. And knowing she goes to a good home . . . and that perhaps this gift may help to bridge the unfortunate gap between our approaches of leading this Council towards a better and brighter day . . . That will set my mind greatly at ease."

Yokum grimaced. "I must always vote my conscience and represent the voices of my constituency first and foremost," he said. "So if this is your way of bribing me into boldfaced agreement with your policies . . . You had best take her home or cast her out."

"No, no! I would never wish to bribe you into agreement. I am only offering you a token of my regard—a present I cannot keep myself and yet wish to not see wasted. If it allows you to see that I hope someday we might have a meeting of the minds, so be it. But if you think it means anything else . . ." He shook his head. "You misread me."

Yokum dropped his head in a sharp nod. "I appreciate the gesture. And I truly hope that the day will come when we can both better understand each other's positions and forge a brighter future for our country. Together. But understand I will not fall silent and let my people be run over to appease your views. And certainly not because you give me a fine gift."

"I do not expect you to. It is very important that the issue troubling us both be voted on and this bill made into law before our citizens are set to cast their votes for the election."

"I am fully aware that is your belief, Councilman Loftkin, but I do not think that voting such a bill into law strengthens anything but our own position in government. What does it do for the betterment of our people—for the good of our citizenry?"

"You said it yourself—it strengthens our position."

Yokum's mouth hung open a moment. "And by strengthening our position we better their lives by . . ." He watched as the Councilman stared back at him. Yokum bobbed his head, trying to lead his fellow into saying whatever next bit was in his mind.

"We are their leaders. We need to remain secure. It's really quite simple."

"No. No, it's not. Our positions in government must be tenuous enough to make us work hard while being secure enough to do our jobs without fear. The balance of power must be in all aspects of government. Checks and balances. What you suggest shifts the power and gives incumbents an unfair advantage."

"We know the system. We should remain. To oust us too soon . . ."

"Why, when you say *know* the system, do I hear *use* the system?"

"Because you see trouble where there is none."

"Or is there no trouble if I simply go along with your plan? Vote the way *you* wish?"

Loftkin folded his arms over his chest. "It would be easier if you trusted in my experience and insight, yes."

"Then I apologize, Councilman Loftkin, because the first thing I was taught was to not trust politicians."

"And yet . . ." Loftkin gestured the length of his fellow and then raised his arm to encompass the Council chambers.

"Yes," Councilman Yokum admitted, "I have become the thing I dare not trust. What delightful and damning irony."

Chapter Seven

Time hath a healing hand.
—JOHN HENRY, CARDINAL NEWMAN

Aboard the Artemesia

Bran had become quieter, slower. He spoke more softly, more carefully. For some women it would have been a welcomed change. But to Maude it seemed all the passion—all the life—had been leeched from Bran Marshall.

He often sat in silence in the small shared room, paging through his journals and shaking his head.

Sad and somehow lost.

Maude found him by the window, staring out at the clouds that nearly always cloaked their craft. He slumped in a chair he'd dragged across the carpet, his shoulder bag on his lap, the bowl-shaped thing he refused to show her a lump obscured by the bag's thin skin of fabric. His left hand rested on the curve of it, his right palm flat to the window's glass.

At his feet his journals were strewn, discarded.

"Might you talk to me about it?"

He startled, caught up in his own thoughts and surprised by her appearance. "Talk to you about what?"

"The thing in the bag that makes you so sad—"

His right hand dropped to better shield the shape that rested in his lap.

"—or anything. About your journals. Why are they . . ." She bent and scooped them up, tucking them against her bosom as if they belonged there, close to her heart.

"There are pages missing," he said, stricken. "Important pages. I have no idea how or when they were mislaid, only that . . . if they are found by the right people . . . or perhaps the wrong people, yes, I think it must be those—the *wrong* people . . . they will have every conceivable reason to board this ship. And a few less than conceivable reasons, too." He lowered his head. "If they find those pages . . . nothing will stop them from coming here. And if they come here, they will find us."

She heaved out a sigh and crouched at his side. "There is nothing to be done for that. They will find them or they won't find them. They will seek out this ship, or they won't. They will find us, or they won't. These are all things outside of your control. There is naught to be done except be as prepared as we might be for discovery by those who would separate or harm us." She snorted out a laugh—a harsh and bitter sound. "By *others* who would separate or harm us," she corrected, looking over her shoulder at where Marion sat across the room, watching them as intently as a hawk above a field freshly cleared of grain.

Her fingers rested lightly on his leg and he twitched the bag and its mysterious contents away from her reach. "I don't need to know," she whispered, cocking her head to the side to peer up at him from beneath her eyelashes. "Tell me or don't tell me. It makes no nevermind to me in the end. But the way you *feel*? This constant and clawing grief you're holding tight to?" She reached up and stroked his cheek with the back of her hand. "That matters more than nearly anything. *You* matter more than nearly anything," she whispered, her eyes narrowing. "Let me help you."

He dragged out a sigh. "I cannot. Not here . . ."

"You cannot *what* here?" Marion asked from beside them.

Maude jumped, clutching the journals even more tightly.

Bran shifted the bag off his lap, turning to address Marion. If he looked small beneath the taller man's shadow already, seated there he seemed even less. He faltered under the glare of Marion's gaze.

Marion swooped down and snatched the bag from Bran's side. "Let's see just what this great mystery is, shall we?"

Maude looked back and forth from one to the other of them, from the younger, bolder, and embittered man who had stolen them from lives they were less than happy with to the slightly older, quieter, and yet equally embittered man she had grown to love. "No," she demanded, reaching for the bag, "you must not!"

But Marion simply swung his arm up and away holding the bag out of her reach. "You forget yourself, madam," he snapped. "You are nothing more than my dear, dear guests. You still exist because, for some godforsaken reason, I wish it that way. For now. So do not expect that you may tell me what to do or not do. Not here. Not now—not ever."

She stood there, as close to face-to-face as a woman a good bit shorter than him could, her upper lip raised in a defiant snarl, her brow lowered.

"Now, let us just see what the good Maker has been

keeping from us. Or shall I play this from a different angle and say there should be no secrets between friends? Would you prefer that, Maude, that I pretend things are different between us? That we are friends?" he said through a sneer. "Because I have needed to be many things in my brief period of freedom from your lover's torture, but I've only recently been forced to be an actor."

Maude ignored him, instead signaling to Meggie, who stood nearby, sniffling at his words. "Come here, little dove. He means none of it," she insisted, leaning over to drop the journals and wrap the child in her arms.

Marion's gaze dropped from Maude's belligerent expression to that of the child, whose nose and eyes streamed as she tried to hiccup her sadness away.

"He means none of it," Maude repeated, hoping her eyes were as fierce as her tone.

He hesitated, his gaze on the Maker's daughter. His voice caught and he denied and confirmed nothing, but said, "Let us see what so much fuss and stress is about," and reached a hand into the bag.

He withdrew Sybil's skull, and for a moment appeared as startled as the women standing between him and the Maker.

Then he laughed, just a brief chortle, but it rolled out of him as he held the skull aloft. "Poor Yorick, I knew him well." He puffed out a breath and his eyes narrowed, his gaze dropping to Meggie and bouncing to Maude and Bran and back to the skull as if he debated something, measured something. "No," he whispered, the shocked expression of his rounded mouth spreading into a slow smile. "A child's skull, isn't it? A child's skull."

He tested the weight of it. "You're toting around the skull of a child. My god. I thought you couldn't be more disgusting. But you proved me wrong. What is this, some sick prize?" He leaned close to Meggie and whispered, "Good thing you're no Witch, isn't it? Heads would roll."

Maude only clutched the girl tighter to her.

"Or was it a friend of yours that Daddy found not sharing well with his little dove?" He snorted at the thought. "Who was she, Bran? Or don't you know? There've been so many of us, I'd wager. We must all blend together. Do you remember the Conductors you Make . . ."

Bran looked away.

"Do you remember the one Topside? The one so burnt out already that he's dying? Do you remember his name? You are what killed him, you know?"

Meggie's sniffling and hiccupping doubled in intensity and Marion froze again. His gaze fell back onto Maude, and it was cold as the first bite of winter. "Take her somewhere else."

"No," she whispered. "We will not leave. We will be witnesses," she said through a closing throat.

"What the hel—" But he stopped the word and just looked at her as if she'd gone insane. "I won't . . ." He tossed out a sigh of exasperation and shook his head. "He will come to no harm. Go now. Such discussions should not . . ." His eyes fell on the child with her hair as pale as moonlight. Or frost on a window. "I am sorry," he whispered. "Such things should never be said before a child."

"You said we are like brother and sister," Meggie whispered between sharp inhales. "That we share the same Maker."

Marion nodded. "Take her now before I say something I'll wish I hadn't."

Maude nodded, spun quickly to plant a kiss on Bran's cheek, and then hurried her small ward from the room.

"If she's smart, she'll find a way to leave," Bran whispered, turning back to the window. "I am amazed she has stayed this long."

"Oh, she's quite smart, that one," Marion assured him. "But she won't go anywhere. Even to save the child. She's in love. It is the one time in their life when a man can easily outwit a woman—when they are blinded to their needs by their desires."

He changed the position of the skull in his hands, cradling it instead of holding it loosely in his palm. "Who was she, Maker?"

"Don't call me that," Bran insisted with vitriol. "I wish for little more than to leave that life behind me. If I could have survived without ever being that, I would gladly go back in time and do so. Be Bran Marshall of House Dregard and nothing else. Just a man."

"And leave all the glory of creation behind?" Marion stifled a laugh. "You were one of the greats. A man without peers! Only your father could hold a candle to your name and he—"

"—killed himself."

"What?" Marion drew up short. "What do you mean he *killed himself*?"

"He stopped being a threat to my reputation when he realized what sort of monster he'd created and so he loaded his pistol, held it up to his head, and he pulled the trigger. Surely that gives a clear enough description of *killed himself* to appease even you."

Marion squinted at the older man. "I . . . I did not know. I am . . . sorry."

"He died long before he pulled the trigger. Some things kill a man well before his brain spatters a wall. Do not ask for any other specifics, please. We kept it from the public record, but it should be shared with you, who believe there is no cost or responsibility we feel for our actions."

Marion stood, mouth agape, as the clouds outside their window parted and a port came into view.

"Now, God willing, you are wrong, and Maude's sight will clear as has ours. If she leaves me—takes Meggie—there might yet be hope for them. They are young."

"So are you."

"But it seems you are determined to not allow me a fresh start. Let them have theirs. Let some good come from all this."

"You—" Marion shook his head. "You astound me."

Bran turned and snatched the skull from Marion's hands. "You're right about many things, Marion. I do not remember everyone I've Made. I do not remember most names, Made or Grounded. Yet that is no excuse." His voice became a strained whisper. "But I remember her. I remember the way she pleaded with me. The way she cried, the way she finally gave up—not the way one gives up to be Made, but the way one gives up to die. I remember all of that and so much more. Her name was Sybil. Somewhere near Boston she was born and had a family."

"Near Boston," Marion whispered. His eyebrows rose high on his forehead, his gaze going in the direction Maude and Meggie had gone.

"Yes. She might have visited the Boston Museum and seen the Feejee mermaid. Sybil might have met a lighthouse keeper," Bran agreed with his unvoiced concern. "She was Gathered in young so I suspect they discovered what she was and turned her in themselves. It's become a common practice. Far better that, they must tell themselves, than fall from grace for Harboring."

Marion looked away.

"Our government has devised quite the societal structure, based around using the most volatile and remarkable of our resources—humanity itself. We make slaves of each other according to the dictates of religion, race, creed, and now—witchery. We judge each other as readily as a farmer judges a sow he wishes to breed. And once the truth is out . . ."

Marion rounded on him. "What truth?"

"That an anomaly has been found."

"What do you mean?"

"Witchery is not dictated by heredity."

Marion was nearly toe-to-toe with him, bent over him. "What?"

"We've been right all along on at least one thing—Witches are Made. They aren't simply born." His voice dropped. "Anyone can be broken to the point of exhibiting magickal abilities."

"When exactly did you learn this?" Marion's breath was hot on Bran's face.

"Making the Witch who suffers through dinner with us every night."

"The Astraea girl?"

"Yes. She should have been an impossibility. Instead, she's an anomaly."

"But if anyone can be a Witch . . ."

"Then our entire societal structure and the source of our energy—for *everything*—is built on a spiderweb of inaccuracy."

"Of *lies*, you mean."

Bran shook his head. "I say what I mean. Lies mean that someone knew."

Marion pursed his lips. "Sybil. It seems she and your daughter are connecting somehow if you are right about Boston. What do you intend on doing with her?" he asked.

"It depends on what you do with me. I promised her—well, *it*—a better burial."

"Hmm. And the rest of her didn't deserve such treatment?"

"The rest of her didn't repeatedly re-exhume herself."

"Oh." He stared at the skull a long moment more before handing it back to Bran. "That is quite a thing."

"Death generally is," Bran quipped, but in his mind he wondered if Sybil was connecting to his daughter from beyond the grave—showing her Sybil's memories—how long until she shared her memories of torture at Bran's own hands?

Philadelphia

Lord Astraea paced the library's floor, hands behind his back, eyes dark beneath his heavy brow. "You have changed," he muttered, addressing the woman who sat, no, sprawled, across the sofa, slurping from her teacup. "I should cast you out. That's what the boys say. Or send you to retire in the countryside."

Lady Astraea belched, clicked the cup and saucer together, and pushed them aside, letting them rattle across the nearby table and making Lord Astraea's teeth clamp shut. "You wouldn't dare!"

"You've no idea what I'd dare . . ." he growled, turning on her. He stalked across the floor to stand before her, and she straightened, her chin up, knees and ankles together, hands falling into her lap to fold there. He placed his hands on either side of her hips, leaning over so he peered into her eyes. "I want my wife back—I want the polite, endearing lady who ran this estate with such close attention and great aplomb back. I want my wife who said please and thank you and fetched me my slippers and paper along with a glass of wine—I want *her* back."

She pulled away on the sofa, crossing her arms. "Is that how you thought of me, as some weak-willed fool?"

"No, never! You were never those things. But a *lady.* You were a grand, grand *lady.* Where has my lady gone?"

"Perhaps your lady tired of your gambling and drinking and lying. Perhaps while you wanted her to look the other way she decided to take advantage of you looking the other way, too, and had some fun!"

"No, not my Cynthia. We always saw eye to eye!"

"It is hard to see eye to eye with a man whose head is stuck up his own a—" Lady Astraea slapped her hands over her mouth, her eyes going wide in horror. She shook her head at him, a terrified *no.*

But he had already stepped back, his eyes cold and distant. "Where has my lady gone," he whispered, staring at her before he turned on his heel and walked away.

Lady Astraea shivered from her ankles to her shoulders and whispered, "But I'm still here . . . I never left you—I never would."

With another body-wracking shudder her demeanor again changed and the other woman sharing Cynthia's body was back. She slouched against the sofa and eyed the teacup on the nearby table. Reaching out a single finger, she pulled the liquid from its cup, making it shimmer and dance in midair before dropping back down with a splash. Then she picked up the cup and swallowed its contents in one gulp.

Aboard the Artemesia

It was as the captain of the *Artemesia* and Jordan's guards escorted her through the promenade for the first time that she was reminded of how few people knew the truth about the life of a Weather Witch.

An older lady, her hair more silver than her original brown, stepped in front of the captain and offered him her gloved hand. He took it, bowed, and gave her fingers a cursory kiss. "And this lovely young lady," the woman asked, "just who is she, one might wonder—seeing her so well escorted."

He smiled at the matron, introducing Jordan. "Why, this is to be our ship's next Conductor. She is completing her training Topside."

The woman clapped her hands together. "Oh, how exciting!" She leaned toward Jordan, her thin eyebrows arched. "It must be thrilling to have Destiny embrace you so young! Knowing how you will live out your life and all the good you will do for others at such a young age! Why, your eyes must be opened to so many things the rest of us never experience!"

Jordan's stomach twisted at the truth in her statement.

"And you get to travel! How wonderful! How lucky you are to embrace your future so very young!"

Jordan lowered her head and sucked on her lips to keep from speaking. But, hearing the child's voice, her head snapped up.

Meggie. The little girl who had argued for her kind

treatment—who had, in her own small way, begged mercy for a stranger.

She watched the child, her hand tucked in the woman's beside her. They paused at the bank of windows, and Meggie pointed out to the clouds, turning to Maude to ask a question. Sweet and innocent, her fingers on the glass, she nodded. They were there only a moment, only long enough to say a few words and for Maude to lean down and kiss the top of Meggie's head.

Then they were on their way, chatting and swinging their joined hands. Behind them stalked the Maker and their strange, tall companion, Marion. There was something about him, Jordan thought, something nearly familiar—as if she should recognize him from more than their regular suppers.

Meggie spotted Jordan and began to drag Maude in her direction.

Jordan froze, Meggie before her. "Hello," Meggie said. Her eyes darted from one of the guards to the other. "You should come with us," she offered. "We're going to the tearoom for biscuits and other tasty things."

Jordan smiled and leaned forward. "That sounds lovely!"

The captain leaned in, putting his hand on Jordan's arm and making her straighten. "But you have other obligations."

"Oh, just this once?" Meggie asked. "I never see Miss Jordan unless she is training."

"It is the destiny of a Witch," Captain Kerdin said, his voice firm. "We must go Topside." He stepped between them, nudging Meggie back. "Take her."

The guards grabbed Jordan's arms and hoisted her.

Feeling her feet leave the floor, she leaned to the side, saying to Meggie, "I wish I could. I truly wish I could."

But she yelped as they yanked her away and Meggie cried out for her.

"Don't hurt her!"

People turned and the captain commanded, "Take her out of here, now!"

Jordan hissed when they pulled on her again and Meggie began to cry, insisting, "Be nice! Why can't you be nice to the lady?"

People began to murmur.

Lightning crawled closer to the windows of the ship and rain fell as tears streaked Meggie's face.

"Nooo," Jordan cried, seeing the rain and the tears and knowing too well they were connected, and that they would show the child to be what she truly was—in public. Then there would be no hiding. No choice except ruining the child to Make her a Witch.

Jordan bit and kicked, twisting free of the guards. She pushed her way to Meggie, grabbed her, and forced herself to cry—harder and louder than Meggie, making the child's show of emotion nothing compared to the drama of a Witch summoning a storm.

Then the Maker was there, urging, "Let her go," and pulling Meggie into his arms, the whole time whispering, "Calm down now, little dear, calm down . . . You must let her go!"

Meggie howled, her hands reaching for Jordan as the guards pulled her to her feet, towing her away. The rain coated the ship's windows, heavy and relentless. Jordan hated the Maker more for taking the child away and making her cry even harder.

And for so much more.

As they dragged Jordan toward the claustrophobic elevator she realized she could do it: she could kill the Maker, and slowly, relishing every moment of the act—taking her time with him the same way he'd taken his time with her—crafting pain like a delicacy to be served at banquet. Her stomach twisted but she fought it, focusing on the hate and pain he'd caused her. She swallowed hard, imagining the bite of the blade into his flesh instead of hers . . . Her gut threatened to rebel and outside the clouds dug at each other and tore each other apart, spitting rain at the windows.

She squeezed her eyes closed and focused on memory. On the pain, the fear, the burn of the blade and the smack of the cat, the scars on Caleb's slender and gentle fingers. No, she couldn't kill. Not for herself. But for Caleb, and most especially for the sake of the little girl—for the sake of the Maker's daughter, Meggie. To protect that towheaded child from the pain Jordan had suffered being Made—for that, she'd kill the girl's father.

As important as having a father was, having one who wasn't the Maker was far more important. It would be better to have no father at all than one who would hurt you to further his own twisted goals.

Aboard the Tempest

The third door down yielded no encouraging clue to Rowen's assignment. He found himself in a dimly lit corridor, pipes and wires and coils of metal running along the oddly curving walls. Peering around, he realized he was in more of a tube than a corridor. The sound of his boot steps echoed back to him and he glanced down at the metal grate that held him suspended above . . . He leaned forward to look and straightened suddenly, realizing that trying to see just how far one might fall was a bad idea. Other tubes or tunnels shot off like dark throats with open maws yawning just beneath the wire walkway, and leading, no doubt, to other sections of the ship's inner workings.

All around him things squeaked, grated, and hissed. The air was thick with moisture, and hot. Already Rowen felt a faint sheen of sweat rising on his face. Soon his hair would droop, his shirt would stick to him, his underarms would begin to be less than delightful, and . . . He glanced back toward the door he'd come through. If he left now what would be the harm? Surely he could determine the right things to say to get back in the captain's good graces and land a more reasonable—a more comfortable—assignment.

He was from a nearly noble family, after all. Certainly there was something he'd learned to say that he could adapt to this particular situation. Something from some etiquette lesson . . . He wracked his brain, knowing he'd need to start with an apology. He hated those nearly as much as asking for directions.

Something rumbled in a tube nearby and steam belched out of a gaping metal mouth. Someone cursed and coughed. And it sounded distinctly as if someone was kicking something. Hard.

Rowen leaned forward and peered down the nearest tube.

A gloved hand reached up out of the shadows, fingers splayed and pressing against the grate a moment before they crept along to the edge of it and slid a bolt aside. With a shove a door in the grate became evident and flipped open on the only quiet mechanism in the entire strange place—a pair of well-oiled hinges.

Rowen hopped back as another gloved hand sought the light and then both held either side of the gap now in the grated catwalk and slowly pulled up their owner, a man of smaller stature than Rowen, but whose body language showed, even as he was rising from the tunnel, that he was not to be trifled with. He kicked the grate's door shut, and it bolted flat. He cocked his head, his gloved hands balled into fists on his hips.

Coated in a thick layer of dirt and grease, the hair on his head spiked out at odd angles, and with far less of his face being what Rowen guessed had to be its naturally pale shade, he wore thick-lensed green goggles, their leather strap worn, its edges split; the rivets holding bits of the thing together were divided between rusty and shiny. If this was the "Ginger" he'd met before . . . Rowen stared. The man wore an apron as dirty as the rest of him and his thick rubber gloves ran halfway up his forearms. Rowen wrinkled his nose at his obvious lack of taste in fashion.

Something chattered behind the man, and a glass and metal spider edged out from his shadow, steam shooting from its belly, its rump a glowing bulb. Rowen shuddered.

"Are you what she sent me?" He shook his head, his lips twisting. "Shite. The woman never listens. I need someone small enough to climb through the tubes and with hands of a size that can actually do delicate work to the mechanisms inside." He didn't bother to hide the fact that he looked Rowen up and down. He shook his head again. "And she sends me a beefy-handed giant. Excellent." He turned his back to Rowen and grabbed a canvas bag that may have at one time been nearly white. Perhaps. Metal clanged against metal as he shuffled through a set of tools. "She hates me. That must be it," he was muttering. "She hates me but she won't say it so she sends me the message"—he turned back and swept a look up and down the height of Rowen again—"loud and clear."

"I'm not thrilled to be here either," Rowen said, eyeing the close quarters and the pipes lining the dim corridor.

"Used to finer digs, are you?" the other man said with a lopsided smile. "Serves me right. Give me someone of rank who doesn't even know what to do with his beefy hands."

Rowen rolled his fingers into fists at his sides. Yes, this had to be the rude redhead he'd met on the Aft Gundeck.

"Not even hands. Mallets, really," Ginger Jack said.

"Then imagine how they'd feel hitting you," Rowen suggested.

"Really. Really?" He laughed so hard he held his stomach and bent back. He stopped, snorting. "You're serious, aren't you?"

The mechanical spider slowly began to climb the wall, its eyes glittering, and Rowen recognized it as the metal Ginger Jack had been toying with in the aft Gundeck.

Rowen stood his ground, his muscles taut, his stance tight with a fighter's intent.

"My god, maybe I've been wrong about her. She must *love* me to send me a treat like this." He tugged off his gloves and tossed them onto the grated floor. "If you're looking for a fight, boy, you've come to the right place."

Rowen looked back at the door behind him, considered the pain of crafting a perfect apology according to a woman's particular standards, and dove headlong at the man in front of him instead.

Because, being raised by a mother like his, Rowen knew that whatever battle he faced with the man before him, it had to be easier and cleaner than doing battle with a disappointed woman. This was bound to be the easier fight to win.

Ginger Jack was not only small, he was also quick, Rowen soon realized, as the smaller man darted around throwing punches that always hit their mark. Rowen snorted in surprise as Ginger worked him over. Rowen had brawled more than his share of times in the taverns of Philadelphia, from the fine ones on the Hill to the dirty and slanted construction by the docks. He had nearly brought a building down once, things got so wild, and Rowen so angry.

But this man—it was more like trying to catch your adversary and *then* fight him . . . He never stood still, he never bothered with a proper fighter's stance, and he always . . . *Oof*! He always managed to place the hit where it hurt most.

He had no sense of decorum. So, struggling to hit a target that moved so fast around him, Rowen decided to level the playing field. Or at least level his adversary.

With a kick, Rowen swept Jack's feet out from under him, sending the man crashing to the grate with a grunt. Rowen dropped down on top of him like a load of bricks and sat on his gut, one hand pressed to his chest.

Ginger Jack kept throwing punches, but Rowen's arms were too long, his reach too great.

The smaller man strained with effort, but each time his balled fists stayed inches from the tip of Rowen's chin.

So Ginger opened his fist and, drawing back . . . landed his fingertips on Rowen's chin.

Rowen snorted and Ginger Jack tried again. And again got the same results.

Rowen laughed.

Ginger Jack groaned, and tried once more.

The same effect was achieved. Nothing more, nothing less, unless one counted the increase in Rowen's amusement.

Because, bruised and battered as he was, he was laughing now.

And suddenly, so was Ginger Jack.

The spider just hung nearby, watching.

They sat there a moment, laughing at the absurdity of it all. Rowen rose to his feet, straddling Jack, and extended a hand for the other man to take.

Jack grunted and accepted the favor, heaving himself to his feet and looking at Rowen a bit differently now—as one might when glimpsing potential instead of problems. Jack's mouth slid from one side of his face to the other. He scrubbed a hand across his chin and finally announced, "Well, lad. You are surely not what I expected, and far from what I'd hoped for, but I think you'll do well enough with some instruction."

Rowen shrugged. "You certainly aren't what I was hoping for either."

"Oh, aye? And just what were you hoping was behind that door?"

"A beautiful girl I'm determined to rescue," he admitted with a wry wink.

"Well, then I am quite the disappointment. I apologize for dashing your hopes," he said with a chuckle. "Perhaps I'll equip you, show you around, and you can entertain me with tales of this ravishing damsel you're seeking to save." Jack leaned into a mess of interwoven wires and slender, wandering tubes and withdrew a set of gloves and goggles. "Try these on. I daresay they might require some adjustment, you being a walking tree trunk and all, but it's better than losing an eye or slicing the hell out of your hands."

Rowen adjusted the goggles' band and tugged it over his head, settling the strange lenses over his eyes, before he snapped the gloves on.

"Good, good," Jack said with a clear look of approval. "Let's get started."

Chapter Eight

Great is truth. Fire cannot burn, nor water drown it.
—ALEXANDRE DUMAS THE ELDER

Aboard the Artemesia

The middle of the day had come and gone and things were no easier between the Wandering Wallace and Miyakitsu than at the beginning of the day. It was like this sometimes. The questions, the shyness, the doubt. "You know why I do it, do you not?"

She tucked her chin against her chest, ebony hair cascading across her face and obscuring it. She muttered something noncommittal and scooted across his lap.

His heart sped in response and he leaned into her, the tip of his nose tickled by the edge of her satiny hair. "It's not just for the Witches, you know. It's not just because of the African slaves. Or the Indian slaves. Or the ones like you—Wildkin. It is because of *you*. It's always been because of you. Because of the place and the way I found you."

She tilted her head back, the black wave of her long hair

dividing to show the softly sloping planes of her face and exposing the curve of her narrow neck. "You rescue me."

"Yes," he said, the breath catching in his throat. "I rescued you." He examined her features, the dramatic slanting eyes fringed with lashes as luxurious as her fox pelt's fur. The low bridge of her nose that only emphasized the dramatic sweep of her black eyebrows, the eyes so dark brown they defied terms like "coffee" or "chocolate" and went straight to making him think in terms of midnight's starless heart.

She was the most magickal thing he owned.

He blinked, realizing the truth of the statement. He owned her. Like the trunk painted with odd symbols and stars in secret patterns. Like the clothes on both their backs—he owned her. The idea was at once repulsive and invigorating because, by him owning her, no one else had any claim.

"You remember now?" he asked, the question clutching his heart the way it did daily. One day he would fail her. One day they would find themselves at this hour, at this most magical moment in their oddly repetitive daily lives, and she would say, "No."

It was bound to happen. He fought a daily and losing battle with time—a battle he saw lost in seconds—precious seconds—every single day.

"Yes. I remember. You come to my land. You find me in house with other girls that English love."

His lips pressed into a thin line remembering the house with its wood-and-paper walls that slid to reveal rooms where beautiful girls—geisha and maiko, they claimed—were kept for the entertainment of men. Then he was named "Hood" because of the sleek fabric mask he wore to do the work only he could easily perform, and he was encouraged to spend time with a girl of his choosing as reward. Uncertain and uninterested, he looked for the one least likely to interact with him.

Quiet, her eyes downcast whenever they did not flit wildly about the room; her demeanor was distant, her body as poised and still as an animal having spotted its hunter. Graceful as a deer, small and lithe as a cat, and feral as a fox, she immediately entranced him.

He chose her from all the girls in short silk robes who stood against the rice paper wall, their pale and perfect legs exposed to nearly the knee even as a coworker of his whispered, "This is no true geisha house . . ."

He was warned against his choice by the house's mother. A recent acquisition to the household with a unique past, she had not yet acquired the appropriate temperament. She had bitten a patron just the other day, the older woman mentioned.

One of Hood's companions stepped forward then, saying he liked his girls feisty.

But Hood stayed true to his decision. There was something about her as odd as his own nature. He knew he must at least keep her from being put in a position where she felt threatened. Regardless of his type of employment, he still understood what construed gentlemanly behavior.

"You say: She is beautiful," Miyakitsu whispered, stretching to accentuate her languid form. "Then you say: I choose her. Her time is mine. My money is hers."

"Yes," he agreed, wrapping his arms around her slender waist. He had told her the tale many times. Every day since the day they'd met. And every night, the moment she finally fell asleep beside him, his arm wrapped round her, her memory was wiped clean of his very existence.

Tabula rasa was what educated people called it. Blank slate.

"You come to my room. I am scared. We sit and watch each other. I remember. I offer tea." She smiled at him, small white teeth perfect between pink lips. Not even the size or sharpness of her canines gave a clue to her more animal nature to most people. Sitting beside him she was utterly human, her human skin a most elaborate and convincing camouflage.

"Yes," he again agreed. "You shook as you poured it." He added with a smile, "You nearly spilled it."

She barked out a laugh. "You nearly bathe with tea!"

"Yes." He touched the tip of her nose with a finger. "And then?"

"Then, you talk. About many things and nothing," she said, wrinkling her nose.

This is how he knew she truly remembered nothing beyond what he'd told her, starting every morning. That simple and damning phrase "about many things and nothing." It was how he summarized that first day they spent together, because the reality of it was much harder to repeat, and ever so much harder to hear.

That first day, before he understood the damage done to her, he explained his every hope and dream to the beautiful foreign girl who nodded politely, listened intently, and forgot every moment that night after he'd left her.

"Then," she concludes, "you leave me, with not so much as a kiss."

"True."

"You come again and again."

He did. She ensnared him that first day. When he returned the next and she acted as if she did not know him, instead of taking it as a rebuff he saw it as a challenge to make her admit recognizing him. When that failed, he fought to make himself more memorable—to be worthy of remembering. Every day he burned his pay whiling away the evening's hours with her.

Every day, as soon as work concluded, he returned to what was little more than a house of ill repute thinly veiled as something far more beautiful, and began their relationship again, determined to not be forgotten.

She was equally willing to try and just as unable to grant him that—his most singularly important wish.

One early evening, his frustration at its peak, Hood sought out the house's Madame and paid for information.

"We know little. Ainu bring her, leave her. Say she work with shaman, magician, traveled. Knows many tricks and skills, but now? They want her no more. Ainu say crazy thing about her being daughter of the night and so she change. Old, crazy Ainu story." She dismissed it with a wave of her hand.

"Tell it true," he urged.

She peered down her broad nose at him. "My time valuable."

He produced more coins, buying more time. "Tell it true."

"Some say Earth and Sky are mother and father of all people as Day and Night are mother and father of all animals. Crazy. But Night," she dragged the word out, lengthening the single syllable and giving him a knowing look, "she share same space as Sky and you know when space is shared . . . more than *space* is shared." She laughed. "She and he make many children, sons and daughters of Night. They fall from Night Sky, always dark, always damaged. Live different life than people. Know different things. Cannot know other things."

He sat back, watching her expression, and waiting for her to explain it all away as some strange joke she played on men recently in port.

"You try and make her remember you, yes?"

He only blinked, but even so subtle a movement told her what she wanted to know.

"She cannot. Maybe she does not want to. Maybe she does. No matter. She is Night's damaged daughter. Every night she shakes off her skin and travels to her parents' realm. Every day she is born anew at dawn. Fresh and clean, no new memory."

"She cannot . . ."

The woman lifted one shoulder in a shrug. "Cannot."

He heaved out a sigh, sinking deeper into both the chair and his own dark thoughts. She would never remember him. No matter how he tried. Hood, so memorable to his other companions, would never be remembered by the most beautiful woman he'd ever met—not after she fell asleep.

"Night always takes her children back. They are special. Like what your people call beastmen . . ."

He bolted upright in his seat, his hands curled around the ends of the carved armrests. "She's Wildkin?"

She laughed at him again. "Yes. You not see it in her? Wild. Dangerous. Crafty."

"No," he admitted. "I had no idea."

"Men. You see only what you want, want most what you fear. Leave her. Find other girl. Less bitey."

The next day he returned and tried to choose a different girl, but still he found himself irreparably drawn to the damaged daughter of the night.

Her voice brought him back to the present. "I am your special girl. And—"

They say the words together in unison, every day at nearly this same hour, "—I love you."

Never had he spoken truer words.

Romance never his forte, the first time she fell into her other form they were both surprised. He didn't shrink away and she didn't slink into a corner. Or bite.

Never before had he beheld such beauty as in the pure black fox with large golden eyes. It was as if she were a song that had just been rewritten. The rhythm—the time signature—remained the same, but the melody twisted, became more sensuous and dangerous, equally foreign and intimate in the shape of its wildly elegant design.

Standing there facing down the very image of the wilderness, he understood then that *this* was what he'd wanted—the magick and mystery this woman embodied.

His paltry illusions paled before magick made fur, flesh, bone, and bitey teeth. He waited out her transformation, patient as a man courting a proper lady should be while waiting for her to be appropriately dressed. When she slid from her fox's pelt, regaining her kimono, he lowered his eyes for modesty's sake.

But his consistent attentions were not overlooked by his peers.

"Other man come for me . . ." It was here that she always faltered, no matter how many times he told it the same way. Something about it lingered in the back of her mind—or her soul—if she had one—if he had one—that made him think she remembered brutality.

The thought gave him as much pain as it gave hope.

He remembered this part of the tale as if they lived it moments ago. The way his coworker—the one who liked women feisty—pointed out that there must really be something amazing about the girl Hood visited so regularly. That she must be tremendously talented. The words were no compliment—fear crept along Hood's gut. The words hinted at intention.

So Hood stretched his legs until they burned in an effort to outwalk the other man, to make it to the house before he did—and stake his claim and protect his interests in the foxgirl.

But it was not enough because, even in Japan, commercialism and capitalism had rapidly become the way of things, edging out older values. And in capitalism there was but one god (a strange contrast to the Shinto ways) and that god was money.

They stood in the same room, two men with different desires, different goals, seeing the small wild woman on the same path they wished to tread. Money was produced by each.

Then more.

The foxgirl shrank back, seeing who had the most, and Hood knew this was a battle beyond his winning. Unless he went all in.

He made the offer that changed his world forever. "She is difficult and dangerous," he said to the older woman looking on, her eyes focused on the money. Only then had Hood truly seen how readily she peddled flesh in her greed. It sickened him knowing he had supported her. "Damaged," he announced, looking at the woman with flint-hard eyes. "She is a liability to your establishment."

The woman hissed at him, her eyes narrow and bright.

"I will take her away from here so that your business prospers."

The woman's eyes did not change, remaining distrustful, dangerous. "What you offer? Make her wife?" She laughed out the rudest, most disgusting noise he had ever heard exuded from any body orifice.

He could not make her his wife, so the woman's words bore little sting. There was too much to accomplish before taking a bride and he came from a modest background. A whore he might take, but a wife of questionable origin? Worse yet, a Wildkin whore?

"I will buy her."

"Buy her?!" The woman snorted and cackled, bending in half as laughter wracked her body. "You cannot even beat his price for one night! How you buy her with no money?"

"Name your price and I will make good on it."

Her laughter stopped so abruptly she sputtered and choked.

He was serious.

Miyakitsu again narrated, saying, "Name your price, Madame, name your challenge."

He nodded; the breath caught in his throat at the way light shone in the unbelievably dark gems of her eyes.

"She names impossible task. A quest no man succeed at."

He nodded, remembering well the dangerous journey he embarked on to save her from enslavement.

"You promise to remind me of adventure?"

"Yes," he whispered, jaw clenched. "Tomorrow." His was the whitest of lies.

She smiled, ready to hold him to the promise made today . . . Tomorrow.

That, he believed, was the greatest of mercies: that she did not know what she could not know.

The only part of the story he can never be certain is true or not, pained him in the guessing.

"While you adventure to save me," Miyakitsu said, "I am well kept, untouched."

He told her that every time, hoping that if he heard it enough, perhaps he, too, would believe it. For to know he left her—with no memory to tell her otherwise—where she might have been ill-used in his absence was too much for a man to bear.

"Madame takes her payment. I am yours. Then real adventure begins!" She snuggles against him, her body fitting into his own, a living perfection.

This was what he waited for every day—what he worked for with unerring consistency and hope—the moment she trusted him again. The moment she knew deep in her shifting bones she could trust him.

These were the magic hours. The brief time remaining before she dozed off and all the progress he'd made slid away in an avalanche.

He had just enough friends to know no other man would do all that he did so regularly, so readily.

He felt sorry for them, realizing, because it proved they had not found true love. For that reason, he hugged her tight and knew that something found could again be lost if one wasn't careful.

Aboard the Tempest

It was as Ginger Jack and Rowen slithered through tunnel after tunnel in the belly of the *Tempest* wearing insulated suits against the heat that Rowen fogged up his mask talking about Jordan. "Is that all you have to talk about?" Jack asked. "This girl? Hammer."

Rowen handed him a hammer. "You started it. You were talking about Elizabeth . . ."

"In a completely respectful and professional way!"

Rowen laughed. "Talking about the shape of a woman's body is somehow tied to the profession of engineer, is it?"

"We have a keen eye for good structure and Evie's built just right," he added with a laugh of his own.

"Jordan is proportioned . . . differently?" Rowen said, thinking back.

"Jordan is a girl, Evie is a full-fledged woman," Jack said. "Therein lies the difference."

"But, if one were to compare them, bit by bit . . ." And so Rowen began to, naming off each attribute in a way so clearly comparative Jack might've drawn a chart. It was as Rowen worked on his own and still rambled on about Jordan that things began to go badly.

First he dropped a screw down a grate. Jack sent the spider to retrieve it. Then Rowen tightened what needed loosening. He scuffed up the paint job on one wall and poured water into a tube clearly marked for oil. The entire time he talked about Jordan.

By the end of their shift, Jack was deciding between ripping out his hair (he eyed Rowen's hair with a mad glee imagining tearing it out instead) or climbing him in order to strangle him. But, exhausted from correcting Rowen's mistakes, Jack decided to let him live.

At least until the next time they had to work together.

Philadelphia

Catrina Hollindale waited as patiently as a member of the Fourth of the Nine could be expected to do at a print shop, mindful of the ink so near the fine fabric of her dress.

Finally the apprentice enquired as to her order. "One hundred posters reading: For the safe return of Rowen Burchette, alive and in good condition, to the following address . . ." She included the address, a reward that made the apprentice's eyes pop, and then described what Rowen looked like for a suitable visual.

When she finished, the apprentice repeated back what she had said, pausing over the offered reward and the number of copies she wanted printed and distributed.

"He sounds like quite the catch," he remarked.

Catrina waved her fan and, stepping out the door, silently agreed.

Aboard the Artemesia

As Jordan crossed the Topside deck for supper her guards guided her onto the Conductor's dais. The captain joined them, watching both Conductor and Conductor-to-be with equal measures of distrust.

The sniper at the Conductor's back shifted on his perch, sensing the unease. He adjusted the position of his gun's muzzle and fidgeted with his powder horn.

The Conductor never paused in his duties but kept moving the intricate bits of the mechanisms that helped keep the ship aloft and headed in the correct direction.

He looked older than when Jordan had noticed him on her first evening aboard. There was more gray in his hair and it warred with the striking ebony that otherwise would have rivaled Miyakitsu's dark tresses. His movements seemed more purposeful, and there was a look of fine concentration rather than near-ecstasy on his face. His lips moved and he sang words she'd never heard before.

The captain cleared his throat. "The Conductor." The captain stepped away.

The Conductor paused in his frantic movements and nodded toward her, saying, "Anil. It appears I am the one to train you. I am not certain how I feel about this fact," he admitted, reaching out to set a group of wheels spinning. The port wing tipped up and cut through the clouds differently. "It is bittersweet, knowing my time as Conductor is nearly over."

Jordan watched the cogs and gears whistle and spin, sensing an odd sort of music in their movement.

"I would have preferred an option of retirement," Anil said, adjusting the main wheel—something that looked tremendously like it belonged on the deck of the Clippers and Cutters Jordan had seen drawn in books. "But that would have required a far different career course."

She found her voice. "Where are you from?"

"Ah. Calcutta."

"In the Near East? Was it beautiful there?"

"It was—in its own way. It was—full—of everything. Both good and bad. It was complete."

"And what would you have done if you had a choice?"

He shook his head, black and silver hair flying. "It matters not one whit. I will retire from my employment here, and soon. My death will finalize it all."

Jordan blinked and Stache wrapped his fingers around her arm, guiding her away from the dais and to the diners' table. Or, more properly, *her* dining table.

That evening the captain instructed the guards to change their tactics with Jordan's seating. The only leather strap was now the one keeping her in her chair—the chair that was bolted to the deck.

Now Mouse grabbed her wrist, spreading her fingers wide. She stared at him as his thick fingers took thin pieces of rope—not much thicker than the floss Jordan's mother used for embroidery—and wrapped them around each of her fingers.

"What—"

Stache did the same for her other hand, and within minutes each of her fingers and her thumbs were tied to separate strings leading away from her table and toward different parts of the ship.

The guards knelt beside her; each grabbed a foot and tugged her recently acquired shoes off her feet.

Jordan's eyes widened, and she drew back from the table as far as she could to see what they were about. But she felt more than she saw as each toe was tied as each of her fingers had been.

Mouse stepped to a nearby lever and pressed it down. There was a faint *zip* and the strings' true purpose was demonstrated and Jordan was left strapped at the waist to her chair, each of her fingers tied to a finer and separate moving bit of the airship *Artemesia*.

Her eyes wide, she felt a tug on her right ring finger and tried to work with it instead of against it.

"This is the finer bit of your training," Captain Kerdin explained. "You understand the basics, now these are the finer points."

Throughout the course of supper Jordan worked hard to learn, to anticipate and coax the ship to cooperate at least enough so she might eat and drink. At the meal's end she felt nearly victorious, having eaten and drunk more than she wore.

The captain stepped to her side, drew a knife, and sliced all the strings with a single move, watching as gravity grabbed and dragged them, hissing, across the Topside floor, until they slithered off the sides of the flying behemoth, disappearing. "Tomorrow you will begin your final phase of training."

Holgate

The Maker's library had been thoroughly gone through, books and papers scattered all over the floor, childhood journals trampled underfoot as the watchmen opened each book's cover, gave it a hearty shake, paged through whatever did not fall out, and tossed it aside if there seemed to be nothing of immediate value.

Exhausted from swatting at suicidal butterflies in the Maker's laboratory, Councilman Stevenson found the library's destruction nearly peaceful. He made a mental note to bring in a crew of low-level scholars to sift through whatever he deemed worthy. They might find things of interest among the rubble he was leaving in his wake, but his goal was simple: find whatever clues he needed to find the Maker.

Surely the Maker made mention of who he was close with, where he felt safe . . . Those were what a man on the run ran to.

The fact the man had the audacity to shirk his duty—abandon his calling—was beyond frustrating.

If he could track him and get his hands on one of the two females accompanying him he could make the Maker obey.

Especially if he got his hands on the Maker's adorable daughter.

He set his hat on the nearby desk and glared at the nearly skeletal man who reclined on the seat, his boots propped on the desk's slightly slanted surface, his long, thin, and spider-like arms crossed behind his head as he stared at the ceiling.

Stevenson cleared his throat. "Are you truly intending to sit there all day as they search?"

"Hmm?" The Tester spared the Councilman a glance. "Why, yes. Thank you for asking. I'm certain you're doing a grand job. Why, if I'd just walked in here I'd look at the floor and speculate on the wildly industrious nature of the hooligans ransacking this room."

Stevenson crossed his arms. "What is your particular problem with the way I am proceeding?"

"Overall, or just here?" He let go of his metal hand and, bringing his arms in front of him once more, reached into a pocket in his voluminous robe. "I believe I started a list . . ."

Stevenson's teeth clamped tight. "Do get up and assist, or leave."

"Fine, fine." The Tester slid his boots off the desk, rose, snatched up the long walking stick that was often close at hand, and headed to the door.

Stevenson kept silent, though the vein near his hairline rose to announce his internal boiling point had nearly been reached.

"One note, though, before I leave to seek out some tea and toast points," the Tester said. "Do consider this . . ." He motioned to the crew of men disassembling the Maker's library book by book. "Are these watchmen truly invested in finding the Maker, or are they simply going through the motions because—let's be honest for a moment, shall we?—Holgate with no Maker means Holgate with no dangerous prisoners and no frightening human experimentation. And, these watchmen? Are paid hourly."

Councilman Stevenson glared at him. "Do tell me why, when there are other Testers in the region, do I keep *you* here?"

"Because I am the best of them all."

It was only after the Tester was out the door, down the hall, and out of sight of the library that Councilman Stevenson sent the watchmen home, and summoned the Wardens and Wraiths.

Aboard the Artemesia

Supper had been consumed, another fine stew with squash and chicken stock and bread baked fresh in their most recent port of call. And so, as all good suppers should end in the opinion of the captain's now regular guests, the Wandering Wallace and Miyakitsu caught everyone's attention for a new illusion.

But before the trickery began, Miyakitsu pulled a pretty little ring box from her pocket.

"Ah, yes," the Wandering Wallace said, smiling. He slid it across the table to Maude. "A mere bauble I picked up on my travels that might be appreciated by a woman of your generous nature."

Surprised, Maude opened the box and looked at the ruby ring. "It is far too grand!" She looked at Bran.

His mouth hung open.

"I cannot accept," she said, carefully closing the box and sliding it away.

The Wandering Wallace returned the gesture, and the box. "But of course you can, and frankly, you must. It would offend poor Miyakitsu if you did not," he explained.

"Oh. Umm . . . Oh," Maude said again, perplexed. "I do not wish to offend . . ."

"Then keep the ring—oh, do put it on now," the Wandering Wallace insisted.

Miyakitsu and Meggie both clapped their hands.

Maude blushed but obeyed. "It is beautiful, thank you both so much."

The Wandering Wallace grinned beneath the mask of a baboon's colorful face. "It is our pleasure." He rose. "Tonight we have brought along a special prop . . ." the Wandering Wallace explained, walking over to the food cart and bending down to grab a bundle of fabric, metal, and wood. Hefting it easily, he brought it before them, unrolled it on the deck, and, with one good, solid shake, he snapped it all together, creating a rigid and thick canvas background.

Miyakitsu did what she did best, pointing to the most interesting bits of whatever he did with an artistic flair and grace that were nearly as wild as his mask.

The Wandering Wallace stood the background up with a flick of his supple wrists and cranked a lever at its side to attach four suction cups firmly onto the smooth deck.

"My lady?" he asked with a gracious bow and a flourish all his own to encourage her to stand before the background.

Bran squinted at the background's image, examining it, while Miyakitsu refused to stand where Wallace instructed. He pointed, she shook her head no and stomped her feet. He pointed and she crossed her arms.

He pointed again and she stuck out her tongue.

Meggie was hysterical.

Wallace strode over to his woman, picked her up by the waist, and tossed her over his shoulder very much like the guards had previously done with Jordan.

Hauled to her designated spot, supposedly against her will, Miyakitsu propped her elbows on Wallace's back and pouted with great determination in Meggie's direction.

Meggie howled with laughter and Bran couldn't stop the smile that tickled the edges of his lips. He looked at her then, his little daughter who nearly glowed with an inner radiance, and he carefully reached his hand out and found hers, wrapping his fingers around her tiny hand.

She startled at the touch and turned to look at him, dazzling him with a grin. Something inside of him melted—exhaled.

Miyakitsu was deposited before the banner-like background, the fabric painted with moons and stars and constellations. Bran guessed that if one knew the stories of the stars, there was quite a tale painted in the swirling and wild colors of the canvas.

"And now, my friends," Wallace said, crossing his arms before him and bending at the waist in a bow, his arms sweeping out as he rose and revealing that he held three knives in each hand. "I shall shoot for the stars and try not to hit the beautiful moon who lives there among them all."

Miyakitsu arched her back, tucked her feet together so that the ball of one nestled into the arch of the other, and raised her arms above her head to grasp her hands together. Stoic and statuesque, she stood there as Wallace found his mark.

The knives glimmered as he threw them, one at a time, like silver stars shooting through the gathered stormy darkness surrounding their ship as the serving girl cleared their place settings and tidied up like nothing spectacular—or even vaguely interesting—was going on behind her back.

The blades hissed into the canvas and stuck nearly as well as they might in wood. Bran squeezed Meggie's hand with each fresh hiss of the blade and she twitched each time, amazed by the weapons whispering past the beautiful girl's body. And the way the girl seemed to not even draw a breath, but made herself even smaller.

The clapping began as soon as the throwing ended, and Wallace strode to the background and plucked the knives back out as easily as one might withdraw a quill pen from an inkwell. He snatched Miyakitsu's hand and raised it to his lips for a kiss.

Then he turned and returned to his spot. "You enjoyed that?"

The clapping increased in volume.

"Let's make it still more difficult, shall we?"

Meggie's hands flew to her mouth and even Maude hesitated a moment.

"Come now," Wallace urged. "Just a *bit* more difficult?"

Meggie slowly lowered her hands and sought out her father's for reassurance. They nodded as one, Bran's gaze holding her own.

"Excellent well," Wallace said. "Do you know the song 'Walk Around'?"

Nods all around except from Meggie.

"No!" Wallace exclaimed, springing over to the table and resting his elbows on it so that his baboon's ridged snout was mere inches from Meggie's button nose. "Say it is not so," he said with mock tragedy. "The Maker's daughter *must* know this song!" He tilted his head away from her then and began to whistle the tune, nodding in time to it.

Behind him Miyakitsu clapped along.

"Good, eh?" he asked Meggie.

She nodded, beaming.

"Shall we try the words? It's simple, really, just a round." The Wandering Wallace clapped a rhythm, repeating the words of the song with only the simplest of tunes. Maude and Bran picked it up, as did the captain, and even the normally dour Marion sang along when coaxed.

Meggie sang out, her voice a trilling and thin soprano that went wispy at its edges.

"Ah," Wallace said, "that is a lovely thing." He straightened and stepped back, dropping the knives so they stuck point down in the wood at his feet.

The captain scowled at the knives in his ship's deck but no one else seemed bothered. He was the Wandering Wallace, after all, and they were well entertained.

"What I need you to do is sing it as a round should be sung. Miss Maude and Miss Meggie together, Marion and Bran working as one, and our good captain—for what sailing man cannot handle his own part of a round?—as our third part. And at every intersection—and you'll see soon enough what I mean—I need you to clap. Let's try one time." And he began to sing in a rich baritone none of them had expected to come from such a slim shape as his. He motioned for Maude and Meggie to join him and then pointed to the others each in their turn.

He was right. The music wove and intersected, and Bran had the distinct feeling that if you rearranged the words at the intersections there was a secondary story unfolding if you went far enough.

"Excellent well!" the Wandering Wallace exclaimed with

a clap in conclusion. "I will give us a count of three and then you will see something amazing! But not at all magickal!"

He turned his back on them then and Meggie nearly fell off Marion's knee in excitement, before settling in to sing.

The Wandering Wallace crouched down, surrounded by his blades, fingers resting lightly on the handles of the farthest ones at each of his sides. "One, two, three!"

The singing started, the clapping joined in, and on every clap he hurled another knife as Miyakitsu worked her way through a precisely timed dance between the zipping blades. She lowered her arms, bent her hands back at the wrists, and extended her fingers so beautifully they seemed to lengthen before their audience, blades nearly grazing flesh. The Wandering Wallace flipped his cloak over his shoulder, revealing a bandolier of knife blades just when everyone thought he'd run out.

With the rising excitement they sang faster, clapped faster, knives flew faster, and the dance became as wild as the blades were deadly and then—

—the last blade flew wide and Meggie screamed as it hurtled toward Miyakitsu's head.

But Miyakitsu disappeared, her beautiful kimono hanging in midair a moment longer, empty, before it crumpled to the floor of Topside.

The song died; no music could be made when so many people held their breath all at once. But the message of the song whispered in Bran's ears. It was no simple round the Wandering Wallace had them sing, but a *catch*, the message only apparent when the words overlapped just so.

Something wiggled in the wrinkles and folds of the silk robe and Meggie screamed again, leaping free of Marion's grasp to wrap her arms around her father's neck. She buried her nose there at the corner of his jaw, and peeked around slowly.

He felt her heart racing.

Just like his did, watching as a dark nose stuck out of the kimono's neck hole, and then a furry head thrust its way free, all black fur, big ears, and bright eyes. With a whimper and a whine the black fox burst forward and leaped into Wallace's arms.

The captain stood, outraged. "How dare you threaten my livelihood—our safety—by bringing magick aboard?! I'll string you up myself!" he threatened, knocking over his chair in his haste to wrap his hands around Wallace's neck.

But the Wandering Wallace was already dancing backwards with the fox in hand and laughing. "Surely you did not think I was so stupid as to bring real magick aboard! Tsu!" he shouted. "Tsu! Step out and save the love of your life, please!"

Miyakitsu leaned out from behind the canvas backdrop and smiled shyly before trotting forward to take her bow. The clapping was loud as the thunder that rumbled in the sky all around them. She stepped forward, dressed in the same kimono which lay empty on the deck. She gave a gracious bow and the captain froze.

It took a moment, but he began to laugh. It started as a faint chuckle, but grew into a deep and riotous guffaw. "You very nearly had me believing that you had brought a magicker aboard!" He let out a deep puff of air. "That was quite the show! Do you not think so?" he asked his guests. "I mean, did you truly see all that?"

But the thing that caught Bran's eye and caused him—the Maker—to carefully unlatch Meggie's arms from around his neck so that he could set her back on Marion's knee was the glint of a large stormlight crystal resting very near Miyakitsu's throat and strung with smaller twinkling stones of the same type on either side. A crystal necklace the Maker thought he would have noticed her wearing before. He looked at her sleeves, but they overflowed in waves of colored silk, swallowing up her arms and wrists so that only the very tips of her fingers showed. Even her socks and sandals barely peeked out from beneath the hem of her kimono.

What he wouldn't give to know if he was correct . . .

Maude reached around behind Marion and slapped the back of Bran's head. He turned and looked at her, eyes wide. "Put your eyes back in your head," she scolded. "You look like you want to undress her!"

He gave her his best look of absolute innocence, but it was not well practiced. And besides, she was correct. He did want to undress her. But not at all for the reasons Maude might suspect.

His interest was sheerly scientific.

Because he had heard such things were possible . . . the rumors flew every time someone of rank had gone missing for a few days or more without telling absolutely everyone in their social circle—as if it was their business. He wondered what would be speculated as a result of his sudden disappearance.

People always jumped to the strangest, most fanciful of conclusions. Surely, it couldn't be . . .

It was impossible, wasn't it?

And yet, aware of the fire burning from Maude's eyes and scalding the side of his head, Bran stared in wonder.

Chapter Nine

The difficulty in life is the choice.

—GEORGE MOORE

Aboard the Tempest

Deep in the gut of the *Tempest* Rowen rambled on about Jordan, Ginger Jack did his best to ignore him, flat on his back and focused on his work, until oil spurted free in a fine plume of black and Jack unleashed every obscene word he knew. Twice. Then once in reverse order and only for good measure.

He slipped down the tube (easier to do now it was well lubricated) to reach a prone sputtering and oil-covered Rowen.

"What the hell are you doing?" Jack hauled out his wrench and began tightening the bit of pipe Rowen had wrongly loosened.

Rowen rubbed his sleeve across his face to clear it, but made an oil slick of himself instead. "I—"

"Enough of this!" Jack snapped. "Enough of the screw-ups,

the poor concentration, the simpering about *Jordan and I this* and *Jordan and I that* . . ." The wrench clattered onto the space beside them and through filthy goggle lenses, Jack's eyes fixed on Rowen. "You love this girl Jordan."

"I do not—"

Jack reached around to cuff him on the back of his head. "You love this girl Jordan. So go find her."

"I do *not* and I cannot. What do you expect me to do? Steal the ship?"

Jack blew air through rubbery lips. "You? Impossible. But even you might manage a pod . . ."

"A pod?"

"We have three of them. Hooked onto the ass end of the ship. You pull a lever and they drop free. Another lever and the wings pop out. Mainly gliders unless you can magick them or get the engine to fire at the right time. But with some ingenuity . . . who knows how far you could get?"

"A pod."

"God, but you're a slow one, aren't you?" Jack tugged a rag from his back pocket and swabbed it across his own face and then handed it to Rowen. "Clean up here and then I'll show you."

It was the most efficient thing Jack had seen Rowen do: cleanup. They dragged themselves free of the tunnels and tubes, stripped off their insulated jumpsuits, and paused in the hallway outside the Mech Deck, filthy.

Jack led him to an area below the Aft Gundeck where three smaller doors, all the same neutral tone, stood side by side. He dug into his collar and withdrew a key that looked similar to the one Evie carried. He popped the lock and swung open the door, stepping onto a metal catwalk enveloped by fabric. The air around them echoed and in three steps, Jack stooped and stepped inside the hatch on a smooth metal hull.

Rowen, hunched as small as he could get, followed.

"Wait!" Jack swung his hands, keeping Rowen in the doorway of the hatch. "There's no easy room for us both, Treetrunk, so just look. And whatever you do, don't touch!"

Rowen leaned inside, seeing a selection of levers, buttons, and dials. The front was made of an assortment of windows puzzled together to create one curving glass surface and the middle was filled mainly with a sloping leather seat. Jack crouched in it, quickly pointing and announcing the names and duties of each part of the ship.

Rowen nodded, struggling to take it all in.

When Jack concluded his tour of the pod, he slipped past the larger man, asking, "Any questions?"

"Yes," Rowen asked, brain swimming. He limited himself to one. "How do I get myself a key?"

"You'll have to take it."

Rowen grinned and pounded his fist into his palm.

Aboard the Artemesia

Rubbing her wrists and ankles to massage the soreness out of them that the strings had left, Jordan expected no one at her door, and certainly no one inside her room—suddenly standing so close to her bedside. She shrank back immediately, seeing Captain Kerdin.

"You are by far the prettiest Witch I've ever had aboard," the captain said, allowing his eyes to roam the geography of her body.

Jordan looked at him, her eyes narrowing so only a glare of color peeked out between her lashes.

He closed the door behind him and turned away from her only long enough to slip in the key and bolt the room from the inside.

Her heart tried to tear through her chest, a wild animal trapped in the cage of her ribs. She read something in the lines of his long and narrow face that spoke of hunger, of predator and prey. He held out the collar of his shirt and let the chain holding the key slip inside.

"You were what? Fifth or Sixth of the Nine?"

Jordan couldn't find the single word to denote her past social standing. Instead she swallowed and took a long step back and away from him and the strange danger she sensed.

"It no longer matters, I guess," he conceded with a tip of his chin. "You're a Witch now. Unranked, unwanted . . ." He undid his cravat.

"What are you doing?" she whispered.

"Whatever I want." He shrugged.

"I don't know what you're intending—"

He snorted. "Yes you . . ." But he looked at her again and his smile slid into a grin. "My god. You don't, do you? That makes this even more wonderful for me . . ."

He grabbed her arms faster than she could pull away and he pressed his mouth over hers to swallow her yelp of surprise.

She fought, kicking, pulling, and trying to get a fist against his face, but he held her tight—his hands like steel bands biting into her flesh—and he dragged her toward her bed.

She fought harder, muscles burning, joints ready to pull free of bone.

He stopped short of the bed and kicked her feet out from under her, driving her to the ground. While her breath was knocked out of her, he gagged her with the towel she kept by her basin and weighed her down with the weight of his hips. Wrapping his long fingers tight around her wrists, he undid his belt with the other hand. He dragged his hips up her body until he sat on her chest.

Then he belted her wrists together.

He pulled up her skirts, took down his trousers and her petticoats, and forced his way into her.

She cried against the cloth clogging her mouth, tears seeping out of her eyes, her nose filled with his breath, her eyes filled with his gaping mouth and glazed eyes, her body filled with his petty desire.

The key swung free of his collar, swinging between them and flashing in the light, taunting her with the lure of freedom she couldn't have.

She closed her eyes, wishing herself anywhere but here, but something bit into her arm and she gasped, her eyes popping open in the shadow of her attacker. Something dug into the flesh of her arm.

Rowen's heart.

She choked on a sob and forced her eyes shut again. She tried not to think of where she was. Or of the hate building inside her, wrapping around the fear, urging dark revenge. Or of what was happening at that moment.

She especially tried not to think of Rowen.

Rowen with his bold laugh and his stunning smile.

Rowen, now bearded and on another airship, who had only shared a glance with her across the distance.

Rowen. Who should have been her hero.

Rowen. Who should have rescued her long before *this.*

She turned her face from the captain but his hot breath forced its way into her ear.

She fixed her gaze on the bed's foot and tried to think of the forest its wood had come from. Wondered what the tree looked like before some man thought to cut it down while it had leaves, and life, and wild untouched potential.

The heart bit into her again and again, dragging her back from the forest to the place reality condemned her to be, pinned beneath a predator. Rage and hate built, squeezed at her heart.

Outside her window the clouds warred, digging into each other's soft guts and dragging out cottony innards to wind around the airship's hull. The sky flickered with lightning and the ship bucked beneath her as she tried to toss him off.

Inside, the second lantern—*her* lantern—lit, flaring and glowing so bright it rivaled the wandering lightning.

Rain sprayed the window in a violent shower, making the world outside Jordan's room run and smear.

No fight left in her, she was filled with only aching sorrow and roaring rage.

Outside, the storm wheezed, falling apart, destroyed with all her hope. And her lantern went out.

Jordan lay broken on her floor as he undid the belt around her wrists and stood.

The door closed, the lock slid into place, and she curled in on herself, pulling her knees to her chest and wrapping her arms tight around them. The shaking that started with his touch wouldn't stop.

Her fingers curled around the heart on her sleeve, the token of Rowen's support even in his absence, and she let it bite into her fingers, forced herself to feel it claw into her flesh, to make even this moment real beyond denial. With a scream she tore it free from her sleeve and hurled it across the room.

Sometimes rescue didn't come.

She slipped back into a fetal position, rocking on the floor and humming some wordless tune she'd heard—somewhere. The place no longer mattered. There was no place but here. No reality but this. No escape from the pain, the fear . . . the humiliation.

She shivered and quaked, her stomach a rioting knot in her gut, her legs trembling, thighs wet. She rolled onto her hands and knees just in time to dump the contents of her stomach onto the floor.

Her hair fell across her face, the ends of it trailing in her own hot vomit. She stayed there, staring at the watery stuff puddling across the floor, arms quivering as her tightly balled fists held her up. She struggled to stay like that as long as she could, staring at the watery bile, because at least she was no longer seeing *him.* Letting the acrid scent cut into her nose because at least she was no longer smelling *him.*

Her gut rioted and her body convulsed, throwing up nothing but stringy spit as she gave in to dry heaves. Her vision shaking, with one fierce push, she shoved herself back, away from the mess she'd made and onto her knees.

Trembling hands pressed her hair back over her shoulders and she waited, gathering herself to stand, finding the strength to pull her way to her feet. She stumbled to the stand where her water basin and pitcher rested and dragged open a drawer, withdrawing the only other scrap of cloth she had.

She grasped the pitcher in unsteady hands and raised it just high enough to pour the water. Clanking against the basin, she chipped the bowl. She no longer cared. A chipped basin, a cracked pitcher . . . She dunked the pink towel into the basin, watching it darken as it soaked up the water—watching as it went to red.

Bloodred.

Her knees softened and she clutched the stand to steady herself. Closing her eyes she focused on her breathing and waited, rocking in time to the movement of the airship.

But the cool water and the bite of Rowen's heart-shaped pin, replaced and again brushing the wounded part of her upper arm, drew her back.

As did the pain between her legs. Gnawing her lower lip, she raised her skirts and ran the wet rag gently along the inside of her legs and the tender space between. She coughed and plunged the rag back into the basin.

Blood spiraled out from the rag into the water and she turned from the sight of it staining the clear liquid.

Regaining herself, she leaned against the stand, wrung out the rag, and wiped herself down again, this time more slowly. She winced, more than her arm bruised.

She dropped the cloth into the basin, pulled up her petticoats, and let her skirts settle back around her legs. She pushed up her sleeve. The spot where Rowen's heart had dug into her arm was as bloody as her thighs and she sighed, seeing the gouge that still wept red. She pressed on it, smearing the blood away to better see the wound beneath it.

It would swell and bruise. Perhaps fever. She knew that from her time spent in the Tanks at Holgate beneath Bran Marshall's cruel ministrations. If she kept it clean perhaps it would not be so bad. She had wondered several times if the filth in the Tanks hadn't worsened some of her wounds.

She wrung the rag out again, and walked the basin to the window, feeling every step differently than ever before.

She cranked open the window and let the water slosh out

and down the side of the airship. The passenger windows were offset, staggered and spaced so that what rolled out of one wouldn't easily roll into another. She pressed the basin to the window's mouth so hard she thought it'd crack. Surely something ceramic would be as fragile as she felt, and if she was as close to breaking as she thought then surely it must give way soon, too . . .

It scraped against the window's mouth and she leaned her body against it, willing it to give, to fail.

To *snap.*

Growling, she pulled it back.

It refused to give.

She hauled it back, setting it down with a *clunk.* Repeating the motions for refilling the basin she realized she didn't feel them the same way—didn't notice doing it as much. Was that the way an automaton was? Doing things—necessary things—but not experiencing them?

She straightened. Was that how it felt to be a Conductor? To be compelled, to connect physically and still be distanced?

She swirled the rag through the fresh water, squeezing out the excess before dabbing it on her arm.

With time and care the wound would heal.

But the wound she wished to never again think of, though she felt it every time she moved? How could she heal from *that*?

Aboard the Artemesia

Long after the news announced Merrow on the move and another steam catastrophe averted, the Wandering Wallace lulled the *Artemesia*'s passengers to sleep with "All around, above with beauty teeming; Moonlight hours are meant for love," and Marion woke to a body silhouetted against their cabin's open door. Rolling out of the bed he had only just begun to use, he slammed his bare feet against the cabin's floor and vaulted at the figure, shouting, "What are you doing?"

Maude screamed in surprise, closing the door to the hallway and shutting them all back inside.

"What the hell?" Marion snapped, grabbing the things in her arms and making the stormlights flare on so Maude shrank back, covering her eyes.

The light showed the truth of it: the fresh bedding now in Marion's arms, the horror on Maude's face at being discovered, and the child, Meggie, standing soaked behind her father, her nightgown dripping.

Squinting, his brow furrowed, Marion stooped down and stalked toward Meggie.

Bran's arms spread wide to keep her from Marion's reach.

"Did you have a wee accident, Meggie?" Marion asked, crouching near the far side of Bran's legs as the child ducked behind.

She peeked out, nodding solemnly.

"That happens sometimes to children," he assured her. "Did you have a nightmare? My little brother had nightmares something fierce," he confided. "He'd wet the bed sometimes, too."

"You have a little brother?" she asked, eyes wide.

He sighed and, standing, rubbed a hand over his face. "Had," he corrected. "I *had* a little brother."

He turned and stretched, rolling his head on his neck. Blinking, he turned back to Meggie. "But, no matter the nightmare, my little brother was never as wet as you are . . ."

He shoved Bran aside. "So, Meggie, tell me what you dreamed about. Was it water, weather, or . . . storms?"

She looked down, hands clasped before her.

Rain spit against their windows and Sybil's skull shivered on the table.

"Oh. Oh, I see," Marion said, his gaze going from the wet child to her father. "Do you know what *irony* is, Meggie?"

She shook her head, eyes still downcast. Her pale curls bounced, shining in the stormlight.

"Perhaps your father will tell you. Because this situation, dear little dove, is a fine example of irony. A fine example . . ." Marion shook his head, hair falling into his eyes. "Change her bedding. Make her comfortable. Her life won't get easier, will it, Maker?"

"No one's life will get easier," Meggie whispered. "They come."

Marion twitched, staring at Bran. Bran did not meet his eyes.

But Meggie did, and the eyes that met Marion's were empty of everything but his reflection, snared in their dark depths. "They coooommme."

Holgate

In the Maker's library, a Ring and more of Wraiths, and a clutch of Wardens gathered. The dark cast of their clothing made an already wretched scene more somber. Their long coats' hems waved lightly in the breeze that always tickled around the edges of any group of them.

The majority of Wraiths removed their tall top hats and the veils that obscured their twisted faces from public view once they crossed into Holgate's walled compound. Some few, knowing outsiders occasionally visited, kept up appearances to quell the natural panic people felt when first seeing a Wraith unveiled.

Though more socially acceptable, Wardens would never be invited to sup at a Councilman's party, not with the tattoos that crawled along their necks and faces, strange colored things blossoming like fireworks as a reminder they had survived Lightning's Kiss. Unable to speak, the Wardens were handsome in comparison to their counterparts, the deaf Wraiths.

Councilman Stevenson cleared his throat and prepared to announce their mission. "This is the opportunity of your lifetime," he said, hands weaving in midair to craft the words Wraiths were unable to hear. "The Maker has abandoned his duties, as we are unable to do."

They hissed, the Wraiths baring needle-sharp teeth between curled and narrow lips. The Wardens clicked the steel-butted ends of their canes in answer, their voices as ruined by Lightning's Kiss as any Wraith's hearing was.

He glanced from monstrosity to monstrosity, no longer flinching at scarred and withered faces or thin tufts of hair remaining after a Making or Lightning's Kiss went awry. "He has disappeared, but I believe a clue to his whereabouts lies within these books and papers. Somewhere in this library. And, as I want so very badly to have him back where he cannot shirk his duty, I will make a deal. Whosoever among you finds the most valuable information used to locate our dear, dear Maker, may have a full hour alone with him to do as you best see fit—so long as it doesn't result in his death."

The Wraiths and Wardens exchanged glances, grins sliding across their uneven faces. For an instant Stevenson was taken back to a brief stay he experienced in Africa and the gleeful hunger on the faces of hyenas the moment before they took down a lion.

One never understood how useful, or determined, Wraiths and Wardens could be until there were things to be hunted—things to destroy. They turned as one, dark coats and cloaks swished like the first whisper of a whirlwind, and they pulled down book after book, flipping through pages with an unexpected military efficiency. Pages flew, discarded and slithering down through the air until they swished their undulating way to the floor, settling with their discarded peers.

A knock at the door signaled a servant requesting entrance. He stepped inside, his eyes widening to take in the mess the room had become.

Was he calculating how long it would take him to clean up such a disaster? Stevenson cleared his throat.

The servant's head snapped up and he presented a petite, ornately patterned silver tray. On it rested a small burgundy-colored box. "What is this then?" Councilman Stevenson asked. "I ordered nothing . . ."

"A gift, good sir," the young man said, lowering his head as he stretched his arms out in a bow to properly present the box.

The Councilman snatched it, holding it directly before his scrutinizing eyes. "A gift, you say? From whom?"

The servant said, "I was simply told to deliver it, good sir," he said, the "good" seeming just the slightest bit strained.

Councilman Stevenson flipped open the folded tag. "Ah. For my wife. Good enough. I shall give it to her upon my return and we can view the contents together." Holding it in his hand, he returned to the task of overseeing the progress of the Wraiths and Wardens.

Nearly an hour into the methodical destruction of the library, all activity suddenly ceased. Wraiths and Wardens stood stock-still, frozen as if they'd sighted Medusa herself.

The Councilman pushed through the line of Wraiths and Wardens building a wall of black between himself and the bookshelves. "What? What is it?" he demanded, shoving between them to stand in their shadows. Behind them at nearly head level stormlights were suspended, their glow seeping onto the scene he encountered: one Wraith clutching papers in his curled and gloved left hand and pointing with a strangely long index finger of the other. He screeched out a word, the tone shrilling in the air between them, and Stevenson snatched the pages out of his hands and, trembling, held them beneath the lamplight.

His finger raced along the lines of script, his mind struggling with what he found. A truth that could not stand—*dared* not stand.

He started at the top of one particular page again, reading aloud as shadows tightened in around him, the Wardens and Wraiths closing in to hear him and see the Wraith who signed as he spoke.

" 'I now suspect Jordan Astraea, Gathered in from Philadelphia, is indeed not a Witch. The fact that the Tester found her to have magick was, at first, the only proof I needed to her eventual Conducting ability. But her heritage is pure, she is more her father's child than her mother's. There is no taint, no history of witchery in her lineage. I am therefore forced to wonder, if the Tester was wrong once, could we *all* not have been wrong once, twice . . . Might we not *all* have been wrong and, if so, how many times? How many wrongs have we done? Would we know if we took the human form to its breaking point—*beyond* its breaking point—and Made something that should have been impossible to Make? Perhaps if I might someday travel abroad to gather in anecdotes to prove or disprove this horrible possibility I might put my fears to rest.'"

Stevenson only had time to look up at the circle of bitter faces twisted in rage worse than the twist Fate delivered through the torture of being Made—only had time to register the sharp design of Wraith teeth, only long enough to hear gloves slide free of taloned fingertips and breathe one desperate "no," before they leapt on him and made his last words the condemnation of his kind.

The box dropped from his ravaged hands, tumbling to the floor and rustling among the papers a moment before a Wraith stooped over and snatched it up. It tore the tiny parchment name tag off of it, letting it flutter to the floor. Popping the box open, the Wraith pulled the ring free of its ribbon, holding it high for all to see.

The ruby caught the light, scattering sparks of red, and the Weather Workers gasped. Wiping off its gore-streaked hand the Wraith slid the ring on its finger and turned its hand back and forth, basking in the glow the stormlights cast. The Wraith shrilled out one more cry—a command of sorts, and the group turned as one, a black line of fury, drifting down the long hallway and to the Tester's apartment. He was dead a heartbeat after opening his door. Down the stairs to Floor Eight they processed.

To the Tanks.

Their kind required no keys, and nearly as few words; the soft touch of their bare fingers caused locks to shroud in ice. With a flick of a Warden's cane, locks shattered, splintering into shards of ice-cold steel.

All along the hallway Tank doors flew open and Witches in different states of Making stepped into the greater light of the hall, blinking, wondering.

As each saw the nearest Wraith or Warden, they shrank together, human and wounded against those who used to be human and were now something somehow both more and less.

The Wraiths looked to their brethren Wardens, and the one bearing the ring on its finger, papers clutched in its other hand, stepped forward—toward the yet unMade.

It spoke in words as clear as it could construct through a mouth that barely survived the glory and spectacle of Lightning's Kiss.

Aboard the Artemesia

"See, the cloud bank parts briefly to confirm navigation and again mere minutes before the dock is expected in sight," Bran asked, pointing out the window.

Meggie pressed closer, her nose nearly to the glass. "Are they being made by Miss Jordan?"

Bran scrutinized the clouds. "It's hard to be certain, little dove. Some Weather Witches have signatures in their storms, but many do not. These clouds could either belong to our Conductor Anil—or Miss Jordan."

The ship slowed beneath their feet, its wings adjusting

for the final coast into the dock. "Oh! I see one of them!" Meggie shouted, slapping the window with the palm of her hand before she yanked it back and pointed to a foot hanging over their window.

Maude gasped. "You could not pay me to climb across an airship in motion." She leaned in closer to watch. A safety rope whispered across their view and cables slapped and slithered against the boat's body, cable catchers leaping after them in a suspended ballet as they snared cables and hooked them to the net of ropes running along the exterior of the ship's balloon.

"Brace yourselves," Bran reminded them, setting his teacup down and wrapping an arm around Meggie for the inevitable jolt that came when the cables went from slack to taut and pulled the floating ship into port.

In such moments Marion left them and they seemed, briefly, to be a family.

The cables caught, the girls fell into him, and somehow he managed to catch them both and keep his teacup from spilling. They laughed, watching as the safety rope slipped up their window and out of view.

"How quaint," Marion said from the doorway.

Everyone straightened.

Meggie skipped across the distance to Marion, looking up at him with doe eyes and dimples and, when she came to a swaying stop, asked, "So where precisely are we?"

Marion barely stopped from reaching out to tousle her pale blond curls. Instead he glanced over the little girl bobbing before him, always so ready to make peace, and glanced at her father and her father's lover. "It appears we are coming into port at Steuben Hill."

Meggie spun around, wrinkling her nose, and asked her papá, "Where is that?"

He raised and lowered his shoulders.

"Ah, Meggie," Marion said, "your father doesn't know things like locations of ports, he only knows how to Make the Witches that power the ships."

"New York," Bran retorted. "Steuben Hill in New York state. Near enough Herkimer for picking up fresh stormcell crystals. You can kick them right out of farmers' furrows in spring from what I've read. *If* stormcells are what your work requires. The crystals are faceted and, here, double-terminated—a rarity. Amazing in their clarity. In Cape May they are tumbled by the sea and smooth as water-worn pebbles. Both can be used to power things if one knows how."

Their view changed, their window coming flush with the wood-and-metal dock on Steuben Hill. The ramp clanked and clattered, lowering and snapping into place, and Marion looked at them each in turn. "Well. Shall we take a turn around town, such as it is?"

Bran swallowed. "Is this it then," he asked, rising to his feet. "Have we come to the end of our journey?"

Maude's expression changed at that, and she grabbed Bran by the arm and pushed him behind her, placing herself between the men. "No. Surely not," she whispered. "We have come so far."

Marion grunted, glancing from Maude to Bran and back. "No. I wish to take a walk. Stretch my legs and see the area. The ship will rest here for a few hours to take on cargo from Ilion and beyond. Come now. I trust you better when I can see you."

Meggie slipped her hand into Marion's, moving around him to stand by the door. "Come along, Papá and Mamá."

Maude stood frozen hearing herself referred to for the first time as Mamá. Bran wrapped his arm around hers. "Come now, Maude, you have been summoned. We shall all promenade through town as if this is not a kidnapping at all, but a pleasant vacation."

She nodded, following him. "Your hat," Bran reminded her. "It looks sunny." She reached over and plucked the recent acquisition—a kindness Marion surprised her with—off the blunted hook mounted high on the wall ("Just out of range of stickin' yerself in the eye if the ship suddenly lurches," one of the mates had said with a wink). She set it on her head and together they stepped out.

Out their cabin's door and down the hallway, they joined other families weaving their way to the dock as well.

They strolled out of the gaping mouth of the ship. Around them people drifted and paused on the dock and were urged to keep moving by the crew.

The Wandering Wallace, donning his braying-ass mask, and Miyakitsu stood at the edge of the dock, propped against a stack of trunks and crates of assorted shapes and sizes. Around them the crowd bustled, grabbing bags and trunks of their own, some making their way to a host of waiting carts, wagons, and carriages and some dragging their items down the packed-dirt path winding toward town.

Marion and Meggie stopped to speak to the entertainers, Bran and Maude close behind.

"Lovely day, lovely day," the Wandering Wallace agreed, flicking a long ear in their direction in such a way it seemed he doffed a cap. "Going into the town, I see?"

Marion nodded. "And you?"

The Wandering Wallace smiled within the confines of his mask. "Waiting on some lovely items we are picking up here from a well-regarded proprietor. Certain things are best to get straight from the source." He leaned over Meggie and gave her cheek a tiny pinch. "Sweet as maple syrup!" he said with a smile. "Maple syrup being a thing you should try while here, my little dollop of adorability. Or maple candy or maple cream—although you are sweet enough without any of the aforementioned products!"

She giggled. "How do you know so much, Mister Wandering Wallace?" Meggie asked with a grin, her dimples going deep.

"Because, dear child, I am a wanderer! I have wandered so far and so wide we had to add it to my name."

Miyakitsu nodded solemnly, her eyes twinkling as she spun a length of midnight black hair around one finger.

"What do you suppose they'll have to put in my name then?" Meggie asked.

"I'd wager it'd be something to do with dimples or sweetness or smiles," the Wandering Wallace said. "But you'd better move along before all the carriages are taken and you have to walk. There are quite a few things the area's known for. Leather, guns, gloves, diamonds, and dimmmmmples." He twisted a fingertip into Meggie's cheek. When he tossed his head, the ass's ears pointed back toward the departing line of wagons and whatnots.

"There are more horses here than I've seen in a long while," Maude said.

"Step lively," the Wandering Wallace warned with a thrust of his chin toward the men who sat beside each carriage's or cart's driver. "More guns as well."

Bran saw it was true. "Are we certain we want to go into the city with the odds of Merrow attack that high?"

"Not Merrow this far in, but other waterborne Wildkin, surely." The ass's head bobbed in a wide nod. "But live a little," he urged. "And stay away from the river and canals." He waved a dismissive hand. "We all must die of something someday. Better an interesting death than a dull one. There are a million worse causes of death than Merrow and company."

"Perhaps I should examine your list of a million worse causes," Bran muttered. "There must be many horrible ways of dying I have *never* considered."

The Wandering Wallace's voice dropped and for a moment his tone went dark and dangerous. "There most certainly are." But then his head bobbed again and he said, "Have a remarkable and enjoyable day. And don't forget about the maple syrup!" he added as they began to walk away.

Marion turned back briefly, tugging Meggie to a stop. "You and I . . ."

"Need to have a good old-fashioned sit-down," the Wandering Wallace concluded.

"Yes. Upon our return?"

"Certainly. Find me when you are back and we shall have a discussion which will surely set things right as rain."

Bran blinked, recognizing the phrase, and peered at Maude. She nodded, having caught it, too. She shrugged. As prisoners there was not much to be done when one heard the rebel phrase dropped.

"But first things first," the Wandering Wallace said, pulling out his pocket watch. "Make sure your timepieces are all set to ship's time. It would make supper far less entertaining if you *missed the boat,* so to speak."

Aboard the Artemesia

Most of the crew and passengers had disembarked to explore the town when the captain made his way into Jordan's room. She ran as far as the walls let her and screamed as loudly as her lungs allowed, but he gagged her again and dragged her to the floor.

Outside her window storm clouds filled in, blocking out the bright light of the briefly blue sky, dragged low to the ground and snaking angrily along Steuben Hill to blacken the world. Lightning snapped out, slapping the sky, as her rage built and she bit back tears. She fought, twisting beneath him and hating him with all her heart, but nothing changed what he did.

And she hated herself for not being able to stop him.

The snap of lightning against her window threw him off of her and he stared at the cracked glass, the scent of singed wood seeping into the room. He grabbed her by the arms and shook her.

"Did you do that?"

She shook her head, a frightened *no,* realizing she *could* be more frightened of him, seeing the vein rise by his hairline, than she had been just minutes ago.

He yanked the gag out of her mouth. "Answer me!"

"No," she whispered.

Lightning flared across the sky again, thrashing against

the body of the boat like an eager dog trying to reach its master.

Captain Kerdin threw her back to the floor. "In all my years I've never seen anything like that . . . Lightning *hunting* you. That lightning hungers for you." He laughed. "You are truly something unique, Jordan Astraea. More wanted than you know. When lightning finally takes you, will its kiss strengthen you or make you Wraith or Warden? Or might you become something else? New and different." Still laughing, he left her, locking her cabin again.

Herkimer Port

After most of the crowd had loaded into carriages and carts and the trunks and boxes the Wandering Wallace and Miyakitsu had been leaning so comfortably against were taken, they settled together in a happy heap, his rump on the wood of the dock, her rump on his lap, her arms wrapped around his neck, and his feet in the first fallen and crumpling leaves signaling autumn's eventual arrival. Her toes pointed and poked at the carpetbag at their side as she smiled into the masked face of the man she once again remembered she loved.

Caught up staring into each other's eyes, it took a moment for them to realize they were being watched by a man carrying a leather bag the size of a small pumpkin.

The Wandering Wallace shifted Miyakitsu on his lap and peered up at the man with curiosity.

"You're he, yes?" the man asked, looking around to assure himself no one else was nearby before returning his gaze with some doubt to the mask. "You are . . . a mule?"

The Wandering Wallace laughed. "Some might say donkey and many would merrily take the opportunity to call me an ass, but all three work and are at times quite fitting. Today though it seems I am destined to be mostly mule." He eyed the leather bag. "And you are searching for—"

The man paused, his lips pursed, taking in the full spectacle of the pair of them for the first time. "—a Reanimator."

"Very good," the Wandering Wallace replied.

The man said, "Strange how all your type goes masked."

"How better to go than masked as bandits, we sly few who steal life away from death. We sly few . . . and the odd assortment of street entertainers, gypsies, and yes, your standard thieves, too," Wallace corrected with a shrug. "It is not as if a mask or other physical trapping defines a person or their station." He tilted his head. "Besides, nearly everyone has either badges or calling cards. Where's the fun in being like the majority? Let the minority go masked."

The man's eyes narrowed further. "Robert said that these must needs reach you."

The Wandering Wallace stuck his hand out for the bag and the man set it in his palm. "Each is whole, sorted and labeled?"

The man nodded but stopped himself partway through the move. "Most, not all."

The Wandering Wallace shook his head. "So I must needs contact a Reader?"

"For a scant handful," the man said, taking his hat off and gripping it before his chest with both hands. "Some were only recently procured . . ."

Wallace reached his free finger and thumb through the mask's eye holes and rubbed around the bridge of his nose. "Recently procured through . . . ?"

"There was a fever outbreak in Utica and you know how it is . . . the regular folk . . . they don't know how the storm-cells work."

"So after they died you helped—"

"—clean the homes. As good Christian folk help each other in a time of sorrow and need," he justified. He rallied, becoming defensive. "We only help ourselves to the soul stones, that's all. And all for the good of the cause."

"Yes, yes," the Wandering Wallace agreed flatly. "All for the good of the cause. After all, what is a little theft when what you're working up to is a full-scale coup d'etat? Some little things must be sacrificed along the way."

Miyakitsu turned to pet the donkey's long silk mane with a tender hand.

"And now I've done my bit . . . ?"

"Yes. Yes, of course." The Wandering Wallace grabbed Miyakitsu by the waist and, moving her aside, rose to his feet, scooping up the carpetbag. "Take us to the one in need."

The man became fully animated then, pressing his hat flat to his head and motioning them along to the edge of the packed-dirt path that led down the face of the mountain. A horse waited in traces for them, its long reins loose as it tugged at the grass now going from bright green to dull at the cool top of the mountain. On the seat of the carriage a man dozed, his arms resting on a handsome rifle in his lap.

Their leader shouted at him, startling both horse and gunman. "Keith, you good-for-nothing lug-a-bed! Look lively!"

The man glared at him with eyes so large they were owl-like. "For heaven's sake, Terrence, there's no need to rouse me when we're so far up the mountain. Only springs up here. Not like a Merrow or pooka's gonna slither his way through the rocks underground just to squeeze out a mountain spring and eat your face!" he added with a wild shake of his open hands.

"Quite true," Wallace added, opening the carriage door for Miyakitsu. "They are not interested in faces at all, much preferring throats and guts instead," he quipped, hopping inside after his lady and tugging the door shut behind them. "Comfortable, Peaches?" he asked as he slid an arm around her shoulders and snuggled her close. "A little nervous, mayhaps?"

She burrowed her nose into the crook of his neck and murmured.

"Well, love, so am I. But. We're a crafty pair. And remember. With Merrow and other Wildkin, it's not necessarily the fastest, the strongest, nor the smartest that survives, but it almost never is the dumbest nor the slowest. So. I do believe we have a leg up on our hosts." He put a thumb under her chin and lifted it away from him enough that he could glimpse her eyes. "Besides. The footman carries a Remington rifle being so near Ilion, I'd wager, and the horse is calm. They usually know if something is amiss."

The other man climbed up beside the gunman and with a crack of the reins the horse began the trek down the hillside and into the bustling town of Herkimer.

The house they stopped before was somewhat bigger than the Wandering Wallace's temporary abode in the Burn Quarter of Philadelphia, and didn't lean quite as far to one side. It was simple construction.

The Wandering Wallace glanced up and down the street. Here there was no laughter, no song, no children playing—no signs of life were evident in the neighborhood at all. He wrapped Miyakitsu more tightly against him and made his way quickly into the house.

He stopped just inside the door, all the humor draining from him.

The body was already laid out on a table in the parlor, the area clean and neat and devoid of any troublesome elements. Like additional witnesses and cats. Cats were quite the distraction for Miyakitsu. Cats and squirrels.

All the appropriate precautions had been taken, but still he dragged his feet forward, because unlike most of the bodies he worked on, this one was quite small.

A child.

It was Miyakitsu who roused him from his sorrow. She tugged on his arm, inclining her head the faintest bit. Without words she reminded him of his duty—of the oath he swore to her every morning soon after she began to trust him and well before she forgot his very existence again. "To save and to serve."

Swallowing hard, he stepped to the table and set down his carpetbag, opening it wide. Withdrawing his apron, gloves, and a length of wire, he asked only the most pertinent questions and quickly set about the task of bringing the dead child back to some semblance of life.

Chapter Ten

> The man that lays his hand upon a woman,
> Save in the way of kindness, is a wretch
> Whom 'twere gross flattery to name a coward.
>
> —JOHN TOBIN

Aboard the Artemesia

The wound on Jordan's upper arm had quickly become nothing but a punctured and angry bruise, now just the most visible reminder of the first time the captain had forced himself on her. It would not be much longer until it was entirely gone, nothing but a violent memory he did his best to relive every time he entered her room, locked the door behind him, and pushed her around until she gave up.

Until she submitted.

Some things were inevitable and some battles ceased to be worth fighting. She fingered the heart pin that still rested in the folds of her sleeve. It was a cold reminder that some hearts were impregnable. Some hearts were too hard to pierce and could only be reforged in the heat of a fire. She slipped it free of her sleeve, squeezing it as hard as she could between her fingers.

If only her heart were as hard as Rowen's.

Funny, the way she thought of this small, shiny, metal heart as Rowen's, as if he'd given her something more substantial than a decorative pin. As if he'd given her his heart. His *heart*. But it was far from the truth. She touched her neck. It was sore from the captain's hands wrapping round it as they had today. She rubbed it gently, wondering if it, too, would bruise.

When he bruised her arm he gave her a new blue dress with longer sleeves. Better to hide the truth. What would he give her if her neck bruised? A scarf? A collar-style necklace? How many ways could you hide physical damage?

Mental damage was so much simpler to obscure.

A Weather Witch was considered unstable by his or her nature. Storms were summoned and released through the wildness of a Witch's passionate nature. She rolled the heart between her palms, walking slowly to the window.

She cranked it open wide enough to dump the water in her basin and pitcher. She could let the heart slip free and plummet to the ground . . . To set it free as she'd set free her hopes that Rowen would come to her rescue. She reached one hand out, opening her fingers so she glimpsed the sheen of the heart still within her grasp.

As she snaked her hand between the window's frame and its glass the wind tore at her, whipping around the ship and slipping through her fingers to tease at the heart—to pull it free from her itself and cast it into the clouds.

She closed her eyes. She could do it: let him go. Let go of hope. Here she was a prisoner on a floating island with nowhere to run. She couldn't just unlock the door, go down some stairs, burst onto a city street and disappear into a crowd.

There was only so far someone could run on an airship before they were caught.

She could let Rowen go. She hated him anyhow. He had been her one hope—her friend who had grown into something more. But he had abandoned her as his parents and nearly every party guest had abandoned her family.

Her fingers curled tightly around the heart and she squeezed it so hard it bit into her skin and dug into her palm like the last thing it was willing to do was go. She gasped seeing the blood well up between her fingers and, pulling her hand and the heart back inside, turned her back on the darkening clouds beyond her window. She slid down the wall, her back against its cool surface, the heart clutched in her bloody hand.

Pulling her knees up to her chin, she rested her elbow atop them, her hand opening, the bloody heart nestled there, smeared with red. Her hand had looked like this before, when she was being Made.

But the hurt had been different.

Outside the window spots of rain pelted the glass, the pitter-patter of drops splashing enough that tiny bits of them spattered inside the open window, chilling her.

She plucked the heart from her hand and tugged open the back of it so the sharp part of the pin stuck out. It was a sharp little blade. She knew from using it before in the Tanks. She brushed its tip against the flesh of her wrist, feeling it tickle.

She ran it along the length of her arm, appreciating a sensation so soft and foreign compared to the captain's rough touch. So light, so gentle, so . . . She pressed down on it, watching it raise a red path in its wake . . . so unlike her reality.

She picked it up and moved it back to her wrist, repeating the action, but pressing harder.

She sucked her bottom lip into her mouth to worry it between her teeth—to gnaw and chew on it.

To feel something.

The heart dug in, blood rising up—just a few drops. Horrified, she dropped the pin to the floor and stared at the slowly weeping beads like tiny red dewdrops springing from her flesh.

This was real. It was pain, but a pain she controlled, a pain she could summon, a sensation to remind her there was something within her grasp—some bit of her existence she steered.

She picked the heart back up, wiping it off on her skirt. It gleamed brighter now. She pressed a thumb on her weeping wound, smearing the blood across her skin. Such a bright red against such a soft white.

She leaned back, letting her head loll against the wall, and closed her eyes, letting the tiny wound weep.

Holgate

Standing stunned and stiff in the sunlight of the main square, dressed in tattered and filthy clothing, the survivors of Holgate's Tanks hailed from all ranks, all backgrounds, and were all yet unMade.

The Wraiths and Wardens drifted around the ragtag group's edges, driving them closer together. People who had been touched by no one but their torturer for weeks or even months were forced into human contact.

It was inevitable that someone would snap out a shout.

"Why have you released us? Why round us up?" the boy with the scarred fingers demanded. "If you've freed us, then *truly* free us. Play no more games. We were all once the same."

The Wraiths screeched, raising bony hands to the sky. One stepped to the center, and spoke in a high-pitched and keening voice. "Freed you to give you purpose. You will find true freedom soon. But first—you will fight!" it wailed, words weaving up and into the air. On a middle finger ruby ring flashed and flared.

Aboard the Tempest

"You know she's nothing but the most beautiful tangle of trouble a man can possibly encounter," Ginger Jack said, the words causing Rowen to straighten. The words by themselves seemed an insult, but their delivery—he eyed Ginger Jack carefully.

Rowen hooked his fingers into his belt and chuckled, glancing toward where Evie stood, a distance farther down the cargo bay.

"What?"

"You're moonstruck."

Ginger Jack's brows pulled tight together. "Moo—"

Rowen's brows raised in challenge. "—nstruck," he finished.

"What?" Ginger Jack demanded, turning from staring aghast at Rowen to the back of the pirate captain where Rowen's smirking gaze rested. "The—the captain? You think I like the captain?!"

Smug, Rowen dropped his gaze to Jack. "No. I most certainly do not think you like her. I know you *love* her."

Jack widened his stance. "Those are fighting words," he said, stunned.

Rowen chuckled again and, resting a huge hand on Jack's face, moved him, sputtering, aside as Rowen walked past him.

Jack looked anxiously from Rowen to the captain he was fast approaching. He jogged after him, pawing at his arm. "Just what precisely do you think you're doing—other than apologizing for this obvious mistake in judgment you've made . . ."

Rowen glanced down at him, not even shortening his stride. One side of his mouth pressed deeper into his cheek and he laughed at the other man from his eyes. "I am merely going to do what any good man would do when faced with a similar situation. You may come or stay—your choice. But what must needs be done must needs be done."

Jack paled a shade or two from his normally ruddy complexion. "You had best not do what I think you are setting to be about . . . *friend* . . ."

"Perhaps what I am setting to be about is precisely that thing that should have been handled a good while ago and I am precisely the man to handle the issue."

"Oh my god, Rowen . . . If you . . ." Jack kept up with Rowen's long strides, staying directly beside him, turned toward the larger man. He sped his pace, getting in front of Rowen and walking backwards.

Rowen's gaze flicked from the captain to him and back again. "If I what?" Rowen teased.

"If you tell her—" His eyes were wide. "I'll deny it—every bit—"

The air puffed out of him when he slammed into her,

and it was only her fist on his collar that kept Jack from falling to his knees.

A grin threatened to split Rowen's face in two.

The captain was significantly less amused. "Deny what?" she boomed out, dragging Jack by the collar so he was no longer sandwiched between Evie and Rowen.

Jack swallowed hard, faced with her obvious dissatisfaction. "Deny that I told him the truth of your ancestry." He crossed his arms over his chest and tipped his chin up, spotlighting the red-gold patch of hair he had carefully cultivated at its end.

She noted it, a brief smile ghosting over her lips, and said with a huff, "You know I told you that in the strictest of confidence. Imagine how I would be judged if every scalawag aboard knew!"

Rowen snapped straight up. "I am not just any scalawag," he grumbled.

She slapped a hand lightly against his cheek, sparing him a quick look. "Of course not, darling," she soothed. "You're a very *special* scalawag."

Jack snorted. "Aye, he is special. You should have seen him try to change the cog on the aft burners!"

She puffed out a breath in amused exasperation. "I can only imagine!"

"Wait—what?" Rowen demanded, realizing how things had suddenly turned on him.

They both looked back at him, laughing in unison.

"He's a giant," she mused. "I have wondered how easily one could shove an entire tree trunk into such tight tunnels as you must work. Do you have to grease him up before you send him in? Perhaps attach a rope to his ankle so you can pull him free if he gets wedged tight?"

Jack bent over, laughing, and slapped his knee. "I'd need to call in an entire team of workers to extricate him if he got stuck! It would be the strangest tug-of-war ever!"

"Well, then, let's try to not put a square peg in places only a round peg should go," she said with a smile. She leaned over, resting an arm on Jack's shoulders.

"None of that has anything to do with why I came over here," Rowen snapped.

Jack froze, staring at him, and Evie adjusted her position, resting her elbow on Jack's shoulder and cupping her face in her hand as she peered at Rowen.

She appraised him with half-closed eyes, the picture of quiet contentment. And very much like the captain Rowen was used to seeing. "And why precisely did you come over here then?"

"I am here to take care of something that is—from my estimation—long overdue." He shot a glare at Jack and the smaller man looked down, knowing his fate was firmly in Rowen's hands.

"And that would be . . . ?" She raised one eyebrow at him. But here and now, anchored by Jack, the woman appeared unshakable.

Jack was in direct opposition to her, his body taut beneath her touch, every bit of his expression tight and frozen.

Inwardly Rowen sighed. "These crates." He reached past Evie. "They are nowhere near where they should be," he grumbled, noting how Jack seemed to deflate in realization. "You told me to move them when I was first . . . *encouraged* aboard and I have not. But it seems a tree trunk is exactly what is needed for such a job."

She blinked. "Aye. A tree trunk, either greased or

ungreased," she added, the edges of her eyes crinkling, "would be the perfect thing to accomplish the task."

Rowen set about the task, noting out of the corner of his eye how the captain straightened up and away from Jack—slowly—saying softly, "Some tasks are better suited to more deftly designed men with great dexterity and intelligence."

She spun on a heel and stalked off, Jack staring after her.

He cleared his throat and stepped over to where Rowen grunted and groaned, unstacking the crates only to move them ten feet and restack them.

"I would like to say thank you for not taking the opportunity to say things that might drive a wedge between myself and the captain and make our working relationship even more difficult than it already is. Things," he paused to stress the word, "which are absolutely untrue."

Rowen adjusted a broad wooden box, scraping it across the back of another until the two were flush. He grunted.

"She loves you, too, you know."

Jack snapped up to his full height, staring in shock. "She most certainly does not."

"Yes, she does," Rowen said, hands on either side of the top crate on a stack, his focus seemingly on shimmying it into place.

"You are so dense!"

He snorted. "There are some who are truly dense—stupid. And then there are some of us—a minority, granted—who appear dense—unerringly stupid—and yet, we are quite perceptive in some ways. I once heard someone say, *it takes a very smart person to appear stupid.*"

"She wants *you,* Rowen—I've seen the way she looks at you—like a starving wolf eyeing a lamb dinner."

"Wants and loves are two distinctly different verbs, commonly, and sometimes tragically, mistaken for each other," Rowen muttered, reaching for another crate. "*Wanting* me is an act of curiosity. Nothing more. Even I understand that. It is a mistake that I will not encourage her to further investigate."

"Why not? She's beautiful."

Rowen paused briefly as he wriggled another crate free like a loose tooth. This was the dangerous moment. To deny the captain was beautiful was to call into question Jack's judgment and Elizabeth's value. But to agree was to reinforce the misperception Jack held in his mind—that Rowen was attracted to her as much as she was attracted to him.

He licked his lips, preparing to navigate dangerous waters. "She is beautiful. But she is not the one I want or love." He froze then, his knuckles whitening on the crate in his grip as he realized what his words meant.

Ginger Jack caught the meaning, too. "So you *love* this Jordan Astraea."

Rowen shifted the next crate, groaning loudly.

"You *love* her."

He set the crate down more heavily than he intended, his head suddenly not in his work at all. Leaning across the crate, his arms straddling its top, knuckles still white, he was nose to nose with Jack. "I shall exchange a secret for a secret," he offered.

Jack grinned. "Oh, I think I would give up two secrets for you to admit this one of yours, Rowen," Jack admitted.

"Fine. You first. Two secrets to my one."

"No, no," Jack laughed. "One of mine, and then yours. If I deem yours worthy, I'll tell you a second secret. If not . . ." He shrugged.

"Deal. You first. What is this secret to the captain's ancestry?"

"An excellent choice!" Jack said with a laugh. "However—she will go insane if you ever mention this to anyone else . . . She says 'those boots are far too big to fill.' So, no using the information except for your own personal and silent amusement."

Rowen nodded solemnly, but one eyebrow quirked.

"Our good captain, Elizabeth Victoria—" He slapped a hand over his mouth. "I wasn't at liberty to reveal her middle name—she's touchy about that, too . . ."

"I won't breathe a word, but that will *not* count as one of your two secrets."

"Ah. Well clarified."

"Elizabeth Victoria: E.V. Now I understand." Rowen grinned. "Do go on with your secrets."

"Our dear captain is directly descended from Calico Jack Rackham and Anne Bonny herself."

Rowen cocked his head and looked at Jack. "Rackham was hung. And Bonny . . ."

". . . disappeared from the records around the time her stay of execution was up. Certain segments of society have speculated quite a bit over what happened to Anne."

"I'd imagine by certain segments you mean, specifically, yours?"

Jack smiled. "Aye. They were quite the couple."

"I seem to remember from my reading there was more to them than a *couple* . . ."

Jack cleared his throat. "Well. That is one of the more lurid stories related to them, true . . . But Jack and Anne had a separate history, you know. Before Mary Read joined the crew. She delivered a child for him and left it on an island with some of Jack's other family to be raised and she rejoined him."

"She abandoned her child?"

"It sounds harsh if you look at it that way. I prefer to think of it as she left her child in the safekeeping of others and went back to rejoin her two true loves."

Rowen nodded slowly. "*Two,*" he said, stressing the single syllable. He winked.

"Yes, *two*. Jack and *the sea.*"

Rowen's grin mellowed. "Fine. Jack and the sea. And our captain is descended from that child?"

"Aye. Imagine being a captain of a ship such as ours—"

"—by which you mean *pirate*—"

"*—trader,*" Jack corrected with a wink of his own. "Imagine being related to not just one famous—"

"—trader?" Rowen tried with a laugh.

"*—captain,*" Jack returned. "Imagine being the descendent of *two*."

"Big boots indeed," Rowen agreed.

Aboard the Artemesia

The Wandering Wallace seemed tired when Marion found him back aboard the *Artemesia* and he was none too eager to have the conversation required of him. But as the ship drifted free of its moorings, the men sat at a table together.

Miyakitsu was leaning against the Wandering Wallace in one of the ship's smaller tearooms, lounging on broad velvet pillows behind a low table. He had exchanged his donkey's mask for that of a yawning housecat, looking in many ways like a much different man.

Marion lowered himself slowly, tucking his long legs under him to make himself comfortable. "I made sure Meggie tried the maple candy, as you suggested. And I found her a pair of leather gloves just right for such a small lady," he reported.

"Good, good," the Wandering Wallace said. "And you, you are—?"

"Right as rain," Marion whispered.

"And yet keeping company with the Maker and his family?"

"More appropriately they are keeping company *with me.* They did not plan this particular journey. It was more of an impulsive agreement we reached."

"Ah. How intriguing." The Wandering Wallace laced his fingers together and stretched. "So the little one . . . she is your most important pawn. The key to your power."

Marion accepted a cup and saucer from the server. "Gunpowder," he requested and she stepped away to return with the appropriate teapot.

"A bold tea choice for a bold young man."

"Not much younger than you, I'd wager." The tea streamed from the fresh pot into his cup, steaming. "Twenty-two."

The Wandering Wallace nodded. "You wager correctly. Not much at all, if any. Might even fall the other direction, depending on month."

"October," Marion specified, taking a long, slow sip.

"Ah. Likely a Libra male. Fascinating!"

Marion stared across the teacup's edge at him as the Wandering Wallace rose and reached behind him to draw the heavy velvet curtains closed. The Wandering Wallace sat back down and adjusted the stormlight so the glow more fully illuminated their faces and cast them in an eerie light. The Wandering Wallace and Miyakitsu leaned in.

Marion did the same.

"If you might indulge me . . ." The Wandering Wallace reached around the table's edge and dug into his carpetbag. He withdrew something carefully wrapped in fine fabric. Undoing a knot, he revealed a small contraption with tiny levers and gears and two miniature bell jars. He set it on the table between them. "I would like to affix this mechanism to your wrist and palm. The nature of our discussion is quite delicate and I cannot afford to risk speaking at length to people of the wrong sort."

"I daresay I understand that," Marion said. "Where and what . . . ?"

"I know the most amazing watchmaker. His talents are frequently overlooked as a result of splitting with a family of relatively notable rank. But he learned his trade from a very talented man with a gift for crafting the tiniest of mechanisms . . ." He motioned to Marion's arm. "Roll up your sleeve, please."

Marion obliged.

The Wandering Wallace next produced a small box. Sliding one part out of the other, he showed it held a scant number of lucifer matches. "Ships are quite particular about the scent of brimstone," he muttered, "as are Christians . . . ready, my love?"

Miyakitsu nodded, cupping a hand as he struck the lucifer, held it between Marion's arm and the first of the two tiny bell jars, and let the flame suck out the oxygen and create suction. Miyakitsu waved frantically at the wisp of smoke left by the burning lucifer, dissipating it. The actions were repeated and Marion soon found himself with the miniature bell jars affixed to his flesh and the device attached to both them and the pulse point of his wrist.

"Now. Are you quite comfortable?"

He looked at the Wandering Wallace, his lips quirking. "Considering the circumstances, yes."

"Circumstances must always be taken into account. This device helps determine the veracity of your statements. If your pulse jumps or speeds, this device reports the variation with noise." He glanced round their shrouded space, clarifying, "A rather discreet noise. Shall we give it a go?"

Marion nodded cautiously.

The Wandering Wallace walked him through a variety of simple questions and answers to test that the machine was appropriately calibrated. Then the real test began.

"You hold with rather abolitionist views. True?"

"True," Marion agreed.

"You believe in the abolition of slavery. True?"

"True."

"You believe that all slaves, whether black, red, or Witch, should be freed."

"True."

"And you are very concerned with the direction this young country has taken. True?"

"Also true."

The Wandering Wallace watched the mechanism attached to Marion's wrist and Miyakitsu watched the place where the curtains had been drawn together but could easily be pulled apart.

"Do you hope for change in this country?"

"Yes."

"Revolution?"

"If that is what it requires."

"Are you in league with any of the established revolutionaries?"

"There are established revolutionaries?"

The Wandering Wallace's eyes never left the mechanism, but he scolded, "We ask, you answer. Are you in league with any of the established revolutionaries?"

"No."

"Are you seeking to start your own league of revolutionaries?"

"I—I don't know . . . I never considered . . ."

"Are you a spy for the Council?"

"No!"

"Are you seeking to uncover information about the revolutionaries so that you may stop their work?"

"No."

The Wandering Wallace flopped back on the cushion. "Darling, please . . ." He waved at the contraption and Miyakitsu used her slender fingers to detach it from Marion's arm, carefully sliding it back across the table to the Wandering Wallace. He leaned over, rewrapped the contraption in the cloth, and popped it back into the bag as Marion rolled his sleeve back down.

"Well, I daresay that is quite a relief," the Wandering Wallace said, letting his arms flop wide open and pull Miyakitsu toward him. "You may close the window, darling. We won't need to escort him out as we did the last one."

Marion swallowed hard.

Miyakitsu rose, cranked the window shut, and locked it.

"We must always think about saving our own skins, you understand? Without us, revolution stands no chance."

"Are you it then, the head of the revolutionary leagues you mentioned?"

The Wandering Wallace shook his head. "I doubt anyone can truly claim that title when a revolution is in the works. I am merely an enabler who is willing to do whatever is required to set this country on the right path."

"And how do you plan to do that?"

"Well, that depends. Are you joining our ranks or simply speculating about joining?"

Marion leaned back. "Have you considered bringing about change from the inside out?"

"Who hasn't?" The Wandering Wallace shook his head and Miyakitsu reached up to stroke the yawning cat's whiskers. "Some things cannot be accomplished from the inside. Where does an apple begin to rot? From the inside out. We must instead make a run at the outside to better find our way in."

"And how do you intend to do so?"

"I must be assured of your allegiance."

Marion rubbed a hand across his forehead and slipped his fingers into his dark hair, combing through it. "What do you need me to say?"

"That you acknowledge there is no path to peace except by complete revolution. You already have the Maker and his family. Imagine what you could do by removing just him from the face of this planet."

"I have imagined. Every night for four years I imagined that," Marion admitted. "But I don't know now . . ."

"Ah. He's gotten to you, has he? He's made you see him as something other than the monster he is."

"He's no monster. There are no monsters. Only men."

"And you think this man should be allowed to continue

what he is doing—Making Witches to power the transportation and luxuries of the wealthy?"

"Of course not."

"Then be rid of him once and for all. Wipe clean the slate and force them to find a new Maker. Make them suffer and slow their ability to produce. Make them Make a Maker!" he said with a laugh.

But Marion's volume dropped and Miyakitsu stiffened, hearing the growl edging up in his voice. "*Never.* I will never let anyone Make another," he swore, his hand clenched around his teacup.

Frost wiggled out from his fingertips, crawling across the china and edging its way to encircle and cool the still steaming liquid. "You would *not* understand," he hissed, his breath coming out in a frosty puff.

The Wandering Wallace poked a finger through the foggy air and gave it a swirl, twirling it. Pulling his hand back, he moved his index finger back and forth and Marion watched, awestruck, as he made the tiny tendrils of fog into shapes and then animals and then, one by one, crystallized them in midair, and let them tumble into Marion's tea where they floated and dissolved.

"Hmm. *Iced* tea. It might catch on eventually, yes, darling?"

Miyakitsu wrinkled her nose.

"Ah well, perhaps. You see, my friend," he said, once again addressing Marion, "I *do* understand. We are not so very far apart in our experiences at all when it comes to magick. I make my living as an illusionist and do what needs doing on the side: the occasional Reanimation and forgery," he said as simply as if naming his favorite colors. "I am no Weather

Witch nor Warden nor Wraith, but I do bear magick. And I recognize that our world would be a sadder place without magick in it."

"Magick is not wanted here," Marion protested.

"Ah. So easily you fall back into repeating the lies they've taught you. Magick is unwanted. That it's some low class anomaly. That it must be quelled and controlled for the betterment of man. And the biggest lie of them all—that magick is what tore all of Europe apart. It most certainly did not. That was the work of greedy politicians and weapon-wielding soldiers."

Marion watched an icy giraffe bobbing in his tea and growing shorter and shorter with each descent. Finally it went under the surface altogether and was nothing but one slightly shinier spot of liquid and then . . . nothing. "Is war truly the only choice? Must it be full revolution?"

"You are quite naive, are you not?"

Marion's head snapped up at that. "No, sir. I am not."

"You seem well bred, but you're a Witch. You've been traveling with the Maker since Holgate and have not yet killed him. You believe the system can be fixed—that the system need not be replaced . . ." He ticked off Marion's supposed offenses on his fingertips one by one. "It all adds up to a certain naiveté."

Marion put both hands flat on the table and pressed down, raising himself up. He peered down at the masked man and his odd foreign bride feeling contempt twist his face. "As my nanny used to say: There is more than one way to skin a cat. Violence might not yet be the only answer."

He turned and stuck a hand between the curtains, only pausing briefly when the Wandering Wallace admitted, "I like his spunk," and then, more loudly, "Do find me when you realize I'm correct!"

The curtains opened and closed and Marion stalked away.

Aboard the Tempest

Jack put his hands on his hips. "Now. Your turn. This Jordan Astraea. You love her."

Rowen smacked his hands together and looked toward the ceiling. Pulling in a deep breath he admitted, "It's worse than all that—I think I've loved her for a while. At least a year or two. Maybe more."

"And you never told her, did you?"

"Of course I didn't. I'm not stupid."

Jack laughed. "And now you find yourself aboard a fine trading vessel and she is . . . ?"

Rowen sucked his lips in and narrowed his gaze. "Aboard another airship."

"Oh, that is good. And do you think she knows how you feel?"

"I don't think so. But women are strange. I'd never admit it to one of them, but I think occasionally they might know things about us sooner than we know ourselves."

"Never again say that aloud. It's nearly treasonous." Jack laughed.

Rowen's brow furrowed, creases threatening to fold it in half. "It may not matter now, though—what she knows or doesn't. I wasn't there when she needed me most."

"Oh."

"She might think I gave up on her. She might hate me."

"You might be correct." Jack rubbed his chin. "And how does that change your goal of finding her?"

"It doesn't," Rowen said with a sigh. "Nothing will change the fact that I need to get to her."

Jack nodded. "You, good knight, seem to have embarked upon the most difficult of quests. Perhaps we'd best hope you are not destined to play Don Quixote in this mission of yours."

"I have heard of that one. Would that not make you Sancho Panza?"

Jack snorted. "I think not. But I would say that tragic love story of yours is worth the sharing of another secret of mine."

"Excellent." Rowen slapped a palm down on one of the wooden boxes. "Just what's in these crates? They're so heavy it's like I'm carrying corpses."

Jack paled a moment. "That is quite a secret you wish to be made privy to. I'll give you a chance to choose a different secret for me to share. For your own safety."

Rowen's expression changed, his focus and intensity narrowing down to hold only Jack and the crates within his view. "For my own safety."

"Aye. There are things aboard trade ships such as ours that are better not known. Sometimes it is the identities of the crew members—"

Rowen fought to school his features as Jack continued.

"—sometimes it is the cargo."

"I want to know."

"If things go wrong, you'll be hanged."

"I expect that is frequently the case for all crew members aboard a—*trading* ship. If things go wrong there, hangings happen."

"Yes. Hangings happen."

"But, if I'm to take such a risk, I want to know for what crime I'd be hanged."

Jack blinked once at him and let the word drop out of his mouth to stand like a wall between them: "Treason."

Aboard the Artemesia

"You," Marion demanded, pointing to Bran when he threw wide their cabin's door and strode in, slamming it behind him. "You are what's wrong with the system. It was through your Making that everything has broken." He stormed across the room, tendrils of fog trailing coldly behind him. "It is only right that you fix things."

Bran blinked. "Meggie and Maude," he said flatly, "to the other room."

Maude only paused briefly, hearing the intensity in his voice. She scooped Meggie up and carried her to the far smaller second room, closing the door behind her.

"Fix it," Marion whispered hoarsely, making his approach. "You are part of the reason the system broke. I want to believe it can be fixed. I want to believe it can all be done bloodlessly."

Bran paled and swallowed hard. "Why now?"

Marion looked away, shaking his head, dark curls trembling.

"Marion . . . why are you asking now—why *now*?"

"I want this to all just go away," he confessed. "You, the girls, the Making . . . I want it to end. You said there were ways, honest, upright, and *legal* ways that I could change things. Ways I might fix the system."

"There are . . ."

"Then tell me and tell me quick, because I need to do whatever I can to make things better."

Bran pointed to a chair and Marion dragged it over.

Quickly Bran walked him through the bits he knew about the government and the harsh reality that, as a man with no rank and few funds, Marion had little chance of achieving his goals. "You are Marion Kruse—unranked, ruined. They will not even let you run for office."

"Then I shall be someone else."

Bran shook his head. "You cannot deny who you are."

"You dare say that when you are as determined to leave your past behind as I?"

"They will want documents—a proper and untainted pedigree showing you are of Fifth of the Nine or better," Bran stressed.

"I will provide them with all they want," Marion promised. "And they will be unable to deny my right to make a grab for power." He was insistent, determined. There was no stopping a man who was both those things and married them to his vision. "I must find the Wandering Wallace."

Aboard the Tempest

Rowen smacked his lips together at the word. He hadn't realized how thirsty moving crates made him. "Treason," he said. "That is most certainly a hanging offense."

"Most certainly." Jack laced his fingers before him and sucked in a deep breath that he released slowly. "So. What secret would you prefer to know in light of that?"

Rowen looked down. "None."

Jack's hands swung loose and he said, "Good enough then. Well. I had better return to that warren of tunnels we call engineering."

"We had a deal," Rowen said sharply.

Jack turned back to him. "Yes. Yes, we did. And you said you wanted no other secret to be told to you."

"Precisely. I still want the one you feel is most dangerous."

"Oh." Jack tapped his fingers across the lid of the crate between them. He nodded to himself. "You didn't tell the captain how I—I mean, you didn't tell her that lie about how I supposedly feel about her . . ." He heaved out a sigh. "I made a promise and I'll keep it. But this means you are one of three aboard that know what cargo we carry."

He reached into his waistcoat's pocket, following the chain that dipped into it, and withdrew his pocketwatch. He tugged further on the chain and pulled out an unremarkable-looking key.

He looked back at Rowen.

Rowen stepped back from the crate, and came around to its front to wait beside Ginger Jack.

"You can still tell me you don't want to know . . ."

Rowen's voice caught in his throat. "I try not to lie."

Jack inserted the key and turned it. The box's surface, seemingly solid, broke into separate and spinning bits, pulling free of each other and rotating until they had spun counter-clockwise a quarter of the way around the keyhole. There was a rattle and a click and the lid released just a hairsbreadth from the rest of the box. "You are certain?"

Rowen simply said, "Show me what's in the damned box already."

"Two things wrapped in one body: revolution and equal rights." He raised the lid and Rowen stared at the thing inside. Calling it a corpse was a fine assessment, because indeed the thing inside was bent up into itself—folded—but distinctly possessed arms, legs, a head . . . And rather than the porcelain and breakable automatons the Council had in Philadelphia thanks to a savvy contract with ceramists, these automatons were sporting shells of—he tapped a finger against a breastplate—thin steel.

He raised his head and looked at all the crates of a similar design and origin—crates capable of holding the same exact cargo.

"It's an army," he whispered.

Jack merely nodded.

Rowen's eyes fell again to the breastplate and the socket there, which was so obviously missing a key component. "All they need is a stormcell . . ."

Ginger Jack slowly closed the box and withdrew the key, allowing the mechanism to click, clatter, and lock once more. "That is why we are headed north to Bangor. To meet someone carrying something even better: *soul stones.*"

Chapter Eleven

Come forth into the light of things,
Let Nature be your teacher.
—WILLIAM WORDSWORTH

Aboard the Artemesia

Led to Topside, Jordan was tethered to the dais not far from the Conductor. Mouse sniffled, rubbing his runny nose with his sleeve, and grunted something at her before walking away. "What?" she asked the Conductor.

He glanced at her, continuing to work his way through the stations that marked the ship's controls. "He has instructed you to pay close attention and learn all you can from me. And he said it so politely," he added, sarcasm tightening his words.

For the next hour the Conductor worked and Jordan watched, learning nearly nothing.

Meggie came up to Topside with Maude and the two sat a distance away, playing jacks. Jordan was certain the child listened and watched the ship's workings, too.

Jordan felt more likely to learn from the child than her

actual teacher. Finally she cleared her throat, asking, "Why keep us aloft? If you want your freedom could you not . . . ?"

The Conductor paused, amused. "Do something drastic? Leave? Crash the ship?" He smiled. "The man at my back is getting nervous from such talk, yes?"

Jordan glanced at the sniper, who now stood, adjusting his gun's barrel to more tightly keep Anil in his sights.

"Yes," she confirmed.

"He need not worry. I will keep this ship aloft for as long as I am able."

"But why?"

His brow wrinkled and without looking, he reached out and turned a nearby dial. "Because they have a power over me."

"What power is that?"

"They have my wife and my son."

"So fly the ship to them. Rescue them," she challenged.

"You are so young. So naive." He said the last word wistfully. From his mouth it came as praise rather than insult. "Rescue—"

"—never comes," Jordan said, looking down.

"No. Not never," Anil whispered. "Sometimes it comes late. Sometimes it is the one waiting on rescue who must rescue herself," he confided. "But in this case—rescue is pointless. They are aboard this ship. They are as safe as I keep the *Artemesia*."

"But—"

"For four hours every day—if the conditions are right and I have filled the crystal to its brim with energy—I may visit them. I set the rudder, adjust the wings for glide, and then I may leave."

"But you haven't left your post once that I know of."

"No. I have been informed that I am not allowed to see them again until your training is complete."

"But . . ."

"It is what it is," he said.

"What it *is* is unfair," Jordan said, standing.

"Do nothing rash, Jordan," Anil asked. "This is the way of things. I obey and by that, keep my family safe. It is love for my family alone that keeps me a lamb rather than a lion. Love hamstrings hate."

She blew out a long puff of air. "I will abide by your wishes. But, if having me trained faster means allowing you to see your wife and son sooner, teach me everything. And teach me now," she added.

He grinned at her and, pointing, he began. "This is a near duplicate of Admiral Fitzroy's Storm Glass."

The big glass tube was filled with clear liquid; crystals like snowflakes and frost pulled free of glass. Large, flaky crystals floated at the top of the stuff.

"See their size and where in the glass they float? That is how we want them to look to maintain the present storm." He dropped his hands to his sides and focused his gaze on the storm glass. "The easiest way to call a storm is through the glass. Imagine moving the crystals and they *will* move."

The crystals shifted position, falling through the liquid to become a thread of floating bits running through the storm glass's center, and a wind rolled across the deck. The clouds began to clear.

"Now," he said, "you try. Imagine coaxing the crystals back to the top . . ."

Jordan stared at the storm glass, willing the crystals to move, but they hung dead in the center, still, though the wind ran the length of the deck. She pressed her lips together and she squinted.

She scowled.

They budged not a bit.

"Better push her into glide," he suggested, pointing to a lever nearly as long as Jordan was tall. "Shove it forward to pop the wings."

She pushed and pulled, but the lever stayed as still as the crystals.

The Conductor peered at her and with a single glance from his eyes the crystals rose to the top once more and the clouds closed in. He sighed. "This may prove difficult," he admitted. "You aren't much like most of us, are you?" He returned to singing his strange songs to the storm glass and clouds overhead.

She flopped into a seated position, glaring at the storm glass. She could not rescue herself and she could not rescue him either. What good was a Witch with no ready power?

Aboard the Tempest

If it was to come to rebellion—or war—Rowen wanted to be at Jordan's side. So in the midst of a friendly discussion with Ginger Jack he reached out with a sly left hook and dropped his friend like a bag of grain. Taking the key from around Jack's neck, he returned to the pods and slipped inside one. He sank into the leather-bound seat, pulling belts across himself to buckle in for safety as Jack had suggested.

He stared at the windows ahead of him and the *Tempest*'s

hull just beside. Resting his hand on the lever marked Release, he took a breath.

Rowen closed his eyes, sighing. What would he do when he pulled the lever? Where would he go? How would he free Jordan if he found her?

With a groan, he leaned forward, resting his folded arms and forehead on the console. He had no strategy, no resources, no support, and no chance of success. He undid the buckles and stepped out of the pod, returning things to just the way they were before he'd opened the door.

Evie paused in the hall outside, her eyes falling to Jack's key in his hand. She nodded. "I believe it is time you and I had a talk about Conducting. And if you still wish to go to her after you know this, I will help you once we meet our contact in Bangor. But be warned, Rowen—the girl you last saw will not be the same one you find Conducting an airship. She will be changed."

"I am not the same boy she last saw, either," he confessed. "We have both changed—for better or worse is yet to be seen. Tell me everything you know. Tell it true."

So Evie did. She told him what it was like to Conduct a ship and to want to crash and kill all aboard just to end the enslavement. She told him of cargo ships and cruisers and great liners like the *Artemesia.* She told him of ruined rescues and Burned Out Witches. And what it was like to be Made. The one thing she did not tell him was how she knew so much.

But he didn't need to ask, watching the light leave her eyes while she told him everything—he knew.

When she finally fell silent, nothing left to share but her sorrow for his loss of Jordan, she asked what he had decided.

"I will find her. Do my best to free her," he insisted. "No one should be treated like that, not as you were."

She snorted and took him to her quarters, where she returned his sword and gave him a pouch of coins "for the adventure yet to come," she assured him.

Then she stretched up on her tiptoes and kissed his hairy cheek, saying, "Boy, you'd best be cutting that mess off before you find your Jordan. She might not recognize you otherwise." And she handed him the things he'd wanted but not dared to ask for—a razor and fine mirror to shave by. "And find Jack before he wakes and goes looking for you," she added with a wink.

Philadelphia

They sat across the table from each other in the Hollindale household, sipping their drinks and watching each move the other made. Catrina adjusted her hand, flexing her fingers in the light.

The ruby in her ring sparked like an angry bloodshot eye and she set down her cup, holding her hand out to showcase the glittering jewel. "This remarkable ring is the most astonishing gift anyone has ever given me. Do tell me what inspired you to give such a thing to me, Uncle Gerald."

He slugged back the whiskey at hand and, smiling, said, "You inspire me in many ways, niece. Enjoy the ring."

"I will, oh, I will," she assured him. "It is just that I have seen a similar ring."

He blinked.

"It seems it is such a lovely ring that every current Councilman's wife has been gifted with one."

He licked his lips and poured another drink. "Is that so?"

"Yes, it most certainly is."

Gerald swallowed the drink, wishing it burned more hotly—that it heated his mind and not just his entrails.

"So," Catrina continued, "the real question is this, Uncle Gerald: where did you find the money to purchase so many ruby rings? Have you been watering down your wine?"

Gerald choked. He closed his eyes and leaned forward, brown hair falling into his eyes. When he looked back up at her, he was grinning. "No, niece. Never that."

Aboard the Tempest

The clouds Evie cast as a precaution parted, the big ship's wings adjusting, light streaming into the windows of the airship, and the captain looped her arm around Rowen's and dragged him to the nearest bank of them. "There she is," Evie announced, "the town of Bangor. Not much to look at yet, started by lumberjacks and built on their stories as much as their industry," she said with a smile. "But it's beautiful in its own way. And filled with creative potential. And that's why we call it home."

Bangor spilled out across a hill, sliced through by high-walled streams cutting neatly around its feet and bridged by equally high lines of tree trunks sharpened at their tops to wicked wooden points and interspersed with narrower wooden stakes thrusting down like cruel fangs toward the water.

"There is so much water here we take extra precautions. The Merrow may not make it this far in from the saltwater easily, but considering the friends they've made of the other water-based Wildkin? We must be cautious."

Rowen nodded, noting the wooden towers marking each bridge's intersection with the land. "Gun mounts?"

She grinned. "Indeed. Sporting a caliber heavy enough to wipe a Merrow ally clean from the face of this earth but not damage the earthenwork walls. Well, not damage them much."

"I've never seen weapons quite like that," Rowen remarked, noting multiple barrels bound together and mounted to a nearly standard cannon carriage.

"The first few did more damage to our kind than to theirs, but our engineers are working on remedying the issue," she added with a shrug. "It's more impressive and faster than constantly reloading, and, as fast as it shoots, precise accuracy matters far less." She let her hand slip free of him. "It's a lovely beast of a gun and shows a great deal of promise for future development."

Rowen raised an eyebrow and considered her a moment. She was everything Jordan was not. Strong, self-assured, powerful, and passionate. She winked at him and stepped to thc horn and flywheel. "Approaching Bangor Port. All hands on deck, eyes sharp, hands at the ready!"

They coasted in toward a heavy-looking stone building near the top of one peak, the wood-and-metal bones of the ship's wings creaking as their fabric billowed, cupping the air below, and they descended in a long, slow spiral to the docks. The last hundred yards the wings shifted, tucking alongside, the ship slowing as it slid by the huge building. There was a *pop-pop-pop* as shots burst from a system of cannons, and Rowen jumped as something shot toward the ship's balloon.

Nets carried in hollow cannon shells caught and held the balloon and they sidled up to the dock with a slow groaning of wood and metal meeting.

Bangor

Rowen followed Evie, Toddy, and Ginger Jack out of the ship and onto the dock. Jack had left the mechanical creatures he often tinkered with behind. Sunlight streamed down on them and Rowen paused, noting the difference of the feel of his boots back on something stable and still. He felt a connection to the ground he had never noticed before standing there near the crest of a hill in Bangor.

Evie and the others turned back to watch him a moment, looks on their faces saying they all once did the same. "Come along," Evie urged. "We are in port until we meet our associate tonight, which is not nearly enough time to explore all there is to offer here." Evie widened her stance, looking him over. "You are a far finer-looking fellow without that thing you called a beard nesting on your face."

"Now, now," Jack warned, rubbing the closely cropped patch of facial hair marking his chin. "You dare not be berating beards, are you, Evie?"

She laughed and reached out, stroking his face so softly Rowen thought Jack would explode with joy. "Of course not, Jack," she replied. "Merely pointing out that some men know how to wear a beard and some men simply shouldn't."

"What is that?" Rowen asked, pointing to the huge granite building behind them.

"Officially?" Evie asked.

Rowen quirked an eyebrow at her.

"Government offices."

His eyebrow rose higher.

"And we, dear boy, are in search of papers kept in the building's very bottom." Evie touched the two items hanging on her belt, asking the rest of them, "Sword and pistol?"

"By my side," Jack responded with a laugh.

"Mmhm, mmhm. Then let us have at it."

They entered the building, walking past the watchmen, who turned to look the other direction as they descended a flight of steps to the right.

"It's very large," Rowen remarked. "And relatively empty."

Evie nodded. "Imagine what might be done with such a grand space! It might just become something amazing, like—"

"—a mansion?" Rowen asked, mentally marking out the spots for appropriate furnishings.

"No, something better," Evie assured. "Imagine a library filling the space."

Rowen's brows tugged together. "It would take many books to fill so grand a space," he muttered, still following the crew.

"Many books would be a fine start for a library."

They came to a door, on either side of which hung an assortment of stormlights. Evie took one off a hook and handed it to Jack, pulling one down for herself as well.

Rowen and Toddy followed suit and Evie warned, "A brief climb now, Rowen, as we enter the Hill King's Cavern."

Rowen's jaw swung loose as Evie opened the door and began to descend a ladder immediately on the other side of the threshold. Jack followed, then Rowen, barely off the last rung when the door closed above and Toddy began his way down. They gathered there, only their stormlights illuminating the area.

From somewhere in the darkness behind Evie and Jack the sounds of voices and music echoed distantly.

"The area is pockmarked with boulder caves," Evie explained, raising her lantern so the light stroked the outline of two huge rocks that rested together at one small spot near the floor of Evie's would-be library. Evie turned and, lantern raised high, began to lead them into the darkness.

Rowen leaned over, saying, "Sorry about hitting you the way I did . . ."

Jack snapped out a laugh. "Did you see how she's been petting me and watching me?" he asked instead. "I am feeling no pain right now . . . All's forgiven."

Evie paused, turning back to face the men.

Jack whispered, "She loves doing *this* . . ."

Evie cleared her throat, saying, "The strongest of all the elements, water, clears the space around the bigger rocks, carving its way through the ground, and creating this—" With a dramatic spin, she held the lantern out and high, lighting the scant distance between them and a glowing and vibrant space below.

Stunned, Rowen joined them, stumbling down a boulder-strewn walkway to come to a place where the ground evened out, widening between soaring rock walls.

It was all at once dark and bright within the mountainside where the liberally aligned traders plied their trade; both sparkling and grim. Stormlights dotted the walls and little pinpricks of pyrite and quartz threw their light back, tossed it onto the dampness creating a slick sheen on the cavern's walls, broadening and strengthening the lights.

For a moment Rowen simply stood there, taking it all in. It was like the Night Market of Philadelphia's Below, but taken to a more vibrant and echoing extreme.

Music reflected off the walls, one tune sliding into another in a riot of sound. Men and women danced between brightly colored stalls hung with tapestries whose patterns made Rowen's eyes ache. The odds and ends of a dozen different cargo runs lay heaped in glittering piles at the base of the tiny temporary-looking shops, brass pitchers glowing beside gemstone bracelets and gaudy rings, scarves of silk waving in the slight breeze that rose whenever someone walked past. The entire market was alive with possibility.

"These are our people," Evie said to Rowen. "*Your* people. For as long as you like."

A man raised a flagon to him and grinned as they passed by, not caring he had a few less teeth than most with which to strain the foam from his ale. A dog raced by, nearly tripping Rowen as it wove between people before bounding up to a wooden crate where it stood on its hind legs. It danced a jig to the tune a lithe violinist played.

"Keep your eyes in your head and step lively," Evie warned from his side. "If they sense you're fresh meat, they'll take all you have."

"But you said they're my people," Rowen pointed out.

"Aye, that I did," she said with a wink. "They'll roll you faster than your elder brother in a mean mood and you'll be lucky to leave here wearing a stitch of the clothing you came in with." She looked him up and down again in that way he found so unsettling. "Or perhaps you'll find a buxom lass and mind losing your clothing not one bit." Evie leaned in. "But remember we're on a schedule. We're only here one night. Just for rendezvous."

Jack laughed. "Had you warned him not to strip to his skivvies with a lass because we only had a few minutes, I think our boy Rowen would still have ample time to pull his trousers up and meet us at the ship."

Rowen bristled at the affront, but Evie was already giving Jack the tongue-lashing of a lifetime.

And Jack responded in kind, hands balled into fists, his mouth fighting to keep back the grin that threatened to impede the sharp words he pushed out as fast as he could breathe.

Rowen shook his head and stepped away from them. They wouldn't notice if he was gone.

For a minute Toddy followed him, murmuring about the price of this or the condition of that, tugging items from his own pouches and the bags he had slung across his shoulders to show, talking trade. While Toddy was politely debating the finer points of belt buckles, Rowen stepped away from him, too.

He walked past a circle of giggling children playing some game and stopped short, realizing they were passing around a sparkling thundercloud the size of a cat.

Seeing they were being watched, one small boy tossed the cloud into the air and winked, as lightning sparked halfway to the ground.

Nearby a young woman turned to scold them like an angry school marm before returning to whatever deal she was finalizing.

Rowen headed for the violinist and her dancing dog.

Wearing a short and colorful vest over a shimmering blouse and a skirt that seemed made of scarf after scarf, the gypsy sawed away at her violin, her booted feet nearly nailed together, hips frozen in place, but the rest of her fully involved in the making of her strange and sad music. The strings sang wordlessly as she twisted in time to the tune, oblivious to the dancing dog who hopped along, barking in time.

She wove a musical spell, things within earshot slowed from hurried to passive, people languishing, reclining on carpets the nearby rug seller displayed. The salesman smacked at loiterers with a reed fly swatter but no one minded nor moved. Everyone simply existed as background accompaniment for the music of the violin.

One last, long move of her arms and she stopped playing, stooped for a moment like a mechanical doll in need of winding. She straightened with a toss of her head, short dark hair flying back from her eyes, and smiled sadly at the clapping and hooting crowd, her expression matching the song's mood. She set the violin aside and raised her hands high, clapping out a rhythm and saying, "You know this one, so I beg you to sing along!"

A voice sang out from the wild blue sea

Recognizing the tune, Rowen jumped in, adding a firm baritone to the mix as they sang:

Echoing well down the deep valley
So sweet and soft and feminine
A fine lure with which to snare young men.

A handsome young prince rode to investigate
Hearing her song put the seal on his fate—

Rowen stuttered, his words no longer matching what the pirates sang. His voice faded away and he listened, curious. The song he'd heard and sung so many times with friends of like and higher rank told a far different story than that the pirates told now. A Merrow princess called out from the sea's depths and a human prince brought her out of the surf to stand beside him.

But in the pirates' version the princess begged to be released—she only wanted to spend some time with a human, not be dragged onto the sand, where, horrified at seeing a tail where legs should have been, the prince sneered and left her to die, not even having respect enough to return her parched body to the sea.

If all stories had stems growing from fact, which one was true? If human arrogance ruined the relationships between themselves and the Wildkin, perhaps the fault of the war rested more on his side than Rowen expected. Perhaps what Evie had said about the Merrow *becoming* bastards was more accurate than what Rowen had been raised to believe.

The song over, the dog hopped down toward the hat by the violinist's feet. He picked it up in his mouth and raced through the crowd, shaking it to encourage the toss of a coin. He paused at Rowen's feet and shook the hat. Coins rattled and Rowen searched himself for the modest stash of money he'd brought along.

The dog growled, its little body shivering with the noise, a small metal tag engraved with the name ZEEKE hanging from its collar.

"Ah!" Rowen dropped a coin in and the dog turned abruptly away, scratching behind it with its hind feet before trotting off.

Philadelphia

The darkness of night in the Below seeped into a man's bones and edged toward his soul if he didn't take care.

George tugged his coat collar closer and pulled the brim of his hat down before sliding his broad-knuckled hands into his pockets. He carried light tonight, his pockets holding only a knife and a Philadelphia Deringer, small enough to fit in the palm of his meaty hand. He'd use neither to accomplish his goal if he might avoid it.

He walked past building after building, pausing outside one that bustled with life and noise, his nose wrinkling at the smell of perfume, alcohol, and vomit.

A woman spotlighted in the glow of the open door turned and, spotting him, shouted, "Come here, love, and enjoy yourself!" She tugged up the hem of her dress to show him the curve of her ankle. "Or, better yet, come here and enjoy *me*."

Shaking his head, he walked on, muttering.

It was the next building he wanted. A small thing squeezed awkwardly between the riotous house of ill repute and the home beside it, featuring the only fenced yard in the area, the plants that thrived there rambling and overgrown. So late at night, flickering candlelit lanterns tricked his eyes and made the weeds there walk.

He avoided both strange buildings, going for the squashed, yet otherwise unremarkable construction between. Since his meeting with Loftkin he had destroyed three contraptions, little things that struck him as remarkably unremarkable, and certainly harmless but if the Council wanted all steam mechanisms wiped out, George would do his best by them so they would keep his family secret.

Because a good father worked hard to ensure the security of his son.

He pounded on the door.

No response and no wonder considering the ruckus in the building to his left. Inside it someone had started to sing, and what must be a huge crowd for so small a space picked up the words and continued, slurring all the way.

He pounded on the door again, harder.

"I hear you have quite the contraption," George said to the man who timidly opened the door to his insistent knocking.

He was a meek thing, a slender man of some height, his shoulders broad and a set of modified spectacles in an array of colors, sizes, and densities suspended from a frame that rested on both his ears and the bridge of his nose. "Oh," he said, adjusting the lenses so he could better see George. "So you've heard. It's no great wonder," he said. "Funny what people think worthy of commenting on."

"That's true enough. I've heard it mentioned in quiet servants' quarters on the Hill and even in the depths of the Below. To have heard so many whispers about the same thing . . . well . . . it must be worth remarking upon, I figure."

The man smiled. "Perhaps. It sprang from an old hobby of mine. If you come back in the morning I will gladly show you my work."

"Ah, there's the rub . . . I won't be in town come morning. Striking out on a journey of my own. Adventuring being one of *my* hobbies."

"Adventuring sounds like a fine hobby. I would show it to you now but—"

George had already pushed his way through the door before his host could say "—the place is a shambles."

"No problem there, friend," he said, taking off his bowler hat. "They say the sign of a clean space is a sign of no imagination, so the sign of a mind cluttered with ideas should be . . ." He glanced around the room, taking in the piles of drawings and designs, the stacks of parts, some metal, some porcelain, some filled with wires and others with tubes and gears ". . . likewise cluttered."

The man stared at him, agape at the intrusion. "I appreciate your willingness to overlook my far less than immaculate living quarters, but I did not invite you in."

But it was already too late, because the contraption, a walking beast much like a medium-sized dog, had already ambled forward to investigate the new person in its home.

"My god. It is as amazing as they say . . ."

Steam burbled out of its metal rib cage and from funnel-shaped leather ears, and the whir of gears quieted as it sat watching the new human. It cocked its head and a pink leather tongue peeked out from between its hinged and heavily riveted jaws.

George raised a hand and it lifted its muzzle up to feign sniffing. Or maybe it did not feign sniffing at all, he marveled, hearing how the matching pair of bellows that were only somewhat obscured by the iron ribs sucked in air, filling their leather bladders and a great bit of the space. The air wheezed back out as he withdrew his hand and a fan kicked in.

Its tail began to wag.

"He likes me," George marveled, trailing his hand along the dog's face.

"No. He doesn't," the other man reported lamely. "He has no emotion. He is a mimicry of life only. He feels no pain or love."

George's hand drifted closer to the contraption's belly.

"Have a care," the inventor warned. "The metal there tends to be a bit warm because of the heat of its heart."

"Steam-powered, is it? Heat from the fiery heart causes . . ." He crouched to better look at the mechanical dog. ". . . water in the glass gut to boil and produce steam that floods the tubes and pipelines . . . like veins, I suppose, and . . ."

". . . activates the valves and pistons that grant it movement."

"So when it sits more steam must be released to depressurize the system appropriately."

"True, true. You have a fine mind for mechanics. You could create such a thing for yourself," he chuckled. He closed the door.

"No. Not within my realm. And why did you build the beast?" he asked, straightening. "It takes more than the interest born of a hobby to create something of this scope."

The inventor shrugged. "Truth be told, there is little profit to be made in my regular ventures as a printer and seller of books. So I thought: what if I created a toy for children before Christmas—now that celebrating the holiday with gift-giving is rising in popularity. Every girl wants a doll and every boy wants a dog . . . what if I combine those dreams and provide them with the best of both worlds? A walking doll of a dog?"

Now he was the one who cocked his head and looked at the mechanical beast before him. "It would be a smaller model, of course. With new safety protocols in place to regulate the temperature of the heart and ribs. And girls would want something prettier. More delicate, don't you suppose?"

"Yes. So I would suppose. And after designing an army of doggy dollies for Christmas, what next?"

The man shrugged. "Who can predict? The science behind such a thing is applicable to many avenues of life—to a multitude of technologies. Why, it's with such little things as these that mankind can make tremendous strides."

George grunted. "That's what I was afraid you'd say."

He reached out and overturned the nearest table, dumping blueprints and notebooks onto the floor.

"What are you doing?" the man shouted, reaching toward George in an attempt to stop him. His hand was smacked away. George bent and, groaning with effort, broke off the leg of the table.

The dog stood, watching the odd scene play out with an unnatural passivity. Its tail no longer wagged, but steam poured out of its ears as it held its position and simply kept watch with dead, mechanical eyes.

It did not even move to defend itself when George began raining blows down onto its body with the table leg. It stood, stoic and still as each blow hit it, the noise of wood on metal a cracking sound that made the inventor cover his ears with his hands and shout at the automaton's attacker.

The shouts began as angry exclamations, demanding a different outcome, but as George continued the violent disassembling of the dog blow by blow, the shouts changed, became cries for mercy and finally—when the dog's segmented spine gave way beneath the force of George's determined swings—muffled sobs of a man who did not understand the violent destruction of his peaceful creation.

The glass gut hit the floor and water gushed out, the fire in the mechanical heart sizzling and spitting before it extinguished, along with the inventor's dream of a profitable holiday.

"Damn it," George muttered between panting breaths, seeing one last gasp of steam ooze out of the beast's heart. "I needed that flame." He looked around and grabbed the nearest lantern. Its candlelight flickered, the glass panes far from windproof. "You'd better get out while you still can," he told the man coolly.

The inventor didn't take long to grasp what he intended to do next. He reached for a stack of papers, but George shook his head. "Trust me. You don't want to take anything with you. Not even memories, if you catch my drift." He swung the lantern in his hand as if winding up his arm for a devastating throw and the inventor rushed from the room—from his small home beside the tavern in the Burn Quarter—with only the clothes on his back.

George grabbed the skeleton of the dog and dug a hand into it to better pull free the rest of its innards. He stepped on them, crushing them under his heel, and the whole time he thought about his boy back home and the threat his heritage hung over his head like the sword of Damocles.

With a satisfied grunt, he reassessed the mechanical dog. It was dead. And with it the most recent threat of steam power shifting the status quo and pounding the comfortable paradigm into dust. Now nothing but a heap of mechanics inside a ruined house, merely a broken skeleton, its bones left to burn and then rust, lungs and heart stripped from it with only the hint of dark smoke smudging the spot where its precious internal organs should have been. It was a dark reminder of the fiery coal-powered heart that heated the watery gut and pushed steamy life into its limbs.

He opened the lantern and pulled out the candlestick. With silent deliberation he touched the flame to each of the nearest stacks of papers.

He stood there a moment while the place caught fire, watching the flames leap and lick while the smoke thickened. He shook his head then, wondering for a moment what amazing things this man might have wrought if life was only different.

But life wasn't. And there were dark things he had to do

to keep them from becoming different. Things that maintained the status quo in Philadelphia, but also, and more importantly, the status quo in his own household—things that allowed him to keep his son.

And to do that . . . well, a good father would do anything.

And George was a good father.

Of that much he was certain.

Chapter Twelve

And binding Nature fast in fate,
Left free the human will.
—ALEXANDER POPE

Bangor

Evie snared Rowen's arm again and led him toward another section of the sprawling underground area known as the Hill King's Cavern. "There is truly something for everyone here. Jewelry of all styles and origins, furniture and rugs of the same, a wide collection of clothing—erm—obtained from a wide variety of sources and through several different methods—always look for tears and bloodstains," she warned with a glib smile. "There are flasks of mead, casks of ale, bottles of wine, and jugs of moonshine. Sugar cane and molasses, tobacco, rice and indigo, silk, wool and muslin, honey and maple syrup, ducks, chickens, hams, lobsters and shellfish, meats salted or smoked, and a variety of baked goods you simply can't find aboard ship. Jade, lapis, amber, and pearls . . ."

She snorted and motioned with a quick move of her head

to a gaggle of women in low-cut blouses and tightly cinched bodices. ". . . and the women to buy them for. Or have them stolen from *you* by—watch the blonde, she has sticky fingers." Then she smiled and wiggled her fingers at the group of them, smiling in particular at the blonde she'd just warned him of.

"I really have no need of—"

But she cut him off with a wave of her hand. "Rowen, you have plenty of needs, you just have very few coins with which to fill those needs. So we should be savvy with our shopping."

He nodded and set his jaw. A nice pair of pants and a good shirt would be a fine start. He had never needed to be a savvy shopper—he had always had more than enough money.

They paused at a tent and the captain sorted through some things, held them up to Rowen to test the size, and in a language he recognized in no way she yammered something at the small woman behind the rickety table. The little woman shook her head no. That much he understood.

Not far from where he stood, men mumbled. "Say the Stormbringer will be the greatest Weather Witch ever. More amazing than Galeyn Turell! That she'll unify the cause and bring sweeping change."

"*She*?" another scoffed. "I heard *he*!"

"All bull and bollocks—prophecies, feh! A lot of hooey and superstition if you ask me."

Evie held up one garment—a muslin shirt that seemed broad enough across the shoulders and chest for Rowen. She eyed the sleeves and the length of his arms and turned back to the shopkeeper. She pointed and again spewed out a long line of syllables he didn't recognize.

The woman again shook her head and Evie shook the shirt, pointing in exasperation to something on its chest. The shopkeeper stepped forward and Rowen bent around Evie to see whatever the captain was so vehemently discussing.

Evie's fingers stuck up through the bottom of the shirt and wiggled out a hole in the chest. It wasn't a wide tear, and easily mended if one had the time and the skill, but it was a tear nonetheless. Rowen frowned. Who would he find to mend such a thing? Just as he readied to tell the captain no himself, she invoked three words that made the little woman throw her arms into the air in exasperation.

"Dead man's deal."

With a huff and one last shake of her head she accepted the terms Evie had worked out.

"Pay her," Evie said, tossing the shirt at Rowen. It took more self-control than he'd expected not to step away from the shirt, but he caught it, fumbled for coins, and paid the woman.

Evie was already outside the tent when Rowen caught up to her. "Is that how you do savvy shopping, buying clothing off a corpse?"

"Don't be so overly dramatic. The corpse that belonged to was nowhere in sight. And it's not like the previous owner will come looking for it—stuck him like a pig, it seems," she said with a toss of her head.

Appalled, Rowen stood gawking after her a moment before he raced to catch up. "This is—"

"Astonishing, appalling, disgusting, horrifying, an affront to modern sensibilities? Or all of those?" She raised one shoulder and dropped it in a shrug. "Apple?" she asked, raising a beautiful red fruit up to his nose. She didn't wait for an answer but tossed a coin to the shopkeeper and threw a piece of fruit at him.

"All of those," he agreed.

Again she shrugged. "It is as it is. This is how most of us live and someday it will be how many of us die." She ran her fingers down the length of an exotic scarf that hung from the post of one stall. "It could be far worse. We are no man's prisoners," she remarked. "Unless you consider us prisoners of our own design." She winked at him and continued up the aisle of stalls, fingers tracing over first one item and then another as she made it her duty to examine and enjoy every moment on land.

"I have to make a stop, one task I must complete," she explained, slipping down a side alley. "There." She pointed to a small flag that sparkled. "This is the place. Come along."

He followed her into a tent and blinked at the crystals sparkling there.

Beside a tiny table sat a wizened little lady with gray hair and matching eyes. She smiled, seeing Evie, and opened a chest by her feet. "You look positively right as rain, my dear," she said, pulling out a leather pouch, its drawstring pulled tight. "As good as a power source can be," she assured, handing the pouch over.

"We are in your debt, Mother," Evie said, but the old woman lifted a cane that rested on the floor beside her and jabbed Evie's leg.

"No, you shan't be. Pay up," she declared.

Evie, chuckled, pulled out a tiny sack of coins. She tossed it to the woman and slipped back outside the tent, followed close behind by Rowen. She enclosed the pouch in a larger bag hanging at her side and smiled at Rowen. "Very nearly there. Now all we needs must do is meet an important man, do our exchange, and make our way with him to Philadelphia."

Rowen balked at the suggestion. "Back to Philadelphia? I—I need to get to Jordan."

"We will determine your lady's next port of call and make sure you reach it, if that is truly what you want after this evening. But I think it is best to maintain an open mind in a place like this—and a close watch on your coins."

"No matter what happens here," Rowen said, "I will be boarding a ship to get to the *Artemesia* and find Jordan—you cannot convince me to do otherwise."

Evie shrugged. "Let's see what Fate has to say about that bold assertion of yours, young man," she said, winking at him. "There is no ship slated to leave Bangor's port until dawn."

Aboard the Artemesia

It was as she slept that the ship first spoke to her. It filled her head with noise, with wind and rain and the cracking of thunder, the shiver of wood, metal, and canvas in flight. It flooded her with sensation instead of words, and Jordan, who thought part of herself dead, was on fire. She hungered and thirsted for the ship—the rough touch of its hidden timbers, the feel of its broad and beautiful sides where wind and weather had worn it smooth as a pebble in a stream bed. She wanted both the warmth of wood and the sharp cool touch of the metal.

In the dream she stood Topside, one hand on the wheel, the sextant Anil had only recently showed her how to use in her other. She peered through a hole in the cloud cover cloaking the *Artemesia* and sighted their path with the aid of the stars. A cool breeze played across her skin and she suddenly realized she stood naked on the deck.

Her chest tightened, her fingers turning to claws on the ship's wheel. Her gaze left the star-filled heavens to search the deck, knowing somewhere nearby danger dwelled and she had not even clothing to keep—her eyes skimmed the shadows, terror growing inside her like an awful flower preparing to blossom—to keep the threat . . .

The breeze warmed and soothed her and her mind grew fuzzy around the edges. Threat? Sharp as the cut of a tiny blade, memory of the threat came back and she pressed her legs together and watched the shadows shift—watched for *him*—the captain.

The ship shuddered beneath her feet and her world wobbled and rippled like water. The scene changed, the dark of night whisked away and replaced with the impossibility of blue sky. Jordan's mind rebelled—there were no airships that could fly without storm clouds swirling around them and tugging them about the heavens.

The moment she doubted, she felt an ease seep into her—first from the air and then from the boards making up the deck of the ship. Her feet tingled and she looked at them, bare and kissed by the sun. They began to fuzz around their edges, to become indistinct. Her legs softened and her knees gave way and before she could scream she was absorbed into the airship like water.

One with the fibers of the wood, she spread like western wildfire, sweeping through the ship, feeling its every pore and splinter. Her stomach dropped, rolled, and she spread her arms wide, fingertips losing form to feel and fill the wings, to catch the air underneath her and ride it like some Old World goddess.

The crack and pop of lightning found her in the dream and struck. Thinking she'd be thrown onto the deck—remade, re-formed—instead she vaulted back awake.

Upright in her bed, she felt her skin crawl with the sensation of a thousand fiery ants walking across it and she rubbed her arms. Outside her window lightning streaked across the sky and curved in its path.

Seeking her.

She pulled the covers tight around her and watched as it flared toward her window before it—in a near-conscious state of self-control—spattered in a spray of brilliant sparks. She waited to smell the singe of wood or see the burst of flame, but nothing came.

She drew the covers tighter—to her chin—and curled onto her bed, watching the lightning dance. Closing her eyes she realized how desperately she missed the sun.

Bangor

"Anything you can find in any major city can be found here, and *more,*" Evie proclaimed boldly. "And things that *cannot* be found in any major city—well, certainly not legally," she added with a wink. "We have the advantage when it comes to trade—whoever controls transportation controls trade. Whoever controls trade controls the economy. And whoever controls the economy . . . well, they control the world."

Rowen snorted. "I beg to differ." He rounded on her, saying, "What of the military? They control the weapons and the fighting men," he pointed out with pride. "From what I see, the military is the most powerful force. Whoever controls the military controls the world."

She smirked. "Your people are slow to lose their rank affiliations, are they not? Perhaps I would have been just as blind had I been born into a more worthwhile rank," she added before continuing with, "however, I do feel it is my duty, as your cap— *hostess,* to educate you as to the real ways of the world."

He raised an eyebrow and crossed his arms over his chest. "Well, by all means—do educate me. Please."

"I shall endeavor to do my best," she assured him. "Though, as they say, you can lead a horse to water . . ."

He snorted. ". . . and see it devoured by Merrow."

"Not the traditional phrase, but true enough." She snagged a long lock of her hair and swished it between her fingers. "You say the one who controls the military controls the world, and yet consider these facts: the military only gets as far as they can be transported."

"Men have legs—the military marches right well and covers great distances when needs be."

"True, true," she conceded. "And they are loyal. But even the most loyal of men have needs that must be met."

"Of course."

"By more than camp followers."

He bridled at the insinuation. "We are fed, clothed, nursed when wounded, and paid."

"And what if that changed? What if the pay went away? Would the military still fight?"

His other eyebrow rose to match the first. "Some might . . ." But his hesitancy marked his argument as failing.

"The economy, which is controlled by transportation of

goods and services, is the thing supplying a military man's pay. And an unpaid military man will continue in his duty as much as an unpaid seamstress continues in hers," Evie said.

"No. Longer." Rowen's voice was firm, the hesitancy gone. "There is where your logic slips a cog. A military man, paid or unpaid, will always outlast the commitment of a seamstress because of one simple thing you have overlooked—believing in a mission. I daresay a soldier will believe in the job he has been set more than a seamstress believes in the stitches she sews."

She winked at him. "A fine point. But if you wish me to believe that the economy does not impact the ability of the military to function . . ."

"No, you are correct. But it may not be as immediate an impact as you believe. How might I expect differently? You are not affiliated with the military and do not understand our ways."

"You, my dear, are also not currently affiliated with the military," she reminded him.

"Location and obvious affiliation are not the only things determining with whom one's heart is."

"Precisely why you dare not say that because I am not affiliated directly doesn't mean I do not feel and understand the things military men do. My men have the same sense of loyalty, face the same dangers and more, because my men might be imprisoned or executed if their true mission is discovered."

"If the ways of government change and a military force finds itself on the losing side, they face the same dangers."

"Yet some military men are awarded the pillage of war," she reminded.

"True," Rowen said, though his tone darkened at the thought. "And some pirates—*traders*—do the same."

She laughed. "Some, aye." She shot him an odd look. "It seems our two sides are not so very diametrically opposed. Perhaps—just perhaps—you, having a previous military affiliation, might yet feel comfortable among people of our ilk. We are kindred spirits."

He laughed. "Yes. I fear we are." He paused, realizing they had outwalked the main bustle of the shops. Ahead of them a crowd milled around a stack of cages. The noise of animals brought Rowen back to memories of the menagerie at Jordan's party. "What is this?" he asked.

"Ah," she said. "The auction. One of the stranger things about the Hill King's Cavern." Her volume dropped and she nearly growled out, "And the reason we have a monkey on board."

Rowen's eyebrows jumped up. "Other than Ginger Jack?"

She slapped his shoulder, laughing. "Yes. Yes! *Other than* Ginger Jack." She headed into the edge of the crowd. "Things can get quite wild when the bidding becomes excited," she explained. "And it is always interesting to see who is here for what purpose." She pressed closer to him to whisper into his ear and be heard above the din of the crowd and the beasts.

"See that man?" She motioned with her chin. "He buys exotic pets for well-known ladies and gentlemen wanting another conversation piece—a living and walking one—Perhaps your family had such things?"

Rowen shook his head. "Horses and dogs only."

"You had horses? I may have a ship, but I think I'd trade it all away for a horse," she confided. "They're beautiful . . ."

"And the fastest way to attract a Merrow attack," he

returned, briefly remembering the fight only he survived when Merrow attacked him and his best friend, Jonathan. "Keep your ship—you're safer being a pirate than an equestrian."

"No worries, you won't find a single horse here. They simply aren't available. And," her gaze returned to the dealer in exotics, "his kind have made bad choices as to who they sell exotics to. Some people simply aren't prepared to keep such beasts. I've heard tales of giraffes breaking free of their enclosures and ruining people's tea parties," she said with a laugh. "What I would have paid to have seen that!" She laughed again. "It was, after all, his kind that thought it clever to sell that pair of red-brown hyenas to the heiress near Gévaudan . . . but everyone makes mistakes, aye?" She stretched to get a better view. "It appears today they have parrots, lions, tigers, and bears . . . Oh!" She grabbed his arm tightly, saying, "My! Look at the birds! And the monkeys," she added with disgust.

He laughed. "You do not like monkeys?"

"When you meet one, you'll understand."

He chuckled, and she leaned around him, her expression fixed on something in a particular cage.

"What is that?" She squinted, trying to get a better view.

"What, don't you have your spyglass? I thought pirate captains always carried one," he teased.

"Good idea! We *traders* often do," she muttered, digging into the pouch slung across her shoulder. She tugged free a spyglass, which she then twisted and adjusted for the distance.

Rowen frowned.

"It's not a *that,* it's a *those,"* she corrected. "Two of the strangest-looking . . ." She passed the spyglass to him and he grunted, raising the eyepiece and trying to see what she was talking about.

"No," she said tersely, "look *here*." She grabbed the eyepiece and wrenched it toward the bent wooden cage that seemed a slightly oversized parrot cage, bowed at the top with a solid bottom. Nestled on the cage's bottom was a bundle of thick red-gold fur, tips of ears sticking out of the bundle, a thick, plush tail tipped with cream twitching at the noise going on all around its quiet cage.

He examined the outlines of the creature more carefully and spotted a second pair of ears and a second tail. A small snout poked out, dotted with a shiny black nose, and the little beast yawned, tiny teeth sharp as needles, tongue pink as fresh rose petals. It blinked large dark eyes and settled its face on the back of its friend.

Ears the size of saucers pivoted and Rowen distantly wondered if the thing could fly with ears so large. One propped paws atop the other, resting its face on its paws which in turn rested on the other's back. Its brethren wriggled about, licking the first one's face before giving a sharp little yip. The first glanced at the other and responded with a piercing bark of equal conviction.

The fur on their backs bristled. Barking and angry howling began and the two oddly proportioned foxes chased each other round and round the tiny cage so fast it seemed they climbed its walls.

"Foxes. Interesting," Rowen said, passing the spyglass back.

She reduced the size of the spyglass and tucked it back into her pouch. "There are many interesting characters in the crowd today."

"Pot calling the kettle black," Rowen remarked.

She snorted. "There—" She pointed. "The one with the very tall top hat. A farmer of exotics. And there." She gestured to another. "A furrier. I've seen him working his way through the stalls. Never seen him at auction . . ."

The auctioneer turned to the cage of foxes and shouted, delivering a swift kick to it. They stopped chasing each other and turned on him, their backs up against the farthest cage wall, tiny faces curled in snarls of rage.

At that moment he switched the order of bidding and focused on the foxes. Slipping thc shepherd's crook he carried through the handle at the cage's top, he hefted it high with a grunt and looked at a paper he had. "Two Fennec foxes straight from the Sahara Desert of Africa to you via Cutter before being—" He cleared his throat. "—intercepted by the good crew of the *Blackguard.* They are fresh, plump, thickly furred with a fine soft pelt."

Beside Rowen, Evie twitched. He glanced out of the corner of his eye at her to see her brow furrow.

"Fine beasts for fun," he shook the cane and the cage rattled, sending the foxes into a fit of snarling and snapping as he swung them over the crowd's head, "or fur . . ." he added with a grin. He held the cage out by the furrier as if to tempt him further with the thought. "Two pelts."

"*Small* pelts," the furrier quipped.

"Quality over quantity, good friend," he said. "And they are soft pelts. Soft as good butter and supple as silk. The two together would make a fine lady's shawl. Or two handsome hats that could become quite the conversation piece . . ." He grinned as the furrier leaned forward to better glimpse the little animals inside.

They snarled at him and he laughed. "No good to be had with them except for the killing. Stitch them together and you might make a decent muff," he challenged with a snort. He waved a hand at them, uninterested.

Evie relaxed just the slightest bit.

"Fine, fine! Not for our good friend the furrier, perhaps, but think of the interest they might yet bring if stuffed and mounted and displayed for show! A scientific curiosity, such foxes! Or use your creative powers to disassemble them, and reassemble them with different parts like the fantastical Feejee Mermaid!"

"Fantastical, my ass," Evie muttered, looking at Rowen. His blank expression made her groan. "The thing's been displayed as part of a traveling sideshow. A spectacle."

"You've seen it?"

She jerked her head down with a quick nod. "A Merrow if ever I saw one. And worse yet . . . a wee one. A babe, nothing more. There's a reason they hate us, you know."

Rowen snorted. "Because of an accident. They hate us because of a tragic accident long ago," Rowen insisted.

"Is that what they tell you? There is always more to a story when it involves such hate."

The bidding had begun on the foxes and was going slow. "Do you know them?" Rowen asked about the participants.

She shook her head. "No. Look like decent folks—as far as our type go," she added with a chuckle. "Good enough they won't go to the furrier, though."

The bidding slowed, the price still low.

The furrier jumped in and everything changed, from the bids, to the auction's pace, to the expression Evie wore. She tensed, the muscles in her body coiled like a spring, and Rowen straightened, watching.

The furrier kept outbidding the competition, coin by coin. Finally his competitors shook their heads and turned away.

"Going once—"

"Dammit," she said.

"Going twice—"

"Why couldn't they be monkeys?" Then she shouted and raised her hand, entering the bidding war for the two fierce Fennec foxes.

The furrier bristled at the sudden unexpected competition, his eyes sparking and his mouth twisting into something somehow even less attractive than the way he had begun.

Partway through the ensuing madness Ginger Jack joined them. "Oh, lord." He craned his neck to see through the shifting crowd. "What on earth is she bidding on now? Another monkey?"

The look she shot him would have dropped a lesser man.

"*Another*?" Rowen asked, lips turning up at their ends.

"She hasn't told you about her previous prize?" Jack asked.

Rowen's eyes gleamed and he said in her direction as much as Jack's. "So the monkey she complained about is her fault?"

She threw her hand in the air to make her next bid and made a distinctly unladylike gesture in Rowen's direction as she lowered it again.

Jack snorted. "She's fiercely competitive, you know," he said around her.

She next shared the same gesture with him.

"Always has to win?" Rowen asked.

"Even to her detriment."

She let loose with a wild whoop as the bidding closed, declaring her the winner. Once more she gestured to Jack, this time with an additional flourish. He grabbed her hand and kissed it, and, grinning, said, "You do that one more time, darlin', and I'll take you up on that offer."

With a growl she yanked her hand free and stalked away to claim her prize. Beaming with pride at the snapping devils she returned with, she thrust the cage into Jack's chest. He grabbed it and they tore round the cage again, leaving even Jack shaken. "You're so clever, Jack. These little foxes will be no problem for the likes of you."

"What are you naming these fine specimens? Demon and Devil?"

She laughed, but her expression was flat. "Of course not. They are Kit and Kaboodle."

"Of course," Jack said. "Fox kits. And a pair this crazy is worth a whole kaboodle. How very clever of *you*."

She inclined her head and mock-curtsied. "That is why I am the captain." With that she began to walk away, but she only got a few steps before she paused, and, looking over her shoulder, said, "Oh, and do be ready to board the ship this evening at nine, our time." Then she left the two of them.

"Right, right," Rowen said, tugging his battered timepiece out. "Our time. What time do you have?"

Jack maneuvered the cage away and dug into his pocket to find his ever-wayward pocket watch. "Ship time is ten past."

Rowen nodded and turned the knob on top of his watch so their times matched. "It seemed so much simpler at home," he said. "We operated by the time the clock in the square rang out. Now I wonder who decided what it was when first set."

"Tricky business, time. The cities can decide for now at least—keep their own time. Set it and run business their way. At least big cities with populations large enough that the government airships can't bully them." He shrugged. "Mark my word, though. Someday someone will want to even adjust our *perception* of time—someone other than the place of the sun in the sky will tell us when noon is."

Rowen laughed. "Noon is noon. If you can't agree on that . . ."

Jack shrugged. "We shall see. I suspect it'll be either the government or a businessman that thinks the sun revolves around them and decides to tell us when and where the sun does and doesn't shine. But for now I doubt if a single major city keeps it the same," he murmured. "Time is as subjective as anything else."

Rowen eyed the engineer, muttering a bemused, "Aye." He reached a finger toward the cage and both Kit and Kaboodle leaped back, snapping like they were the Merrow themselves. "Someone once told me that dangerous things should be kept in cages," Rowen added.

"I agree with whoever that was," Jack said, holding the cage as far away from his body as he could. "Because there's no way I can possibly see how the decision to bring these two rascals aboard could *possibly* go wrong . . ." He shook his head. "Hungry? Look for the tent with 'brownies.' Like a chocolate cake that fell."

Rowen snorted, turning back toward the stalls, but his nose caught the scents of cooking meat and vanilla pastries that drifted from . . . He had no idea, but the sudden rumble in his stomach guaranteed he would find out.

Aboard the Artemesia

Anil's hands moved more slowly over the ship's controls, cloud cover scattered and patchy to the west, lightning sparkling in the distance, a weak glint. Jordan sat by his bare feet watching and wondering how much time he had. His eyes were no longer glazed in the strange ecstasy they once had but were clear and sharp. He was slower today than yesterday and slower yesterday than the day before. And his songs worked as slowly as his hands.

His complexion had paled, his normally rich brown skin ashen and his hair without luster.

He was dying and she wasn't ready to take over.

She couldn't grant him more time with his family, though she tried.

Not far away Meggie and Maude sat on the deck, playing pick-up sticks while Meggie's stuffed dolly, Somebunny, slouched nearby. Topside had become Meggie's favorite place to play. Before meals, after meals . . . whenever. And every time she sat positioned so she could watch Jordan and Anil.

And listen.

And every time Meggie was nearby the storm cell crystal tucked in Jordan's dress warmed like it sat in sunlight.

Jordan scooted closer to where Anil stood, giving her full attention to everything he did, hands folded in her lap as she watched the intricate movements of a man keeping an airship from the one thing its captain claimed it truly wanted: the ground.

"Here." He nudged her with his toe. "Come stand beside me. You have watched enough today. Now is the time for doing."

At the supper table the standard guests prepared to eat and drink, and occasionally turned to look at how this new phase of Jordan's training was going. No longer tethered or tied to the ship, Jordan knew what each bit of the ship did—how it all felt and moved and worked in wind and any sort of weather.

She rose and he took her hand and laid it on the wheel. Her eyes never left his as he grabbed her other hand, placing it on the wheel as well. "You know what each part does, yes?"

She nodded.

"And you can call a storm?"

"Yes, but . . ." Out of the corner of her eye she saw people at the dining room table shift.

"Then you are ready to fly the *Artemesia.*"

She opened her mouth to protest but Anil stepped away, his hands touching no part of the controls. The floating crystals in the storm glass began to shift and Jordan saw the clouds start to clear.

"Fly, Jordan," he commanded. "Light Up."

"I can't," she protested, eyes widening as light began to pierce the veil of clouds. "I can't fly . . . I can't call a storm without the proper trigger," she said, the words strangling in her throat.

"Then pull the trigger," Anil said with a shrug.

The clouds wisped away and Jordan heard Meggie say, "I can see the sky!"

The ship shivered under her feet.

Then they started to fall.

"Light Up!" Anil shouted. "Or we all die!"

"I can't!"

"Yes, you can—I know you can, lightning hunts for you, hungers for you! Now call the storm!"

"I can't!" she shrieked, anger rising to twist around her growing terror. "You don't understand . . ."

He laughed at her. Leaned into her face and laughed at her. "Then we'll *all* die."

The captain jumped to his feet and the wind, now whistling around them as they glided down, faster and faster, tore his hat away. He cursed and Meggie screamed, catching a nearby chair lcg.

"She's not ready," Bran shouted.

"No one's ever ready—to *die*!" Anil yelled. "I wasn't, you aren't—but it's too late!"

"You bastard," the captain shouted.

"Mamá!" Meggie screamed and Jordan turned to face her, seeing how Maude gathered her in close.

Jordan's hands clenched the wheel and she said in a very clipped tone, "I *hate* you," to Anil.

The emotion she named bubbled up inside her like a heat sizzling in the space between her skin and muscles.

The clouds began to gather. They popped into existence, sizzling with lightning the way Jordan sizzled with emotion, and she adjusted her grip on the wheel, felt her lip curl in a snarl, and she pulled the clouds in tighter, made them thicker, made the winds in their bellies blow out to fill the *Artemesia*'s wings, and they were caught up in the power of the clouds as they closed in around them.

Anil laughed harder. "So that's your trigger? Hate?"

She shot him a glare in answer.

"I'll take the wheel," he said amiably.

She smacked at his hands.

The captain laughed and leaned across the table to the Maker. "She was ready. Some things even the Maker doesn't know!"

"What?" the Maker snapped, his arms around Meggie and Maude. "You *planned* this?"

The captain nodded. "Well, not the loss of my hat, but, yes." He laughed.

Jordan heard and she hated even more.

"You don't need to trigger with hate," Anil whispered, slowly stepping close to Jordan and the wheel. "You only need to connect with the weather through strong emotion to call the storm. Love your power. Let it sing out of you. Sing it out. Go, Draw Down."

"No," she whispered her jaw set as she stared straight ahead.

"Draw Down," he said again, his eyes meeting hers. "This is not worth killing yourself over. Little is." He moved to pry her fingers off the wheel but there was a flash of blinding white light and Jordan was on fire, licked by lightning from the crown of her head to the tips of her toes.

Every one of her senses was on fire, lightning screamed in her ears, her fingers fountained sparks and her vision flared, everything glaring white before going black, and Jordan fell to the deck, destroyed.

Chapter Thirteen

When the fight begins within himself,
A man's worth something.
—ROBERT BROWNING

Bangor

Past the tent where pillows were strewn across foreign-looking carpets Rowen went, only slowing to take in the sight of the men reclining by low tables, pressing their lips to a narrow hose they passed from one to the other and exhaling the smoke that came from inside a strange metal-and-glass device. Unlike the Below sprawling at the feet of the Hill, there were no signs to better educate the wayward pirate on his first time into the caverns carved into the heart of Bangor. But truly no signs were needed.

Rowen had spent enough time in the taverns and darker bits of one of America's biggest cities to know an opium den when he saw one. The pipes themselves were not the danger, as he'd been told; it was what was put inside the pipes for smoking. Still, Rowen steered clear, preferring the one poison he personally understood—alcohol.

But at the moment he had no interest in that. He followed his nose, and found meat. Pork, painted with coconut milk, roasted on a spit and still sizzling and stuck on a stake. He paid for the thing and sat down. He had barely managed to down three bites when he heard the man speak up.

"Hey, I've seen that face before . . ." someone said, loudly enough that everyone in the modest (and temporarily erected) establishment turned to look at the man, and more importantly, at Rowen.

He stopped chewing; the meat went dry in his mouth. He tried to swallow, but it wedged in his throat and he coughed, recalling the fact that he was still a wanted man. Yes, within a nest of other wanted men and even women, surely, but—how did these things work themselves out? Did the one with the highest ransom on his head assume the greatest risk?

Worried he was about to find out exactly what happened in such situations—firsthand—he choked.

"Aye, I seen him, too!" another proclaimed.

Rowen managed to swallow the bite of food and turned about, looking as if to see who they might possibly mean. He set the stake on his plate and calmly wiped off his hands. He might need to firmly grasp his sword's handle in a moment and grease would do him no good.

"And me!" a third voice shouted.

So it would be a bit of a competition. He turned back, giving them his very best *you can't possibly mean me* look.

"I seen him first!"

Hands shot out and grabbed him, hammy fingers digging into his biceps and securing him.

An argument broke out. Who saw the wanted man first, who should claim custody, who should he be turned in to (as it seemed three separate entities were now in pursuit) and should the money be split between two or three of the finders? The restauranteur stepped in and suggested he be granted a finder's fee as it was at his fine establishment that Rowen was in fact found.

The arguing died away and Rowen heard the familiar sound of Evie's boot steps. "Just what is going on," Elizabeth Victoria, using a voice Rowen had barely heard before—a voice that spoke of power—asked. She slowly tugged off her gloves, folded them together, and hung them through her belt. She cocked her stance, crossed her arms, every bit of her body language warning them that here stood a woman not to be trifled with. "This is my crew man. He is signed up aboard the airship *Tempest* in service to the Killpoint fleet. What business do any of you claim to have with him?"

The first claimant stepped forward, short and nearly as wide as he was tall. He dug into the pouch hanging at his side and pulled out a crumpled piece of paper. Though it was bent and folded and appeared nearly gnawed at the edges, when he unfolded it and pressed it flat on the nearest table, Rowen saw it was the same poster that he and Jonathan had seen as they rode hard for Holgate.

Captain Elizabeth Victoria glanced from the produced paper to Rowen and back, her jaw set, her eyes hard. "It does bear a striking resemblance."

He purpled at the statement, his fingers rolling into fists as he motioned toward the offensive image with his chin. "That looks nothing like me," he snarled.

His captain blinked rapidly at that particular complaint. "He makes a good point. It bears little resemblance to the man we see before us now—"

"Rowen Burchette!"

Rowen's head snapped around in the direction of the call and Evie groaned.

"But then there's *that* . . ."

The caller grinned and stepped forward with a wanted poster of a different variety. "I would say that recognition of such an uncommon name as his should count as proof." He held up the poster. "As he responded definitely to me, I claim him as mine."

"You cannot claim him like some lost dog," Evie protested. "He is already mine." But she eyed the posters with quiet curiosity. No, Rowen realized, she eyed a very specific part of the posters—the reward.

"As I have said, he is a member of *my* crew."

"The crew of an airship that is going nowhere near either of these ports," one of the men pointed out, shaking the poster again. "If you wish to retain him so you take the reward, you will have to either hold him for a long enough period that you risk them no longer wanting him or you will need to diverge from your standard path and take on additional costs and risks. Is keeping him in your care worth the loss of your contracts?"

"Well, I am the one who brought him here after all," she stated simply. "I should at least receive a delivery fee." She shrugged and said to Rowen, "I knew you were quite wanted, but I did not imagine even men wanted you . . . pretty though you are . . . What's the top ransom, boys? Show me *all* the wanted posters."

Quietly the crowd tightened in, peppered heavily with crew members from the *Tempest.*

The ransoms were quite impressive "—and not a one does

your face true justice . . . how sad," Elizabeth Victoria remarked. "A captain could refit an entire ship with that ransom. Or purchase the guts of a thermoacoustic engine . . ."

"Get me out of here, Evie," Rowen whispered.

"And just why should me and my men fight all of our friends to keep you safe? Seems more headache than it's worth." Still, she unsnapped the frog holding her sword's scabbard and let the scabbard drop into her left hand.

Ginger Jack slipped up beside her, the cage of foxes slung across his back. He rubbed his hands together, weighing their would-be opponents.

"Why save me and take me with you? Because I have connections. I can help you unify the rebel cause in Philadelphia."

She laughed and the crowd rippled with the sound as well. "You think the rebel cause can unite? That there is a single leader to this mess calling for change?" She shook her head. "There is no true leader. No unifying chapter organizing any of us."

"Then become one," Rowen said, challenging her with his eyes. "Be the leader they need. Be the change you want to see. Get me out of here safely and you'll have the things you need to unite the rebels."

She pressed her lips together, a fine line forming between her eyebrows as she considered.

"And if I do not prove my value in short order," he said, "turn me in to the person offering the greatest ransom."

She sighed. "You have a way about you, Rowen Burchette," she admitted. "Boys," she shouted, "let's get him to the ship!" She winked at him as she kicked aside the men holding his arms and drew her sword. "Besides," she mused, "what crew doesn't want to talk about their last fight while they sit in the comfort of their airship drinking? At least until the vomiting ensues!"

Rowen drew his sword, standing with Evie and Jack. The wayward crew of the *Tempest* gathered, slung their belongings over their shoulders, and leaped into the crowd.

Swords clanked against each other and Rowen swung and slashed at his opponents, keeping his back toward his friends, guarding theirs as they guarded his. Out of the corner of his eye he caught glimpses of Jack and Evie taking out entire groups of men as they worked together, him knocking men to her with his fists where she kicked them onto their rumps or knocked them out with a strike from her sword's pommel or the scabbard she wielded like a club. The rest of the men played cleanup crew to the team of captain and engineer and, groaning with effort to keep his attackers at bay, Rowen grinned, knowing he had been right about the *Tempest*'s crew.

Together they fought their way out of the Hill King's Cavern, back to back, with Fennec foxes included. Boarding, Elizabeth Victoria called a storm, and the *Tempest* tore away from the dock, snapping nets and cables alike.

Aboard the Artemesia

She woke in her room, her body stinging like a winding trail of fire sprouted on her hip, then wound around her back and neck and onto her left cheek. Her ears rang from the blast. She opened her eyes slowly, her vision hazy and uncertain.

She worked breath into her mouth and down her throat, feeling it burn its way into her lungs.

She coughed.

The noise echoed in her ears.

Parched, her tongue rattled against split lips. She moaned, aching, but she rolled far enough out of bed that she could grab the water and drink. She took down her fill, emptying the pitcher. Her belly tight with water, still she wanted more.

She rolled out of bed and went to the door, pounding on it and calling for Jeremiah.

He appeared with fresh water, his eyes never connecting with hers but staying stuck to her stinging cheek.

"I've never seen one quite like that," he whispered.

"One?" Her fingers flew to her cheek and she flinched away from her own touch. "One what?" she asked.

"Lightning's Kiss. That's—" His hand stretched out, his finger nearly touching her cheek. "That's what that mark is."

"A mark?"

"A scar."

"Scar?" Her voice rose and she forced her fingers to touch it—to brush lightly across the raised surface. "It hurts . . ."

"Here," Jeremiah said, "I have something that should help. Wait a moment." He disappeared out her door and was back quickly, holding a small jar. "It's an anything salve."

"An anything salve?"

"Good for anything," he explained. "Rub a little on and you'll be right as rain." He stiffened and she looked at him. Not many used that phrase—her family frowned on repeating it as much as on cursing. Some things were simply not said if you were of her rank.

Were of rank.

"Right as rain," she agreed in a whisper, accepting the salve. "Thank you."

His gaze trailed down her neck and shoulder and he looked away. She would have sworn he blushed if his skin tone hadn't already been so dark. "You had better look yourself over thoroughly," he suggested. "I brought you this . . ." He handed her a mirror. It wasn't large or tremendously beautiful and it certainly wasn't as grand as the ones that were once in her bedroom on the Hill, but she hadn't had a true mirror since she'd been dragged out of her seventeenth birthday party.

"Thank you," she said. "Thank you."

He bowed and stepped out of the room, closing the door behind him.

A scar? Trembling, Jordan raised the mirror to inspect her face. Pink and angry-looking, something patterned like a snowflake rose from her skin in tiny blisters. She gasped, lowering the mirror.

Her father had made it clear the only two things she had to her advantage were her rank and her beauty.

Now both were gone.

She sat down hard on the edge of her bed, letting the tears flow. She was marred—inside and out. When she had finished sobbing, she raised the mirror again, determined to see the full damage of Lightning's Kiss. Blinking rapidly, she looked, seeing how it spiraled down her neck, and when she slipped out of her dress she saw it continued, twisting across her shoulder and back to end on the front of one hip—a long rose-colored cane dotted with something that was part exploding fireworks and part drifting snow.

Experimentally she dabbed salve on the burn on her face. The pain eased and she smeared the salve everywhere she could. There were some places she could not reach—some places destined to hurt—but by the time she finished, she felt physically better.

She didn't hear him walk through the door.

"Look at *that,*" Captain Kerdin said.

Jordan jumped, grabbing her dress to hide herself in the folds of fabric, but he tore it out of her hands.

"I have never seen so much scarring on anyone but a field slave," he muttered. "Who would ever want you *now,* scarred as you are? Not me. Not *now* at least."

He left her, untouched, and strangely—crying anew.

Aboard the Tempest

In the heart of the *Tempest* Evie was making plans. "Take the foxes," she said, pointing to Toddy. "Give them to Cookie. Tell her they aren't meat, but they can be used to turn meat on a wheel—like a proper household would use a turnspit—if she's clever. Unfortunately no one gets a free ride here. You'd best make good on your promises, Burchette," Evie muttered as she headed for the horn and flywheel.

"I will," he promised, "I will."

She spoke into the horn. "Direct line the Wandering Wallace," she said, tapping her foot as she waited for someone on the device's other end to do . . . something. Rowen had never bothered to wonder about the mechanics of such things; one merely lifted the one part, set the wheel to spinning, watched for the crystal to light, and spoke into the horn. Someone else made it *work*.

Evie growled. "I am not certain," she said, "just make it

happen. Aye, you're a modern miracle worker." She nodded as if the person she spoke to could see her as well. "We left our designated rendezvous port early," Evie snapped into the horn. She slid her gaze to where Rowen sat, slouched against the ship's wall, fingers woven into his hair. "There was some unexpected action. Aye. I have them, but we still require your stock to run the entire crew. Aye. Your next port? You're in our path. We will intercept and take you and yours aboard."

She nodded again and yanked the flywheel to a stop. She counted to three, moving her lips as she did, and then spun the wheel again. The stormcell blinked and she said, "Adjust course to intercept the *Artemesia.*"

Rowen's head snapped up at the statement and he jumped to his feet. "The *Artemesia*?"

"Aye." She set the horn back in its place on the wall. "It appears Fate is allowing you to have your way after all. Let us all just hope Fate feels kind in letting you get what you wished for."

He grinned.

She shook her head. "Sometimes, love," she muttered, "what we get is exactly what we wished, but not what we really wanted. Are you ready for that possibility?"

"I am ready to see Jordan. That much I know."

She nodded. "Then, while we wait, start to contact these friends of yours. We have many things to make this little venture a success, but we will need money. Get us that and I won't need to seek creative means to get it for us." She tossed one wanted poster at him.

The sum offered at its bottom made Rowen's eyebrows rise. A small fortune—perhaps even enough to finance a band of rebels. Rowen looked at the hardened and lean men around him, each a specialist in his own specific field.

There was Ginger Jack, ship's engineer; Toddy, who knew the ins and outs of the *Tempest* like few others; Bertram, who had used a plate and tankard to take down five rival pirates; Sam, who specialized in munitions; and . . . the list went on.

They were quick, they were efficient, they were fighters.

They might be all he needed to get the money.

He read the poster again.

And, oddly, perfectly legally.

Aboard the Artemesia

The lightning had changed every bit of her. Long sections of her hair were frayed, ends split, curled, and fragile. Running her fingers through her once lovely dark mane blackened her fingers, chunks of hair falling free between them. Jeremiah again came when she called, and when she actually asked for something other than water, he simply asked, "Do you need anything else?"

She shook her head. What she needed most he could not provide. He locked her door as tightly as the captain did. She hadn't asked him to do more than he normally did.

Other than this one, small thing.

She looked at the scissors in her hand. Good, strong, sturdy, and most importantly, sharp. They were exactly what she needed at the moment.

She pulled free of her dress and set it aside. Kneeling by the window so she could watch the burst and burn of lightning as it lived and died in the dark nest of stormclouds, she reached up, grabbed her hair, and cut huge chunks of it off, letting it drop around her like it was nothing. She hacked off section after section and with each cut she imagined she was cutting away the last bits of who she once was.

The job done, she ran her fingers through her hair, letting it stand. She crawled into her bed, pulled the covers up tight, and waited for sleep to steal away her senses.

Aboard the Artemesia

That evening many men had eyes only for Jordan of the fallen House Astraea. Scarred by lightning's ravaging kiss, her hair shorn short and topped with a boater's hat in blue, she sat stiffly at the lower table and although she was free of tethers and strings her movements were palsied and she focused hard on the simple task of feeding herself.

The Topside staff had changed again, cycling through servant after servant so all could say they had served both the Maker and the Wandering Wallace. There had also been a few servants who were turned away at the elevator, their noses red, voices hoarse. An illness was spreading among the crew.

"Not long until we see port in Salem," the captain called to Anil, pulling his gaze away from Jordan.

A servant woman whose hands shook as much as Jordan's did poured wine into the Weather Witch's goblet, sloshing it enough that Jordan looked up into her face. The woman drew back, ducking her head, and Jordan blinked as she stepped quickly away. Finishing filling diner's drinks, she was finally allowed to serve the Conductor and his ever-present would-be murderer.

Bran was torn between watching the coffee-skinned servant woman with hair as dark and straight as Miyakitsu's slipping free of her large cloth servant's cap and Jordan, as the captain circled her like a predator stalking prey.

Bran thought he'd seen something before in the unspoken body language between the two, and now . . .

He squinted. Something about Jordan had changed—not just her face, nor her hair. Something cast a pallor across her features, like she'd lost the glow of life from deep within. And it was a change he'd glimpsed in small ways since before they landed in Herkimer.

Yes.

Across the table the Wandering Wallace shifted in his chair and Bran noted he paid close attention to the servant woman carrying wine to the men on the dais.

"I like your new hair, Miss Jordan," Meggie piped up. "Might I have mine done that way, Mamá?" she asked Maude.

Maude petted Meggie's curls but said, "Whatever you like, my dear. Only not today nor tomorrow." She frowned. "And probably not the next day either."

Bran's gaze flicked back to Jordan in time to see the captain touch her arm—no, not *touch* it—*stroke* it. Jordan didn't react. She didn't wince or flinch or glare. She didn't pull away. She slumped there, shoulders rolled forward, eyes downcast until the captain bent by her ear and whispered. She rose, so like a puppet controlled by unseen strings that Bran caught himself checking her unfettered feet and fingers.

The captain had released her days before from the strings, and whereas Bran might have expected more life from her, now it was rare he even got a glare from her dull eyes. Something had happened. *Had been* happening. Something out of view of the captain's supper guests.

Something more dark and damaging than even he, as Maker, had done.

He watched the pair of them walk to the edge of the deck's platform, the captain striding, Jordan dragging her body along by her feet, head hung, gaze staying just a step ahead of her. She did not push the short strands of hair back from her eyes when they flicked into her face in the slight breeze that teased along the edges of the airship.

She stopped a half step short of the banister.

Captain Kerdin leaned against the banister, watching the roiling clouds that followed the ship. He slouched there, let his spine slip, and looked at Jordan as she stood so stiffly beside him, grinning at her with a look that made something twist in Bran's gut.

The wind shifted and voices carried to the people remaining at the table. Bran straightened. It was a strange thing to happen—the Conductor controlled air flow so well, what was heard at one part of Topside might appear to be nothing more than moving lips when viewed from another vantage. But the seated diners all heard when the dark-skinned and fine-featured servant woman said, "Bring us down."

They turned to her, seeing her face so close to the Conductor's, her lips intimately near his ear.

"Bring us down," she begged, wrapping her fingers around Anil's arm. "He is dead. Our son is *dead.* Bring this whole ship down."

The sniper tugged at his ear and leaned in to try and catch a conversation the wind wisked away.

Maude clutched Meggie tight and looked to Bran, eyes wide. Bran swallowed, feeling his own eyes grow equally large.

But it was the Wandering Wallace, today masked as an exotic bird with drooping and colorful plumage, who stood, and dashed toward the embracing pair. In his wake a napkin dropped and turned into a robin, flying away.

The sniper stood, the muzzle of his gun moving between the two lovers as he decided what to do. His mouth moved as it seemed he shouted to the captain, begging for guidance, but his words were whipped away by a flick of the Conductor's hand.

Anil raised his head from where it rested against his woman's neck. His eyes flashed so brightly they flared from brown to polished bronze.

He raised a hand to halt the Wandering Wallace while the sniper made a choice and set his finger to the trigger. The Wandering Wallace shouted, "Behind you—" and Anil flicked his fingers, letting the wind tear the man from his perch, tossing him overboard. His gun clattered to the deck's boards.

"Where is the child?" the Wandering Wallace shouted. "I might yet help—where is the child?!"

Marion set a broad hand on the table. "Stay in your places and have faith. If anyone can talk a man onto a particular path, it is the Wandering Wallace."

Bran swallowed again, but nodded, hoping the drama on the dais was as well-contained as the players' words, but the drama playing out at the edge of the ship's Topside deck . . . ?

He refocused his attention there. To Jordan and the captain.

Jordan slapped her hands onto the deck's well-polished rail, her fingers wrapping like claws around it. From his place at the table, Bran knew they whitened. Jordan pressed her hips against the banister and swayed forward, looking out into the distance. It was not a playful move. No.

It was a *calculating* move.

"It is too late," the servant woman wailed from the dais,

Anil allowing the breeze to carry her words to the table but no farther. Distantly Bran wondered why. "He is three days dead—too far from this world for Reanimation . . . Bring us down," she begged again, her strained voice ragged.

Jordan swayed back and then forward again. This time she paused, fixing her sights on the clouds obscuring the world far below. She swayed back, straightening once more.

Considering momentum and gravity.

Bran stood.

Marion raised his hand off the table and brought it back down with a slap. A demand—a reminder of who controlled whom in the strange gathering. But Bran had seen enough, and with a certainty that chilled his gut he realized why Jordan—who had fought him long and hard and always shown spirit—was no longer the Jordan he had battled so fiercely to Make.

Bran strode forward, swallowing the space between himself and the girl standing so near their world's edge.

Behind him things at the table shifted, chair legs scraped across the platform, cups settled on the table with a clatter.

But Bran began to run, his arms outstretched.

Still he could hear Anil and his wife. "He would not let me tell you," she said. "The captain would not let me come, but I found a way." Her tone toughened. "Now, so close to your end," she said, "take me with you. I will not suffer life without either my two loves. Bring down the ship!"

The Wandering Wallace—the Reanimator—whoever the hell he was, hiding in the shadows of his masks—said nothing. What could a man say to *that*?

Jordan swayed back and pitched forward . . .

. . . as Bran's feet kicked up, nailing the railing; he bent at the waist, his hands grasping her arms as his body straightened and he yanked her back from the edge, throwing her onto her rump and landing nearby on his own.

Captain Kerdin straightened.

Bran rose and stuck out a hand to Jordan.

She refused it and stood.

Bran met the captain's eyes and, if he'd had any question about what he'd done to Jordan, it was burned away in that instant. Bran reached out to topple the captain, to throw him over the edge of the ship, but a wind tore across the deck and did it for him, Bran's fingers only brushing the man's coat as he slid his way, screaming, down the great balloon's side.

The scream became nothing but the rush of wind and then—

—there was no sound Topside except Bran's ragged breathing and silence where the tick-tick-click of the Conductor's wheel should have been.

Jordan looked at Bran, something burning up from the depths of her eyes like hate twisting into a growing cyclone. He realized how very close they stood. And how close he was to the railing and the edge.

And how off-balance.

But the fire in her eyes fizzled and she turned away, staggering one step back.

Bran gasped and grabbed the rail, realizing how easily Jordan might have gotten rid of both her torturers. Dread, a fist squeezing his heart, made him turn to watch what all other eyes were fixed on: Anil and his woman.

New streaks of silver cut through Anil's hair like the lightning he called from the sky—the lightning that was growing more sporadic as thunder began to growl in the heavens.

Anil was losing control. He was Fading. Fast.

His woman held tight against him, now more a crutch holding him up than an equal partner. Anil tilted his head and regarded his Maker coolly before addressing Jordan. "There is not much I have controlled in my life and my time grows short."

Jordan stepped forward, one word on her lips. "Don't."

"I would be a poor man to leave my love behind in so cruel a world," he said, "especially when she asks to accompany me beyond it. You are the *Artemesia*'s Conductor now."

"No," Jordan said, the word more a plea than a demand. "I do not even know all the ports . . ."

"You will set the right course and you will find your way without me—without any of us. Of that I am certain. Do you not see?" he asked softly, his lips brushing the frilled linen cap his wife wore. "You are free now, Jordan Astraea, ranked Fifth of the Nine. Free to captain your own ship. I beg that you return the favor—grant me my freedom—let me end as I wish. Do not make me fight you to earn this one last thing I can control."

Nodding, she stepped back. They all moved back.

"Summon the storm inside you, Jordan, but find with it joy equal to its power. Put aside hate for something stronger: love." He tipped his chin down and said to his wife, "Hold tight, my love."

She tucked her head against his chest.

He wrapped both his arms around her so that his wrists crossed and his palms lay flat on her shoulder blades. "Are you ready?"

She nodded and he closed his eyes, his mouth moving as he began to sing. The rest of them watched as the wind built around their feet, playing with the hem of the woman's heavy skirt before working its way around them, tearing along faster and faster, in time to the increasing pace of the song, fire riding its edges as it twisted heavenward and then, with a *woof*, it consumed them both.

Lightning cracked and a burst of brilliant light shot out of the clouds and filled a nearby stormcell crystal, knocking everyone back with its power. Glowing green, it barely steadied before the Wandering Wallace popped it out of its lantern and slipped it into his pocket.

It took a moment before Jordan realized they were falling.

Her short hair tickled around her ears and, feeling everyone's eyes upon her, Jordan stepped up and took the wheel. Emotion warred across her face—joy at her freedom obtained by Captain Kerdin's death, fear at the loss of the Conductor, and hate—cold and clawing hate—stiffened her features, glowed in her eyes.

Snarling, Jordan pulled the clouds together so fast they were all briefly blinded by a thick and all-consuming darkness. Thunder rolled, deafening as war drums on the march.

Something warm touched her arm, pulling her out of the cold and swirling heart of the storm. Looking down through the clinging tendrils of black and reaching clouds, Jordan saw the gentle upturned face of little Meggie, her large and shining eyes seeking Jordan's.

Meggie smiled and the small blue crystal in Jordan's bustline, the stormcell she had found in Tank 5 in Holgate, warmed against her flesh in something like recognition.

Meggie slipped her tiny hand into Jordan's free one and Jordan's face changed, reflecting back the child's faith. Jordan's heart hammered.

The lightning tore at the sky as bright as cannon fire at midnight and then it changed—became fireworks and colorful rockets spattering the sky with the most amazing light show. The inky clouds reflected a rainbow's worth of fleeting colors. The thunder softened, receding as Topside cleared, mist and darkness crawling off the dais and across the deck to creep down the balloon's colorful fabric like curling ribbons of oil, finally dripping off the ship's lowest level and dissipating into the sky.

The Wandering Wallace brushed his hands down his waistcoat's front and then ran a finger along the edge of one sleeve. "Quite an eventful dinner," he murmured. Then he raised his head and raised his voice to match. "What say we make things official?"

Jordan cast him a wary glance. "What?"

"The captain and his man are dead, as is our previous Conductor and his lady love . . . It seems to me, milady," he added with a courteous dip of his head, "that the *Artemesia* is truly *your* ship."

Always one for drama, he paused.

"At least Topside. But there are stacks of cabins below our feet and many staff and crew. Perhaps it is time to . . . change the status quo?"

She quirked an eyebrow in his direction and turned the ship's wheel slightly, worrying her bottom lip between her teeth.

"It is simple, really," he assured her, "securing our position. Shall I demonstrate?"

Marion rose from the table.

"Have no fear, Lord Kruse," the Wandering Wallace said, raising his hand.

Marion froze at mention of his surname.

Jordan's head turned slowly in Marion's direction. "House Kruse of Philadelphia?"

He nodded and Jordan released Meggie's hand and returned her focus to the sky and the storm brewing all about them.

She nodded. "Yes," she said vaguely in the direction of the Wandering Wallace. "It is time to shift the status quo. Secure our position," she commanded him.

The Wandering Wallace grabbed Meggie's hand, and swinging her arm in time with his, began to rock back and forth, watching her mimick him. Together they skipped across the deck, swinging their joined hands, until they stopped by the ship's intercom system. The Wandering Wallace leaned in toward her, beckoning her closer. "This is the way I sing to you every night," he said.

She laughed and rolled her wide eyes. "You sing to *everyone* every night."

He looked over her head at Bran and Maude and he winked. "No, little lass. I sing for *you*."

Miyakitsu made a show of stomping her way across the deck, her hands balled into fists, her lips puckered as she scowled at him.

"Oh," Wallace whispered, his mouth's shape mirroring the single syllable. In a stage whisper he declared, "I'm in trouble now!"

Meggie giggled.

"And of courrrrse," he said, stretching the words out, "I sing for *you*, my true love."

Miyakitsu nodded sharply and unrolled her fists.

"Would you like to help me secure the ship?" the Wandering Wallace asked Meggie.

She nodded.

"Can you whistle?"

She tried, producing a thin wisp of noise.

"Well, that is a fine start. Now, when I spin this flywheel you do that into here," he tapped the horn's rim, "and then I shall do *my* part."

He cranked the handle and set the wheel to spinning. Pointing encouragingly to the horn, he watched through the eyeholes of his mask as she whistled her best bit into the contraption. Then he leaned in and whistled the tune by which he was known in alleys so dark and dirty the only way one could recognize a person was by sound or scent.

He stopped the wheel from spinning and straightened, grinning and knowing that in the guts of the ship his men and women were reacting to the cue he gave.

On floors throughout the great airship *Artemesia* men like Stache the guard, and Jeremiah the powder monkey, and women like the serving girl who was unimpressed with the Wandering Wallace's napkin-to-bird trick disarmed and rounded up the men and women who were not recognized dissenters and locked them tightly into elegant rooms.

Screams echoed up to Topside as rebellious supporters of the status quo were thrown from windows.

Meggie blinked but Wallace just grinned and swung her arm until she, too, smiled again.

Marion paced between the dining room table and the Conductor's dais, his eyes darting to Meggie, the Wandering Wallace, and Miyakitsu as much as to Bran and the cloud cover coming under the Conductor's control. What the Wandering Wallace had just done was beyond Marion's control—most of what was happening was. But some things he still could manipulate and work. His gaze came to rest on Bran. "In light of what you did with Jordan and the captain, I think we have finally come to the end of our journey."

Maude stood, pressed her shoulders back, and, tilting her

head, stuck out her jaw. Her eyes pinned Marion to the spot. "He saved her, Marion," she said, her voice strong but soft. "And he'll do whatever he must to keep Meggie safe, too. Do not do anything drastic . . ."

Marion snorted, shaking his head. "Of course you think the worst of me. I cannot blame you. But I intend no harm, Maude. The opposite, actually. Your tickets aboard this ship are open-ended. We will be in Salem shortly, where I will disembark and begin a much different journey of my own. It is an election year, I am a young unknown with a freshly forged pedigree and a desire to change our country in the very best of ways. I will make people listen to me."

Bran stood. "You will bring change legally?"

"I will."

Maude stepped forward, moving between them to protect her lover. But this time she walked forward until she spread her arms, wrapping Marion in a hug. "You will be a man remembered for great deeds—and a forgiving heart," she whispered.

"I hope you are correct," Marion said, wrapping his arms gently around her as well.

"I apologize for ruining your political aspirations, good Lord Kruse," Jordan called, "but I am afraid we will not make port at Salem."

Startled, Marion stood silent.

"We," Jordan clarified, looking at Marion, "are going home."

The Wandering Wallace laughed. "To Philadelphia? How fortuitous! That is precisely where we need to be as well."

The top edges of the three elevator walls pierced the deck and inside stood Jeremiah and Stache. A broad grin on Jeremiah's chocolate-colored face made even the most tentative among them smile in response. "The ship is ours," he reported.

"Excellent," the Wandering Wallace shouted, grabbing Meggie's hand to tug it into the air as if she were a boxer who'd just won a fight.

"But something is approaching."

"Another ship?" Jordan asked.

Before Jeremiah could get the words out, the Weather Workers punctured the *Artemesia*'s cloud cover and rained down on them.

Chapter Fourteen

An institution is the lengthened shadow of one man.
—RALPH WALDO EMERSON

Philadelphia

A Ring of Wraiths, a handful of Wardens, and one dour-looking Tester stood in Councilman Yokum's doorway. He straightened, eyes weighing them. Realizing at that moment he had made his choice, he had stuck to his guns and stood with his vote against Councilman Loftkin and now he would pay.

Now Yokum would lose everything.

Voting his conscience would cost him.

He nodded, looking at his butler, stoic as ever. "Fetch our newest maid," he said.

The girl was marched out from the hallway by the pantry and she dug her heels in the moment she saw them waiting for her. "No. No, mister," she insisted, looking to Yokum for support. "I'm no—"

He shook his head and pressed his lips together. "How

old exactly are you, child?" With her soft and rounded face and her flat hips and chest he had presumed her to be fourteen at most. But he knew reality would show her to be older. He braced himself for the truth.

"Seventeen and three-quarters."

"Of course," he muttered.

A few of the servants had already begun to sneak toward the door and others had gone missing—likely packing their belongings. No one lingered once a household had fallen from grace. Unless you were a member of the faithful skeleton crew still employed at the Astraea household. Yokum had not yet earned such loyalty. He had acquired the Kruse house (and seemingly all the figurative ghosts that went with such a purchase) inexpensively enough. Now he would lose it all.

Perhaps some things, like a man's honor, simply came at too high a cost for someone striving to live cheaply.

Aboard the Artemesia

The Weather Workers burst through the *Artemesia*'s cloud cover like spears through fresh bread, tearing apart the atmosphere as they descended on flying machines of a design so strange the crew Topside on the *Artemesia* were stunned to silence. Big enough to hold three people, and each with a Warden or Wraith as driver, the open-topped ships came.

They made one swooping pass and disappeared back into the cloud cover on Topside's far end.

"What do I do?" Jordan shouted, eyes searching for signs of their return. "What do they want?"

Everyone turned to look at Bran. The Maker. The one whose life's work had ruined so many. He clutched a chair to keep standing and, catching his breath, stumbled across the deck toward Jordan. "Don't watch for them," he suggested, "listen. The machines make noise as they near. Keep us as far from the noise as you can."

She pressed her lips together and concentrated on sound. She reached out to the ship—closed her eyes and reached *into* and *around* the ship, using it and the storm to feel out the vibration of the lightships' noise before they were upon them again. She turned the ship's bow away from the noise and toward Philadelphia in a weaving pattern, and pushed the ship faster.

"Draw Down," Bran demanded, handing her the nearest tankard.

She sucked the liquid down and shook her head. "Water only."

Bran motioned to the others and they checked the goblets and tankards and brought her all they could.

The lightships burst from cover again, too small and fast against a cumbersome liner-class vessel.

"I cannot," Jordan apologized. "We must stand and defend . . ." She closed her eyes a moment. "Ah! Step lively, all," she snapped. "I am about to try something new . . ."

Bran opened his stance to steady himself as Jordan reached a hand into the swirling darkness not far overhead, spreading her fingers wide. Lightning snapped and arced between her fingertips and she drew her arm back and threw the living ball of light toward the first lightship she saw.

The fireball smacked into the ship, sending it careening back into the clouds, listing to one side as it limped into retreat.

"Clear the clouds, extend the wings full-out for a glide,

and give us a chance to shoot the bastards down," Stache yelled from his place by the elevator, watching wisps of moisture float haphazardly across the deck.

Bran nodded. "I find myself partial to *that* idea . . ."

The lightships burst through again, spotting him. Six ships circled the Maker and the Conductor, buzzing close in recognition before zipping away again.

"This is it," Stache said, raising the gun he carried and sighting along the end of its barrel. "They'll take him this time if they can!"

They returned so fast Stache barely finished his sentence. One lightship zipped between Jordan and Bran, a hand reaching down, blade glinting, to slash at the Maker.

Jordan gasped, recognizing the hand.

It was strange the things one remembered about someone when you'd never seen them face-to-face.

A single, scarred hand told much about its owner.

"Caleb," she whispered.

Jeremiah handed a gun to Marion, but he would not touch it and turned away. The Wandering Wallace accepted it in his stead, saying, "Sometimes the thing you wish never to do is precisely what needs doing."

"Eyes steady, sight, and shoot when you've a clean target," Stache commanded.

They were a gathering of statues, watching the tunnel of sky in which their ship rode. Then they heard them—the sound of an entire hive of bees descending.

Jordan slung out one arm and wiped the sky clean of clouds as she threw all her weight behind a lever. It ratcheted its way forward, the *Artemesia*'s wings popping into their most sustaining glide position.

The lightships buzzed in and zipped away to a greater distance, gaining a higher altitude, seeing their advantage stolen away.

"Oh. Oh, no," Jordan whispered, clearly seeing the Weather Workers in their fine cloaks or tailed coats and sharp hats steering the lightships with young men and women riding behind them—dirty and ragged and probably still wearing the clothes they were Gathered in. Jordan looked at Marion, shouting, "They're our people! From Holgate's Tanks—the unMade! They are *our* people!"

"Don't shoot!" Marion roared as a lightship soared overhead, circling.

The knife in the unMade's hand glittered and Jordan mouthed, "No—" even as Caleb dropped from the lightship with nothing but Bran filling his eyes—

—and was caught by one ankle by the Wraith steering. "Heeec must liiiive," it snarled.

Caleb arched his back, swinging his body up, and sinking his knife just deep enough in the Wraith's hand that it shrieked and let go. He fell, tumbling toward the dais and Bran Marshall.

Jordan jumped in front of Bran, knocked him to the wooden floor, and screamed the only thing that might make Caleb pause. Turning her head away, she threw her hands up as a shield against the impact of the boy and his knife—

—but it never came.

Jordan blinked and turned her face back to the threat that hung, suspended in a cushion of air ten feet above her.

Caleb squinted at her. "*Take the tea?*" he repeated, confused. He blinked and whispered her name. "Jordan?"

She nodded.

The soft expression on his high cheekbones and perfectly sculpted jaw hardened and he looked as if his gaze would pierce her if his knife could not. "Let me finish what I came to do. Let me mark him up the way he marked me." His hands trembled with a rage he struggled to keep in enough control that he could still speak.

The first time she had ever seen Caleb's face, she gasped. A network of scars made his flesh a grim patchwork.

"No," she whispered. "We should not fight each other."

"Then don't fight *me,*" he said with a laugh. "Set me down and let me take him. Let him pay for what he's done to us. To *all* of us!"

Above their heads the lightships hummed, circling.

"No," she insisted, the word softer now.

"You would save the man who ruined us?" He swung his arms and kicked his feet, but gained nothing.

Meggie broke free of Miyakitsu's grasp at their place near the ship's intercom and raced to Jordan and her papá's side. "Leave them alone!" she shouted into the sky. She stomped her tiny foot for emphasis and the clouds snapped back, becoming nearly impenetrable as Caleb was hurled to the deck a half-dozen feet away.

Caleb dropped the knife and scrambled backwards, away from them all as lightships plummeted all around them, slamming into the Topside deck and throwing some riders to the floor, pinning others beneath wreckage.

The Wraiths crawled forward, watching the child with the platinum-colored curls as much as the bold Conductor who toyed with the lightning snapping between her fingers. The air smelled of lightning and rain, but the day stank of prophecy.

Aboard the Tempest

"I see it, I see it," Evie murmured as she lowered the spyglass. Never had she seen such before, though. The way the clouds fizzled away and then slammed back into existence around the ship they approached, like a huge black box smacking shut its lid on a toy. "Most powerful Conductor I've ever seen," she muttered, eyeing Ginger Jack.

"You've heard the prophecy," Jack said.

Rowen nodded. "At the Hill King's Cavern. It seems a very popular theory among—liberally aligned traders."

"What if it's more than a theory?" Jack asked grimly. "What if we're about to meet with Destiny himself? What if that ship holds the future? What if that there's the Stormbringer?"

"It might give us the greatest weapon to use against the Council . . ." Evic whispered.

Rowen shook his head. "It might not come to all that."

Evie leaned into the horn and said, "Bring us alongside, boys—and try not to get us killed in the fireworks."

They raced forward, straight for the heart of the storm.

Philadelphia

In the Council, Loftkin instructed the leading men of Philadelphia's military. "Yes, yes, of course kill as many of the bloody Merrow as you can," he said, his expression droll. "The seas are teeming with them."

"What if we find the seas no longer teem with the Merrow

threat? That the tide of the war (if one might pardon the expression) has turned in our favor? Do we kill them with the same fervor?" The leader of the country's air force asked.

Nearby, Gregor Burchette, proudly representing both the local militia and the army, rubbed his hands together and kept his eyes fixed and cool on the Council.

The Council whose membership seemed to change with the wind—only a few members staying through both Hell and high water.

"Yes, of course. Kill all of the bastards," Loftkin snapped. "They are our enemy."

"And when we run out of this enemy?" Councilman Mendelheim wondered aloud. "What happens when our superior firepower and technology brings this war to a bloody end? What then?"

Councilman Loftkin said with a sneer, "What you really want to ask is, once the Wildkin threat is ended, how do we continue to galvanize our people into one cohesive country? With such a diverse population of immigrants, how can we possibly and accurately bear the title of the 'United States'? The good news is that we were wondering that shortly after the war began all those long years ago." He stood, smoothing his cravat and straightening his waistcoat. "But a good war . . . and yes, every politician worth his salt knows there are such things as *good wars*—a fruitful war—can last for decades, generations! If you are wise enough to pull the puppet's strings at the right times—and not too hard."

Gregor Burchette swallowed hard.

"So the threat of abolitionists pulling the fabric of our country apart . . . ?" a Councilman to Loftkin's left muttered.

"No threat at all so long as the Wildkin threaten," Loftkin answered with a grin that made Gregor's gut flip.

"And if there is a sudden peace between the Wildkin and we brave Americans? If they beg a truce?"

The grin became sly and dark. "You do what we did some years ago. Kill the peace bringers and send the adults' pieces back to their leaders. Take the wee babe they brought along and stuff the thing. Put it on display like a tattooed woman and let it tour the country so everyone can see just how horrible the creatures look when out of the briny deep long enough. Let our people judge their intent based on their looks. Tensions rise. The war goes on—appears insanely rejuvenated—as a result. Our citizens are horrified when the Wildkin react in kind, the belief they are savages incapable of being trusted is renewed, the focus on problems on the Fringe and not within our borders is renewed, and the status quo maintained."

Gregor cleared his throat. "Why not be honest with our citizens?"

Councilman Loftkin nearly choked. "Be honest with our citizens?" He shook his head. "I have to continually remind myself how young you are in the face of politics." He dabbed at the corner of his mouth with his napkin and took another long sip of tea before continuing. "We are the elite. The educated few standing atop a mountain of savages that wear similar faces to our own. They do not have the knowledge, nor the inclination nor ability to obtain the necessary knowledge to comprehend the way in which a government must function to succeed. The moment you remove the threat of the Wildkin, our savage citizens will look for something—or someone—else to tear apart. It may be their neighbors or, God forbid, it may be *us.* We are a judgmental species, regardless of what the Bible warns of judging others. We find fault in each other far more readily than we find it in ourselves. If you study the human species, you will discover that our favorite pastime is raising someone up to better tear them down. Consider how far you and I might fall if we give the mob a chance."

Mendelheim nodded. "So we keep the war going and the more obvious threat supercedes the supposed threat the abolitionists claim slavery is."

"Slavery and the rank system," Loftkin agreed. "How they hate that. But it works well."

"For *us,*" Councilman Mendelheim said.

Councilman Loftkin picked up his teacup and peered over its rim at Mendelheim. "Does anyone else matter as much as we do?"

Aboard the Artemesia

Jordan felt its approach in the air before she saw it through the haze of clouds. Another ship was cutting through their airspace and angling up alongside them.

"Below deck," the Wandering Wallace shouted, "get everyone below deck until we identify them . . ."

Maude grabbed Meggie and Miyakitsu and headed for the elevator as the first grappling hooks flew, snaring banisters and railings and dragging the dinner table a few feet before it overturned, glassware and fine china shattering.

"*Identify* them?" Jordan shouted. "What if they are more of the same?" she asked, looking at the broken lightships and the Weather Workers and unMade who still struggled to untangle themselves from the wreckage, all under the watchful eyes of the Wandering Wallace, Stache, and Jeremiah.

And their guns.

"What if they are *pirates*? They don't need to be identified!"

"Maybe they are not," the Wandering Wallace said.

Jordan glared at him. They were under attack again. They might be taken prisoner this time. Or worse.

And there was no rescue coming.

There never was.

Unless it came through *her*.

"Ready your weapons," Jordan demanded.

"Be at ease," the Wandering Wallace urged, looking over his shoulder in an attempt to identify the ship.

Jordan reached into the sky, drawing the lightning to her hands and turning it between her palms, solidifying it.

The fireball glowed and snapped, making her fingers twitch, and Jordan dropped her left hand, rolling her right shoulder back, and hurled the ball of light at the neighboring ship.

It landed, skidding and popping its way across their deck and leaving a trail of fire in its wake.

Jordan leaned over and fought to catch her breath, licking her lips.

The fireball hadn't stopped them.

They were boarding.

Aboard the Artemesia

Leaping from one airship to another could not even steal Rowen's breath away as much as the sight of the woman at the ship's helm did. Tall and slim, she stood at the wheel.

The lightning threw fleeting shadows over her, flashes of its bold white light played across the tips of her short hair creating an ethereal nimbus.

He landed in a heaving heap on the deck of the *Artemesia.* The deck was littered with small aircraft—not pods like the *Tempest* sported, but something else.

Something mostly smoking and broken.

Behind him he heard Evie and Ginger Jack talking in oddly congratulatory tones, but he paid them no mind and strode forward, his gait lengthening to allow him to cross the deck in only a few paces.

Swallowing hard, he stood before the woman at the ship's wheel and the child standing nearby. Jordan raised her hand, her face contorting in a snarl, lightning falling from her fingertips and sizzling on the wood floor.

"Jordan?" he whispered, stepping around the wheel and mindful of the sparks.

She blinked and stumbled back a pace, her hand falling to her face in awe, the lightning nothing.

Nearly toe-to-toe with her, Rowen lifted his hand, reached out to touch her face and paused there, letting it hang in midair. Overhead lightning threw them both into stark contrast and his eyes traced the strange pattern still fresh and pink on her face. The scar. "You have—"

"—been kissed by lightning," she said, looking away. "Much has changed since we last saw each other."

The world went wild around them, guards pouring onto the deck to be greeted by friendly shouts and traders bearing gifts.

A little girl slid up beside Jordan, her hand grabbing a pleat of fabric at Jordan's waist.

Lightning vaulted across the sky, but the black clouds softened, grayed, and a sad and somber mist pervaded Topside.

"Yes," Rowen agreed, his voice going soft and low. "Much has changed." His fingers brushed her cheek and she shrank back. "But not everything," he said, "not everything," he assured her, his eyes searching her face. "You are still the most beautiful girl I know."

She looked down and closed her eyes. So much had changed. He read it in every move she made—and the multitude she dared not.

This was not the Jordan he'd allowed the Wardens and Wraiths to drag away on the night of her birthday.

This was a far different girl.

In the flicker of lightning flashes, Rowen saw before him a shadow of the girl he had known.

And *loved.*

A distant stranger who pulled back from his touch.

There was a squeal and a yip-yip and a blur of red-gold. A fox kit zipped past Rowen, tiny feet scrabbling, stomach hitting the floor as it turned too quickly and dove behind Jordan. Not far behind, Rowen heard the angry bellow of Cookie and the stomping of heavy feet as she shouted for her spit-dog.

Jordan jumped, spinning to look behind her for it, but as she turned it followed the train of her dress, and for a moment they both spun, Jordan laughing, and Rowen watching them play.

Jordan stopped suddenly and threw a hand out, catching Rowen's arm to steady herself. His hands shot forward and he grabbed her shoulders, bracing her. She raised her eyes slowly and met his. His breath and hers intermingled, his gaze and hers locked. They stared at each other as the color drained from her cheeks again. She looked away.

"Where is that beast?" Cookie growled, barreling toward them.

Jordan peeled finger after finger off Rowen's arm and straightened. A brief glance passed between them and she tipped up her chin and flipped her skirts out to cover the frightened little fox.

Rowen's heart stuttered in its beating—for a moment catching sight of the old Jordan.

No, he corrected himself. Of the real Jordan.

Cookie roared past them, never seeing the very tip of the fox's tail peeking out from beneath the hem of Jordan's dress.

The second fox raced to join its sibling, moving so fast it bolted beneath Jordan's skirt and knocked into her legs, sending her toppling into Rowen.

For a moment the world disappeared and she leaned against his chest, her ear resting by his heart.

Slowly, carefully, he reached out and wrapped her in his arms.

Jordan sighed.

And there she stayed in Rowen's grasp.